# The Quest
# for the
# Flaming Pearl

## Tales of St. George & the Dragon

written and illustrated by

# Edward Hays

Forest of Peace
Publishing

Suppliers for the Spiritual Pilgrim

## Other Books by the Author:
(available from the publisher)

### Prayers and Rituals
Prayers for a Planetary Pilgrim
Prayers for the Domestic Church
Prayers for the Servants of God

### Contemporary Spirituality
The Lenten Labyrinth
The Ascent of the Mountain of God
Holy Fools & Mad Hatters
A Pilgrim's Almanac
Pray All Ways
Secular Sanctity
In Pursuit of the Great White Rabbit

### Parables and Stories
St. George and the Dragon
The Magic Lantern
The Ethiopian Tattoo Shop
Twelve and One-Half Keys
Sundancer
The Christmas Eve Storyteller

# The Quest for the Flaming Pearl

copyright © 1994, by Edward M. Hays

Library of Congress Cataloging-in-Publication Data
Hays, Edward M.
    The quest for the flaming pearl : tales of St. George and the dragon / written and illustrated by Edward Hays.
       p.   cm.
    ISBN 0-939516-25-X : $10.95
    1. Spiritual life—Fiction. I. Title.
PS3558.A867Q4 1994
813\.54—dc20
                                   94-35481
                                        CIP

*published by*
Forest of Peace Publishing, Inc.
PO Box 269
Leavenworth, KS 66048-0269  USA

*printed by*
Hall Directory, Inc.
Topeka, KS 66608-0348

1st printing: October 1994

*The parable "The Lighthouse" is reprinted from Edward Hays' Parable Preface in* **Sacred Dwelling** *by Wendy M. Wright.*

# The Quest
# for the
# Flaming Pearl

# Rationed Reading

is recommended for the parables you will discover herein. Rather than reading rapidly from entry to entry, the reader should use special "Sea Reading Glasses" and allow time for personal reflection and application of each parable.

If you are on a quest, the purpose is not to finish the book but to find the *Pearl*.

Dedicated
to
David de Rousseau
loyal friend and
companion
on the quest

# Publisher's Preface

## The Background of Igor's Return

In the mid 1980s, we had the good fortune to come upon a journal manuscript written by a certain St. (which stands not for Saint but for "Sent") George. You may be familiar with our publication of that diary that tells of George's experiences in the remodeled toolshed behind his garage where he retreated to find peace and quiet. While there he was providentially befriended by a flaming-red Chinese dragon named Igor who among other things was a spiritual master. Together they went on a quest to find the Holy Grail. George's progress on the spiritual path was guided primarily by Igor's parable-stories. That manuscript ended when Igor disappeared after having led George to the end of the first stage of his quest.

Some six years later, we received in the mail an account of the second stage of Sent George's quest. George had taken a sabbatical from his work and home to deepen his spiritual life. Instead of retreating to some exotic monastery, he was strangely "sent" to a boarding house run by a wise woman named Mama Mahatma who hired him to do cooking and domestic work. His time with Mama, as well as his attempt to balance his daily duties and his inner work, kept him on the razor's edge of this stage of the spiritual journey. George gained insights into his quest not only from his disciplines but also from his new friends and fellow boarders, Father Fiasco and Inspector Bernadone. George was again aided by means of parables that this time unfolded from an old Edison Magic Lantern in the attic. This Magic Lantern account of his sabbatical ended as George returned, renewed and deepened in spirit, to his work, his home and to his wife, Martha.

We at Forest of Peace Publishing were amazed and delighted recently when a brown paper package arrived at our office. Inside was another journal manuscript, accompanied by an unsigned note. It stated that the manuscript had been found in the drawer of an old desk purchased at a garage sale. The anonymous sender had been told by a friend that we might be interested in publishing their "find."

This third journal marks the return of Igor the Dragon and is in the form of a ship's log with accounts of weekly hermitage experiences. Each entry gives the month and the day, but no record was made of the year in which it had been written. Two different styles of handwriting appear after the log heading, *Officer at the Helm*, one belonging to Sent George and the other to his wife Sent Martha. Her entries, we feel, have greatly enhanced the document's value. George had spoken of Martha and her interests in the two previous manuscripts, and now we had a record of their mutual adventures with Igor as they alternated days in their hermitage.

This book, we believe, is only part of the original manuscript. The first log entry is dated August 26 and implies earlier entries. Missing is information about George's return to his work, home and family, as well as how it came to be that George and Martha began to alternate time in the hermitage.

With this background, it is now time for you to begin the journal-log of Sent George and Sent Martha.

# Ship's Log

**Vessel:** *THE HERMITAGE*

**Officer at the Helm:** *GEORGE*

**Date:** *SATURDAY, AUGUST 26*

**Time:** *2300 HOURS - 11:00 P.M.*

On this warm late-summer evening, I chose to sit outside the toolshed hermitage on the old porch swing that hangs from the oak tree next to the garage—it was cooler there. Because I got a late start, this had become a hermitage evening rather than the usual hermitage day.

The lightning bugs had appeared, transforming our backyard into a wonderland. It was as if small sparkling stars had fallen to the earth and were dancing on the blades of grass or playfully somersaulting like circus acrobats high above the lawn. I was so enjoying their flickering performance that I surprised myself: like a child, I asked myself aloud, "I wonder what makes the lightning bugs glow?"

"Midsummer's magic!" came a voice from behind the creaking swing. "Magic, and a little chemistry brewed up by the original Alma Mater."

I knew that voice! My heart exploded with joy like a birthday balloon popping. It was Igor! The air was pungent with the smell of fireworks as I whirled around and saw my old mentor, Igor the Dragon. He was standing behind the porch swing with arms folded, causally leaning against the oak tree. I leaped to my feet as Igor came walking around the swing, and we embraced each other.

"Igor, after all these years, you've returned!" I said, my voice electric with delight. "Oh, Igor, my beloved old dragon, how I've missed you. Here, sit down, please. Where have you...I mean, what have you been up...No, don't say anything about the past. It's just good to have you here again. You and I could spend the rest of this night visiting."

"It's good to see you too, George. Thank you for that welcome—it's warmer than this August day. But, George, you look so tired! Isn't it about your bedtime?" he asked with a humorously wicked smile.

"My bedtime? No way, Igor! Seeing you—having you sitting here beside me—I'm not the least bit sleepy. I usually do go back to the house at sunset, but Martha won't be home till late today so I decided to stay out here. Join me here on the swing."

As we glided back and forth on the swing, the night breeze had begun to cool things down after the sweaty heat of the summer day. Far off in the distance, dark clouds exploded with flashes of light. Igor asked, "How's your quest going? Are you still as enthusiastic about your spiritual journey as you were years ago?"

Not wanting to face that question head-on, I pointed to the far-off electrical storm and said, "When I was a kid, my Grandfather called that 'heat lightning.' But I would say that they were giant lightning bugs zigzagging in and out of the towering clouds. It's nice to have two light shows," I added, motioning to my little friends hovering above the lawn.

"Ah, the mystery of glowing lightning bugs!" he said, graciously not pursuing his question about my spiritual discipline. He slipped a large dragon paw around my shoulder as he continued, "It's magic and chemistry. As I understand it, lightning bugs spend their days eating pollen from flowers, and at night they cruise around looking for someone to love. In the Midwest they're called lightning bugs;

in other places they're fireflies or glowworms. Their lights flash on and off because certain chemicals in their bodies come in contact with other chemicals, causing those beautiful little blue and white lights you see. Then another kind of chemical in their bodies causes the light to go out. Some lightning bugs seem to light up as they ascend and dim when they descend. They glow again as they repeat the upward arc of their flight cycle."

"Thanks Igor, I appreciate that bit of dragon knowledge. I know it's growing late, but it's been so long since I've seen you, and I'm hungry for one of your stories. You don't, by any chance, know any parables about lightning bugs that would challenge an old student like myself?"

"The Master of the Occasion," he said as we rode side by side in the old, gray porch swing through the early evening darkness. "That's the name in the Orient for storytellers who are supposed to know an appropriate story for every situation or need. They're as important in many villages or tribes as all the doctors of mind and body, legal advisers and wisdom-dispensers combined. You're lucky, George, that I have a doctor's degree in MOO!"

"Moo—as in cow?" I kidded him.

"No, MOO as in Master Of the Occasion," he replied as he jabbed me in the ribs with one of his five claw-fingers.*

"Now, with any luck I should be able to dig down deep into my bag of tales, legends, myths, rhymes, riddles, and odds and ends of parable-stories to find a parable about lightning bugs."

The old porch swing creaked as Igor searched through his file. Then he said, "Sorry, can't find a single story from any tradition listed in my directory! So, I guess that Igor Dragomirov, M.O.O., will just have to *create* a parable for this occasion.

*Readers of **St. George and the Dragon** will recall that Chinese Celestial Dragons of the Jade Throne have five pronged claws since they are royal. Ordinary, run-of-the-mill dragons have only four.*

# Once upon a time, in- or out-of-time,

out there at the far edge of your back lawn there lived a young lightning bug named Lucky Lux. Like the other lightning bug children, his bedroom walls were covered with pictures of heroes and heroines, their heads encircled by rings of golden light.

His parents read to him legends of how these Shining Ones had fearlessly flown into the Empire of Darkness to do battle with the forces of evil. Lucky knew by heart the stories of their flying feats and daring air battles. Each night as twilight descended and darkness crept over the world, Lucky would dream of the day when he also would fly in battle against the Empire of Darkness.

On his eighteenth birthday, Lucky left home to go to flight school. His parents and teachers knew that he would do well. He was good—and lucky—in everything: his studies, sports, the arts and particularly in his ability to glow. With nothing more than an old battered suitcase and a few belongings, Lucky arrived at the Light of the World Flying School.

Beaming with anticipation of great adventure, Lucky soon apprenticed himself as a student pilot to a luminous master named Photon. Lucky's teacher, like the quantum of electro-magnetic energy with the same name, seemed to have an indefinitely long lifetime. No one at the school knew how old Photon was, but he seemed, to Lucky, ageless rather than old.

Photon was always surrounded by a cloud of light that shone with blinding brilliance. Lucky loved to simply sit in his teacher's presence. Accomplishing each difficult assignment given him, the only reward Lucky sought was a smile from the old master. As the months of schooling passed, a bond of love deepened between master and disciple, delighting both of them.

Lucky quickly moved to the head of his class. While his flying was brilliant, it was still not consistently luminous. Lucky's light would blaze brilliantly at one moment, and then suddenly go out! There were flashes of greatness—he would soar heavenward, his long white silk scarf trailing behind him, light blazing forth from his plane with blinding beauty.

However, right at the peak of his ascent, surrounded by luminous splendor, his light would suddenly completely go out.

Each time this happened, Lucky would vow to double his disciplines. He prayed hours longer than required and took upon himself numerous three-day fasts, drinking only water. He changed his diet, eating only foods that the ancient books said would increase one's light. He made pilgrimages to the shrines of the Shining Ones. He knelt in prayer at their icons and kissed with devotion their relics. Lucky longed to be a champion, to be a carrier of light, to be extraordinary. Daily he sat with the other student fliers at the feet of his teacher, Photon, listening intently for any wisdom that might enhance his capacity to always be luminous.

One day in the middle of a class on flight preparation, Photon said, "You must be holy and blameless. You must be full of love."

Lucky's heart exploded with excitement. "Of course, that's the reason my light is not consistent: I'm not *full* of love!" From that day onward, Lucky tried to fall in love with every person he met. He had an army of friends, yet his pursuit of becoming full of love went beyond people. He attempted to love every book he read, every tool he used, the food he ate, even his dirty laundry. Somehow or other, the word *love* managed to find its way into every conversation. Despite all these efforts, Lucky's flying still failed to be consistently illuminated.

When the days of his training were completed, Lucky and the rest of his classmates were given their silver wings as pilots and were assigned to various fighter squadrons. With youthful enthusiasm, Lucky couldn't wait to enter into combat with the powers of darkness. Each day as the sun slipped beneath the horizon and darkness crept silently across the earth, sucking up in great gulps the fading daylight, the fighter pilots would come to kneel before Photon for a blessing and perhaps a word of inspiration. Thereupon, they'd eagerly race across the field to their planes. As ground crews pulled away their wheel blocks, one by one they would roar down the runway to rise up luminous into the darkness.

Within a short time Lucky Lux's flying was generally acknowledged as superior among all the fighter pilots. He was a champion in combat, and everyone began calling him "Ace." While he was a true force of light in air battles with the enemy, sadly he was unable to maintain constant illumination. At times his light would fail, even completely disappearing into the darkness. When this happened, Lucky would find himself engulfed in the moist, alluring embrace of darkness whose seductive touch frightened him.

Lucky grew frustrated at the failure of his efforts to always be ablaze with light. As the months grew into years, his personal periods of darkness also grew. He found those eclipsing embraces easier and easier to accept—and more comfortable than his difficult disciplines. Lucky even began to enjoy the times when darkness would stroke him, causing his heart to pound with excitement. While he still observed his spiritual disciplines, he did so only halfheartedly.

He even stopped visiting with his mentor Photon. He was ashamed, and he feared that his old master, being so wise, would know immediately that his disciple's dream of becoming perpetually luminous had become a casualty of the war.

Lucky no longer wore his white silk scarf. He acknowledged to himself that he wasn't a true ace—so why dress like one? While he continued to fly nightly against the enemy, he had to admit to himself that he was only average. Sadly, he embraced the dull pain of living only an ordinary life.

While he had abandoned his passion to become one of the Shining Ones, whose heads were encircled in light, the echo of his dream continued to haunt him. His deep-seated desire to be a hero would quicken in the middle of watching an adventure movie or listening to a moving song. Strangely, it would be strongest when he was erotically wrapped in the intimate embrace of darkness!

Yet his growing love affair with darkness progressively plunged him into inner turmoil. Had he not from childhood been dedicated to becoming light, to being counted among the Shining Ones? The real battlefield was now not in the night sky, but in his heart. There light and darkness twisted and turned, dove and barrel-rolled with each other.

The constant conflict further crippled Lucky's will. His fellow pilots began to notice his lack of zeal and enthusiasm. When they asked him the reason, Lucky would complain of war nerves or a lack of sleep.

One dark moonless night, the air raid sirens screamed out their call to the pilots to do battle against the forces of darkness. As they raced to their planes, Lucky remained behind, saying he had come down with the flu. It wasn't sickness of the body, however, but the soft, seductive voice of darkness that kept him grounded as the sirens called the brave to battle. That voice from the shadows whispered its tempting promise of peace and comfort. Lucky did not resist the visitation.

Near sunrise when his exhausted comrades returned to the barracks, Lucky pretended to be asleep. He lay with guilt as biting as if he had been wrapped in thorns and thistles. Prickly guilt tormented him all through the day, until it pushed him to do something he had needed to do for a long time. When the sun disappeared behind the horizon, ending that painful day, he resolved to visit Photon and make some changes in his life.

Wrapping his white silk scarf around his neck for good luck, he knocked at Photon's door. His old master seemed as ageless as ever. In Photon's presence, Lucky faced the painful truth of his life. Fueled by the converted energy of his guilt, Lucky poured out his heart to Photon. He spoke of his sorrow over his shattered dream and his shame at his easy acceptance of being only ordinary.

Photon listened to Lucky with great attention. Photon's face was aflame with affection and the usual cloud of light that clung about him glowed like the sun at high noon. Photon's love for Lucky had not dimmed over the years. He continued to cherish his young disciple, even as he watched him slip deeper and deeper into the embrace of darkness, watched the glowing radiance slowly fade from his eyes.

15

"It grieves me, Lucky," said Photon, "to see the most promising of all my students so sad."

"Yes, Master," replied Lucky, "I am sad because I've failed. I haven't been able to achieve constant illumination in flight, and I've lost my dream of being one of the Shining Ones, a true hero." Lucky became silent for a moment as the reality set in. "But damn it, Photon, even when I was completely faithful in practicing my disciplines, I wasn't able to shine constantly! It's hopeless; why even try to be a Shining One?"

Through the large window directly behind Photon, Lucky could see squadron after squadron of luminous planes flying off into the darkness of the night. As he watched them brightly ascending into the night sky, Photon asked, "Why do you believe, my young friend, that it's possible for anyone to glow *constantly?*"

Lucky looked at Photon in disbelief. "Because, Master, the legends about the Shining Ones tell us that they were full of love and light. And you, my mentor, always shine with such great beauty each time I'm in your presence!"

"Yes," replied Photon, "that's true, but it's because of my great affection for you! Indeed, whenever I am with you, I do shine. But, Lucky, you are not around all the time! As regards the lives of the saints, the Shining Ones, remember, Lucky, that those who wrote the stories of their lives always wrote them backwards."

"Backwards? Master, I don't understand—their lives were written in reverse?"

"Indeed, Lucky, the saints died full of love and light. Their beauty at the time of their death greatly influenced how people have remembered them. Each time the lives of saints and saviors—or any of the enlightened in history—are retold, the periods of their darkness shrink and shrink, until their lives are remembered *only* as light."

Lucky went to the large window that looked out upon the Kingdom of Darkness, now under full attack by the hundreds of flashing explosions of light. Photon slowly rose and walked over, placing his arm around Lucky's shoulder. He spoke softly, "Look inside yourself, Lucky. You, like each of us, are made of a combination of contradictions that interact like chemicals upon one another. Each time you ascend, by a thought, word or deed of love, you glow with great beauty. Ah, what beauty! It's a splendor like that of the sun! That moment of ascent, however, is usually soon followed by one of descent, and your light goes out. But don't lose heart, for the light has disappeared only temporarily. Be humble, my young friend, be humble. Remember the laws of gravity!"

"Gravity, Master? You mean like the earth's field of gravity?"

"Yes, Lucky, life is like the earth. It too has a field of gravity. In daily life, each ascent is usually followed by a descent. The temptation, when you're descending, is to crash dive into the darkness. It's easy to be held down by the guilt that you have failed. Be humble: embrace with hope your slow growth in becoming light. Remain steadfast in your disciplines, and slowly, I promise you, you will become so light-hearted that you will no longer be affected by the downward pull of darkness."

"Like a feather's ability to float—or, better yet, a cloud!" replied Lucky with his former enthusiasm.

"Yes, exactly! But you must be patient, my friend; it takes a lifetime. Besides being hopeful and humble, you also need faith—faith in the Spirit of Light. Have faith that if you keep your heart ablaze with the dream of greatness, each time your light is extinguished, the visits of darkness will only be temporary."

The two stood in silence at the window, watching the night battle between light and darkness. Photon spoke softly, his reverent words bridging the silence between them, "Look out there, Lucky." Photon pointed a luminous hand toward the darkness, now filled with beautiful explosions of light. "We are gifted beings. If taken one at a time, we are nothing! Each of us is a mere speck of splendor in an ebony ocean of darkness. Ah, but when we come together in great clouds of light, forgetting about being "aces," willing to take turns at being light, then the night is *filled* with light."

Photon's arm tightened around Lucky's shoulder. "While some of our friends out there are ascending, we see their light.

Yet at their shining moment of beauty, others are descending. In those places we see only darkness. At any given moment, we see only about half of us, only those who are ascending and, therefore, luminous. Oh, my young friend, how I long for the day when we can all come together. I don't mean four or even forty squadrons, but one great luminous cloud composed of *all* of us. Then the night shall become like the day—there will be no need even for the sun or the moon!"

Photon playfully began to tie a loose knot in Lucky's long, white silk scarf. "The first thing we need to do, Lucky, is *light*en up! We can't take the great battle so seriously. Earnestly, yes, but not too seriously." Then his words began to flow like liquid lava. "Listen, Lucky, the night calls to you. It calls you not to be darkness, not even to attain light, but to *be* Light. The Shining Ones, the heroes of your youth, were champions because they bore with patience the same frustrations you are suffering as they endured their periods of darkness. In that way they moved beyond the polarities of darkness and light."

Lucky looked into Photon's eyes, now deep as blue lakes and glistening with a hint of tears, as the master continued, "Lucky, the Shining Ones realized that this seeming burden of rising and falling actually is the Dance of Light. Yes, the interacting contradictions within you are part of a grand ballet, a grand design."

Adjusting Lucky's white scarf securely around his neck, Photon added, "Go now, Lucky Lux, you've got an important duty to perform. Keep your dream perpetually aflame as a sanctuary lamp in your heart. As you go about your duty, strive to rise ever higher and higher. Bear with great love the play of the forces of gravity within you—those conflicting forces that have been given to each of us for a good reason. Go now, my beloved student, my friend. Take up your dream once again with humility and passion."

Lucky's eyes were full of tears, but his lips were frozen. No words had yet been created to express how he felt, being encircled by the love and light of Photon. He embraced his old master and kissed him on the cheek. Then he saluted

Photon, turned away and walked briskly toward the door. As he opened the door, Photon called after him, "God go with you, Lucky! Remember, before time began, before the world came to be, before even light and darkness were separated, *you* were designed to be Light, chosen to be *full* of love!"

Igor was silent at the end of the parable. The only sound was the creaking of the old swing. My heart was full of joy. Igor had returned, and with his serpentine wisdom, as a true MOO, a Master of the Occasion, he had created a perfect parable for me.

"I'm like Lucky Lux," I said, breaking the silence. "I too have drifted from my original desire to excel in the spiritual journey. During the time when you first led me on the quest, I was faithful to my practices. Even later, after you had left and I was on my own, I was disciplined for a while. But then, sometime after I returned from a second quest, I didn't seem to be making any progress. Like Lucky, I essentially gave up and made compromises. One of the reasons, Igor, is that there's just so little time. Years ago, when you first visited me, I had more free time, more leisure to use for my spiritual pursuit. Now it seems that, for me at least, earth's most endangered species is time. Minutes, hours, entire days seem to disappear into some great invisible black hole."

"Perhaps, George," Igor said, "it's not just a matter of losing time but of losing perspective. Like Lucky, you've gotten bogged down because you've perceived the quest as a

19

solo flight, like a new Charles Lindbergh in your own *Spirit of St. Louis*. Photon was right; the quest is one of love, and love involves companionship. Ours is not an age for solo heroes in holiness. Sent George...ah, indeed, 'Sent!' You are sent along with others to climb the heights, sent in the company of others to light up the world."

"That's one part of the quest, Igor, in which I do feel blessed. Martha is now a serious spiritual pilgrim and has been on her own path for years. You know, Martha and I have decided to share time here in the old toolshed, and we're traveling the way together. She and I have been alternating Saturdays using the hermitage. Do you think, I mean, would you..."

"Also drop by to visit Martha—is that what you're trying to ask?" Igor asked, smiling broadly. With a nod of his head, he said, "I'd be glad to, George. In fact, over the years I've really wanted to meet her. I need to ask, however: she won't be afraid of me, will she? We dragons, after all, are only big snakes."

"Perhaps a bit startled at first sight of you—as I was! But Igor, you're a charmer, and I have no doubt that she'll fall in love with you as have I."

"All right, then, next Saturday I'll drop by here and meet her. But now, George, you really are beginning to look sleepy."

"I know it's late, but it's so good having you back in my life. If I didn't have so much to ponder with the Lucky Lux parable, I'd ask for a bedtime story."

"That's wise, George, one parable story at a time. If you get greedy, you won't go deeper than the surface of the story. With questions, pick and ax and dig your way from one level to the next. The questventure is about being your own archeologist. I promise that if you dig deeply you'll discover a rare treasure buried beneath the surface, the pearl of great price, the flaming pearl of wisdom. Chew on the Lucky Lux parable. Especially when it comes to soul food, we must chew our food slowly."

"Well, I do have a lot of digging to do with *Lucky Lux*, but it's not over, is it? Maybe it's because I want to see how *my life* comes out, but isn't there more to the tale?"

"You have to write the ending to your own story, George. As for Lucky Lux, all stories have to end sometime. They can't go on and on, or else you'd never get to bed! I'm surprised that Martha hasn't come home yet. She could have liberated you from this old storyteller." With that, Igor fell into silence.

In the silence, all I could hear was my desire to listen to more adventures of the greatest ace in the war between Light and the Empire of Darkness. As the old porch swing creaked in chorus with the crickets, I closed my eyes to imagine Lucky Lux soaring through the night sky in luminous splendor.

I must have fallen asleep, for I suddenly awoke with a start—to find I was alone on the porch swing. Igor was gone. At first I was afraid that everything that happened was only a dream. When that flickering doubt disappeared, I eagerly went to the hermitage and have recorded all that this evening held. I conclude this log entry with a final observation. While Igor's departed, I'm not sad since I know he'll be back again— if I'm faithful to my hermitage times.

All the entries in this ship's log—which Martha found in a secondhand bookstore—have listed the *vessel* as "the Hermitage." Tonight I realize how appropriate is a ship's log for this journal since Martha and I have now set sail on the "Voyage of the Red Dragon." No question about it! She and I have left the quiet harbor of our lives to embark on a great adventure, a questventure. That's also a term Martha and I coined for our journey since we now share the quest for the Holy Grail—or in this case, for the pearl of wisdom—and the search for the Holy is the greatest of all adventures!

All's quiet as the stars in the clear midnight sky seem to be dancing. So is my heart! Igor, my own Photon, has returned to my life, and now Martha, whom I so love, will have the opportunity to know and love that old dragon as do I.

# Ship's Log

**Vessel:** the Hermitage

**Officer at the Helm:** Martha

**Date:** Saturday, September 2

**Time:** 1500 Hours - 3:00 P.M.

A warm but good day here in the hermitage. I've especially needed this time alone. I've felt so exhausted. I wanted to take a nap in the old easy chair in the corner, but I was afraid I'd miss Igor. George told me all about his return last Saturday, and about the story of Lucky Lux. I was so excited that Igor agreed to visit me, but now three-quarters of this day has passed without a sign of him.

As is our pattern, I'll return to the house to share supper and the evening with George. We call it our Islamic prayer day. Like the Muslims who pray from sunrise to sunset, we've given a similar structure to our hermitage times. Today, however, it feels as if I could use more time.

The fatigue I'm experiencing is more than just physical weariness. I feel worn down at the soul level. Too much to do, too little time in which to do it. My job, my volunteer work and my ministry at church are all pressing in on me. I thought that once the children were grown and gone I'd have more time, but I still have so precious little. Being tired in body and spirit makes it difficult to relish the quest. I even find myself daydreaming about cutting back on my ministry and volunteer work so that I can challenge myself to put a little newness in my spiritual life.

"Burnout!" said a voice I didn't recognize. I looked out the window and saw him. He was peering at me through the window as he hung upside down from the roof. I was startled and jumped, dropping my pen and logbook. After all, right in front of me—and upside down as well—was a large and glorious red dragon! His great serpentine body was covered with scarlet scales that glowed orange and yellow-red. Great puffs of smoke issued from his mouth, giving the impression that he had swallowed a carton of lighted cigarettes.

Then he addressed me, "*Ciao,* as those dashing Italians say. *Ciao* and *pax tecum,* peace be with you, Martha! But why the surprised look? Were you expecting the Loch Ness monster?"

I laughed aloud, not only at his line about the Loch Ness monster but also because of his smile, which made his dragon teeth look like a wide white picket fence. "Hello, Martha, I'm Igor Dragomirov, alias Celestial Dragon of the Jade Throne, the Imperial Treasurer of the Chest of Wisdom, the Master of the Occasion. I'm also known as the Benevolent Guardian of Children, Seekers of Truth and Pilgrims—of whom, I might add, you are one! Last but not least, to coin a cliché, I'm your husband George's old friend. I hope I didn't startle you?"

"Well, yes, a little bit, but I was expecting you. George told me you had agreed to visit me here in the hermitage. I'm honored that you would; thank you! To be honest, though—not that I'm usually dishonest—I must confess that having a dragon as a...er, spiritual director is a bit unusual!"

"First, it is I who thank you, Martha, for it is my pleasure to visit you. I have been eager to meet you for years. Excuse me, but I'm getting a bit light-headed hanging upside down. Would you mind if I came inside?"

"Yes, of course, Igor, excuse me, please come down." As I spoke, with the agility of a young yogi he swung down from our hermitage roof, doing a complete flip, landed right-side up and strolled through the doorway.

"Would you care for some iced tea?" I asked. "I believe

there's at least one large glass left in my thermos."

"It's kind of you, Martha, to wet the whistle of an old dry dragon," he said, raising the thermos to his lips and draining it. He wiped his lips and said, "As far as having a dragon for a spirit guide—it's not at all uncommon. In China of old, the Taoists considered dragons to be symbols of the Way, which they said reveals itself momentarily only to vanish mysteriously in an instant. Dragons, as you may remember from childhood tales, guard hidden treasures. Mystical dragons guard—or seek —another treasure, the flaming pearl—or as you might say in the West, 'the pearl of great price.' The pearl is the oriental symbol for the goal of everyone on a quest: perfection, the mystic center, divine wisdom.... Martha, I'm certain that I'll enjoy accompanying you in search of the flaming pearl."

"Thank you, Igor, you are kind to ease my anxiety. You're as gracious as George said you'd be.

"When you first spoke to me, you used the term 'burn-out.' I hadn't thought of what I'm feeling in that way," I said, "but perhaps you're right. Do you think that's the reason why I feel so depressed and exhausted?"

"Martha, I'm no medical doctor, only a dragon. Still, feeling 'burned out,' drained, exhausted—'in the doldrums,' to use an old sailing expression for dead calms which were the bane of sailors—yes, it's frequently the source of being dispirited. Take heart, though, you're not alone. It's a very common affliction today when the gas tanks of most people register on empty. It's also difficult to be enthusiastic about life and the spirit quest when the people you live and work with are also in the doldrums. It's a pilgrim's woe—no wind, slack sails, dead in the water. In the doldrums, coworkers or shipmates who have lost hope in the future can be liabilities."

"I know you're not a medical doctor or a miracle worker, but does a wise celestial dragon like you know of any good Chinese herbs for burnout?"

"Martha, I don't have any herbs for that fatal fatigue. However, I think I do have another kind of cure here in my back pocket, a tale about Robin Hood! Now close your eyes and relax. Allow your imagination to let the tale unfold as if it were a motion picture."

As I closed my eyes, I saw Igor lean back in the old easy chair. Then he verbally began to massage my weary, sagging spirit:

Not that long ago,

in a city not that far from here, Robin Hood jumped out of bed as soon as he heard his ringing alarm clock. He began his customary morning ritual. In the predawn darkness he took a shower and quickly dressed for work. He hummed a little tune as he slipped into his red vest and brown coat. Then he grabbed his worn leather satchel, closed the door of his one-room flat and, whistling, skipped down the street toward the bus stop.

Boarding the bus, he greeted its half-awake passengers with a cheery "Good morning." The bus was full of black-and brown-skinned housekeepers and other servants on their way from the inner city to their work in the suburbs. They welcomed Robin with smiles as he came dancing down the aisle. His arrival on the bus always changed the drab predawn mood to one of joy.

Robin got off at his usual stop and headed for work. He again began to whistle as he walked down the street with its beautifully landscaped homes. All the lawns in the suburbs looked like golf course greens, so plush and free of weeds. Robin arrived at his place of work, a lovely home, just as the great red ball of a sun was climbing over the edge of the horizon. Robin stood in wonder; it was so beautiful and *new*, just like the first dawn of creation. His heart was full of joy as he opened his satchel, taking out a sailor's straw hat and a bamboo cane. Robin proceeded to jump out on a tree branch and begin singing,

> *When the Red Red Robin*
> *comes bob-bob-bobbin' along, along.*
> *There'll be no more sobbin'*
> *when he starts throbbin' his old sweet song.*
> *Wake up, wake up, you sleepyhead!*
> *Get up, get up, get out of bed!*
> *Cheer up, cheer up, the sun is red!*
> *Live, love, laugh and be happy!*

A ringing alarm clock inside the house was greeted with grunts and groans. Minutes later, with Robin still belting out his song, a sleepy-eyed man in a terry cloth bathrobe opened the curtains and stood looking blankly out into his backyard. If Frank heard Robin, there was no indication of it on his sleepy, sad face. Undeterred, Robin went right on singing and dancing as Frank showered and dressed. There was much rushing around in the house as Frank and his wife Claire prepared to leave for work. As Frank stood tying his necktie at the window, Robin put all the zest he could into his song: *"Wake up, you sleepyhead! Live, love, laugh and be happy."*

"Hurry up, Frank, or we'll be late for work," came the standard cry from somewhere deep in the house. Frank closed the curtains and was on his way.

Robin quickly packed up his gear and raced as fast as he could to the tree outside the *7-Eleven* store. Frank and Claire would sometimes stop there for gas and coffee on their way to work. Sure enough, in a moment they came driving up to the pumps. Robin filled his lungs with air and began,

> *Happy days are here again.*
> *The skies above are clear again.*
> *Let us sing a song of cheer again.*
> *Happy days are here again.*

Frank, however, was deaf to Robin's song as he filled his tank and raced into the store to pay for his gas. Soon Frank's car roared off into the river of rush-hour traffic. Robin sang to several others as they made pit stops at the *7-Eleven* store, but, like Frank, they were all deaf to his song. Robin packed up his gear and moved to his next stop. Each day, for years, this had been his routine.

When the day's work was over, Robin and his friends stopped at a bar for a drink. The Nest Bar was crowded with Blackbirds and Blue Jays drinking and talking. At a table in the center of the bar, Robin and his companions took stock of their day's work.

"I've got about a minute and a half," said one Robin as he emptied his day's takings onto the table.

"I've only got forty-five seconds," said another Robin.

"I was able to get four minutes," said another, "but it was from a small child."

"You know that doesn't count," the rest of the Robins kidded him.

A black Crow walked past the table. "Hey, Robin Hood, you and your merry band still working for peanuts?"

Robin looked up and laughed, "Yeah, usual day. We've only been able to steal a little sadness—a minute here, a few seconds there—but that's show business!"

The Crow cocked his head and said, "Why don't you and that merry band of yours come and work for us Crows and Blue Jays? We're picketing and demonstrating down at city hall and the courthouse. No one pays any attention to you and your happy songs. Today it's the croaking and squawking of demonstrators that makes the evening news and talk shows. I bet you've never even been on TV. Come and join us—take up a cause, carry a placard—it'll give your life some meaning, and the pay is much better than what you birds get."

"Thanks, brother," said Robin Hood, "but we've got a cause, and even though we're poorly paid and aren't very successful, you might say it's a way of life for us."

The next morning Robin overslept and, being in a hurry, forgot his lunch box. He did his song-and-dance numbers outside the homes of the sad folks of suburbia whose lawns looked like golf course greens. Around noon Robin became hungry and regretted that he had forgotten his lunch. Spying a nice large earthworm crawling through the green grass, he swept down to feast on it.

That night, he didn't stop by the Nest Bar, being tired and not feeling like having a drink. He awoke in the morning feeling sick with the flu or some virus. For the next few days it required real effort to sing since he always felt sick to his stomach. So on the way home one day, Robin decided to stop and visit his friend Doctor Duck.

After all the usual tests had been taken, a nurse ushered Robin into Doctor Duck's office. "Sorry, Robin," said the doctor, "I'm afraid that you have cancer."

"Cancer!" gasped Robin. "That's impossible, I don't even smoke!"

Doctor Duck shook his head. "Our tests show heavy traces of herbicides in your blood. What have you been eating lately?"

"I follow a strict diet, Doc. I only eat health foods," said Robin. "Ah, but there was that worm I ate about a week ago. I'd spotted it in the lawn where I work."

"That's probably it," said Doctor Duck. "How do you think they keep those lawns looking like golf course greens? Herbicides! I'll bet that worm was covered with the stuff!"

Robin sat in silence for a few minutes and then said, "How much time do I have left, Doc?"

"At best," said Doctor Duck, "I would guess four to six weeks. If I were you, I'd retire today and enjoy the little time that's left."

"Thanks, Doc," said Robin, "I'll consider that."

However, Robin didn't retire or take it easy. Instead, he plunged with even greater energy into his work. While the cancer ate away at him, each day he sang his song, "*Wake up, wake up, you sleepyhead. Live, love, laugh and be happy.*" Still, no one listened to him. Oh, they heard him all right, but they never listened to his song. Robin thought to himself, "My life's ending, and there's so much sadness in the world—and I've only been able to steal little bits of it here and there. Yet while I haven't changed the world, at least the world hasn't changed me!"

Two weeks after his visit to Doctor Duck, Robin's alarm clock filled the predawn darkness of his one-room flat with its shrill call. It rang and rang and rang, but Robin didn't hear it.

Two hours later out in suburbia, as the sun was rising in splendrous orange glory, the branch outside Frank's bedroom window was vacant. Frank opened the curtains and looked out, rubbing his sleep-filled eyes. His mind was crowded with the business of the coming day, but a thought nudged its way into the maze of problems and worries: "Something's missing this morning...but what?"

He showered, dressed quickly and stood once again at the bedroom window, as that haunting thought once again drifted through his mind. "Frank, for God's sake, hurry up or we'll be late for work," came a loud voice from the front door. Frank picked up his briefcase and headed for the car. As he locked the front door, he was surprised to find himself softly singing, *"Happy days are here again. The skies above are clear again...."*

Claire, with both hands gripping the steering wheel, was gunning the engine as he opened the car door. She looked at him in astonishment. Frank was wearing something she had *never* seen him wear to work—a smile!

As I opened my eyes, I too was humming "Happy days are here again." Then I noticed that the easy chair was empty! Igor had disappeared. George had warned me that Igor often would be there one moment and then would be gone in the wink of an eye. As Igor had said, dragons are symbols of the Way, which—how did he say it?—oh yes, which 'reveals itself momentarily only to vanish instantaneously in mystery.' I wonder how he does that, I mean disappearing almost before your eyes? The next time he comes I'll ask him to explain not only how, but the *why* of his magical exits and entrances.

Igor's parable-cure may not have magically made my burnout disappear, but it is having an effect. I sure know how it feels to be in a rut like Frank and Claire in the story, robot-like going from one activity to the next, morning till night. *I need a Robin Hood to come into my life and brighten it up, to help me change my perspective on my daily activities.* I know that everything I'm involved in is important and valuable work—even the simple and mundane tasks. But it's so easy to feel overwhelmed by the sheer volume of the demands. That's the very reason why I started coming out to this hermitage every other Saturday—to add enough inner spaciousness so that I can keep my perspective, so I can hear the "song" that underlies the daily grind.

After sitting quietly with those thoughts for a few minutes, another parable-inspired question occurred to me: Am I, like Robin, a songbird of Good News? Regardless of the shape of my day, do I want to sing with zest, "Happy days are here again"? Recently, at work and here at home, my song's been more like the old classic, "Stormy Weather." "Don't know why there's no sun up in the sky, stormy weather...."

God knows, in our world today we've got more than enough gloom and doom. It's not the wedding march but the *marcia funebre*, the funeral march, that's become the world's background music. Little-but-mean wars are festering everywhere, exploitation of the poor goes on all the time, and there's been so little movement in overcoming discrimination. Personally, as a woman, it's easy to fall into feeling powerless: we're still second-class citizens in society—and especially in the Church. Most of the time there seems to be so little hope of anything changing. Even when the faces change, the status quo seems to be firmly entrenched. But I realize that I can't help anyone, especially myself, if I join the crows and blackbirds and *only* complain.

Igor's parable certainly helps me see how my theme song of late has too often been "Stormy Weather." It also puts me in touch with my deep desire to be like Robin and his merry band, highway robbers who daily steal gloom and despair from other people's lives. It's an interesting twist: to rob the poor to make 'em rich! But how to do that?

How did Robin in the parable remain hope-filled even when no one listened to his song? I wonder if that's what good prayer is about, to help keep us connected to the source of the song? Communion with God is communion with hope and promise.

Along with communion, I think that community is an essential ingredient on the questventure. Just as Robin Hood was part of a merry band, it feels important for George and me to have friends who can share our voyage and join us in "singing" the Good News. I really value the spiritual community I have with George, but we'd both like to expand it to include a "band" of like spirits.

My brief time with Igor also makes it clear that those who search for—who even catch a glimpse of—the prize, the flaming pearl, are energized by that search, and so are full of joy. I know that the Gospel has always been a song of hope and joy sung in dark times, including darker times than these in which I live. That song acknowledges the darkness and evil in the world but sings of the triumph of the light. I think of the song, the Magnificat, of Mary the mother of Jesus (I almost wanted to say Maid Mary, reminded of Maid Marian from the original tale of Robin Hood). While Mary was no more than a second-class citizen in her day, she sang of God casting the mighty and powerful down from their high places and all the poor and powerless being raised up. That's the essence of singing an upbeat song: that God will lift up those who are beaten down.

Igor's tale of Robin Hood has sown a seed. It makes me want to write my own parable, my own version of Robin Hood! My Robin could be an inner-city heroine who lives among the homeless. I'd call her Robin, the Homelesshood. I don't know the rules for creating parables, but I'd like to experiment with pretending to be the character in my parable. That insight helps me formulate my intention for the next two weeks.

Intention: In the coming days I will try to strengthen my sense of communion with God through daily prayer and my sense of community with George, and possibly with others. I will also pretend to be Robin Homelesshood, the great thief of sadness and gloom. I will steal as much gloom as possible as I draw attention to the good and positive in the world. As part of my personal creed, I now add the following dogma: I believe that light is more powerful than darkness, and that while evil abounds today, grace and goodness abound all the more.

That sounds faintly like a line from St. Paul. If so, I give Paul the credit for it. I conclude this hermitage time and this entry in our questventure log with a prayer:

O God of thieves and pickpockets,
    make me one of heaven's holy robbers
    whose vocation is stealing the blues
    from those who live down in the dumps,
    whose lives are empty of hope or promise.
With a smile, a laugh, and love for all I meet,
    may I rob the poor of heart
    to make them rich of spirit
    with the song "Happy Days Are Here Again"
    playing in my heart.
O Musical God,
    you who gave each species of bird a unique song,
    give to me the Song of Songs,
    the anthem of the new reign of God.
Amen.

# Ship's Log

**Vessel:** THE HERMITAGE

**Officer at the Helm:** GEORGE

**Date:** SATURDAY, SEPTEMBER 9

**Time:** 1300 HOURS - 1:00 P.M.

I start to record this log entry as the day is half-spent. Last Saturday night at dinner, after she returned from the hermitage, Martha shared the excitement of her first experience with Igor. We discussed his Robin Hood parable and how we can maintain a healthy and positive outlook on life, one of hope. She observed that hope is often an attitude associated with youth! The older we grow, the more cynical or pessimistic we often become. We concluded—over a third glass of wine— that staying youthful is at the heart of remaining positive. So the trick is to not grow old, even while aging. Just what is the difference between aging and growing old? We both agreed I should ask Igor what he thought about this—we agreed that, for an old dragon, Igor was still youthful. I note this observation in our log even though I suspect Igor will not easily be induced to share his secrets of how to stay young while aging. Martha also said I shouldn't ask him his age.

I know that, after sitting with the parable of Lucky Lux, I feel renewed—like a young buck—in my enthusiasm for the adventure of the quest. I feel a little like Lucky did at the end of the story, after he left Photon.

Earlier today I counted the knots on the cord that hangs on the wall. While this converted toolshed hermitage is land-locked, it seems very much like an explorer's vessel on the high seas. It's our own questventure Ship of Fools. I've placed a brass compass on the desk. The knotted cord hanging on the wall reminds Martha and me that this is a vessel of passage.

So far we've placed fifteen knots in that symbolic cord that measures our speed. It sounds humorous to think in terms of speed on the spiritual quest, but it's fun to monitor our progress. In the old days of sailing, navigators gauged speed and distance by dragging behind the ship a piece of wood, a log, to which they fastened a cord. That log-line was knotted at intervals. A knot became the universal measurement of speed, and a log became the term used for the record of a ship's speed.

The piece of wood attached to our knotted log-line is a replica of the old ones on sailing ships. It's six inches in radius and the shape of a quadrant, so it could float—if we were on water—perpendicular to the vessel. This ship's logbook, our questventure journal, is like the later nautical books in which "logs" were entered to record not only the vessel's speed but the general proceedings on board. The captain wrote in it such things as the weather and the behavior of the crew. The expression "to be logged" meant to have your name recorded in the ship's journal for some misdemeanor or offense. The log also recorded unusual sightings (like sea dragons?—those old sea charts of unexplored areas frequently pictured sea dragons).

Today, I'm on deck at the helm (the Officer at the Helm) for my day on the questventure that Martha and I share. Since Igor told me the parable of Lucky Lux and talked about the need to form a community of light, I'm even happier that Martha and I can share our mutual quest for the sacred. We've both discussed whether we should expand to include others in a support community seeking the Sacred.

"The Sacred?" came a voice from the open doorway. "I

35

hope that doesn't mean *just* the spiritual." Igor was leaning against the door frame, looking as casual as Gary Cooper. "*Ciao*, greetings! *Como esta*, George? How are you, and how is your quest? I hope it's a quest for the fully human as well as the fully holy."

"Igor, welcome! Before I answer your question, thanks for visiting Martha last Saturday. She told me your healing-parable about Robin Hood. Both she and I are reflecting on its deeper meanings. As for your question about the quest— yes, I hope I don't fall victim to some spiritual path that denies the natural. I want to be as fully human and holy as was Jesus. I'm hungry for the fullest measure of the holy and the human that's possible in this life."

"Good, George, I'm glad to hear that you don't want to be half-alive. That's not easy in your society since a large number of people, especially men, surrender part of their humanity for—"

"'Half-alive,' you say? Oh, I feel a tale unwinding. Igor, I'm ready and hungry for another adventure on the quest."

"Well, George, you're right. Today I have a strange tale about a young man and two clever doctors, Franken and Stein.

He was only fourteen or fifteen

the day he visited the clinic of Doctors Franken and Stein. Their A & C Clinic was located near the lad's high school, down a dirty alley just off Wall Street and Broadway.

Doctors Franken and Stein were identical twins, known widely in the trade as "the twin surgeons of success." Over the doorway of their makeshift clinic hung a sign that read:

DRS. FRANKEN & STEIN
ABORTION AND CONTORTION CLINIC
ADJUSTMENTS AND ALTERATIONS—CHEAP
FREE POSTOPERATIVE GIFT

No kid that entered their clinic ever came out the way he or she went in; that is to say, by the front door! They all left by the back door that led directly to Broadway, Wall Street or Grand Avenue. Time, and the mercy of the mind, had dulled the young man's memory of the day he went to see the twin surgeons of success. As best as he could recall, its events took place like this:

He walked into the clinic and took a seat in the waiting room whose walls were lined with photographs of famous men and women, those who had made it. The door to the back room opened, and Dr. Stein, wearing a blood-splattered white coat, stuck his head out and shouted, "Next!"

The lad stepped through the door into a crude operating room where two identical-looking doctors, in matching blood-spotted coats, stood smiling at him. In perfect unison they asked, "What can we do for you?"

He answered, "I've, ah...come, ah, for an operation, for an adjustment. I...I..." Both doctors smiled and in one voice spoke again, "You want to fit in, right?"

"Yes," he gulped, "you're right."

"We're always right, kid. That's our business! We're specialists. I'm Dr. Stein, the abortionist, and this is my brother, Dr. Franken, the contortionist. Together, we guarantee that when we're finished with you, kid, you'll fit in perfectly!" Then the two doctors winked at each other.

Dr. Franken produced a strange looking garment from behind his back. "Try this on, kid; see how it fits."

The young man slipped into the oddly shaped garment that didn't fit at all. "See, Doctor Stein, he's like all the others. It just doesn't fit him."

"Not so, Doctor Franken; don't forget the four percent for whom it fits perfectly!"

"Doctor Stein, my brother, the perfectionist. Precision, precision in all things. All right, yes, for a mere minority our services are not needed—that famous four percent who don't need an adjustment or alteration for *it* to fit. This kid, however, obviously isn't among that privileged group. Look at the way *it* hangs on him. It's too small here, see? It's far too large over here, and on this side as well."

"You're right, brother. It's obvious he'd never fit in without our expertise. OK, kid, lie down on the operating table. Together, my brother and I will grant your heart's desire."

He laid down on the stone-cold operating table. Doctor Stein stood over him, grinning, as he produced a coat hanger from behind his back! "Take a deep breath, kid." The teenager screamed in pain as Dr. Stein wildly slashed this way and that inside him with a bent, razor-sharp coat hanger.

"There, finished! All that prevented you from 'fitting in' has been successfully cut off or cut out of you. Your turn, Doctor Franken."

As Doctor Franken leaned over him, the lad pleaded, "Don't I get any ether or gas? This is so painful!"

"Like the sign outside our clinic says, 'cheap.' We can't afford anesthesia and still offer you kids cheap surgery. Now, since you're too short in some places, we'll need to make a major adjustment. The abortion is over, son; now comes the contortion!" Leaning close, he smiled down at the lad, saying, "Now, take a deep breath."

Doctor Franken seized the bent coat hanger and began stretching the teen this way and that, pulling on one part of him and then another. The young man screamed with pain as he felt himself being stretched beyond his limits.

"Complete!" cried Doctor Franken at last. "Look at that, Doctor Stein, another perfect contortion! Stand up, kid, let's see how it fits." He stood up and the two brothers slipped the odd garment on him. "Look at that, *it* fits perfectly! Kid, you're now fitted out for a life of success."

"Not so fast, Doctor Franken," said Doctor Stein. "Have

you forgotten that he's a boy? Unlike our girl patients, he'll need one extra treatment. Lay back down on the operating table, kid, this will only take a second." The young man hesitated, eyeing the back door. Seeing his hesitation, Doctor Stein said, "You want to fit in, don't you? Just lay down and be a big boy. This is all included in the cheap price. Nothing more for this small operation."

Doctor Franken quickly yanked a large industrial-tank vacuum cleaner from under the operating table. Doctor Stein pushed the end of the vacuum cleaner's hose over the teen's nose and eyes saying, "Now, take a deep breath."

As the young man did, Doctor Stein shouted, "Step on the gas, Doctor Franken." Suddenly a surge of unbelievable pain shot through the young man.

"Done!" cried Doctor Stein. "All your tear glands have been sucked out of you! Now, around mid-life they *may* grow back in again. Don't worry, though, Doctors Franken and Stein guarantee their work. Kid, you just come back to us, and we'll suck 'em out again!"

A bit dazed, the teenager stumbled off the operating table and staggered toward the back door when Doctor Franken called out, "Hey, kid, don't forget your free postoperative gift!" He and Doctor Stein grinned from ear to ear and handed it to him. It was beautiful. He felt so proud as he stepped out the back door of the abortion and contortion clinic and headed up the alley toward Wall Street and Broadway.

At the end of the alley he joined with the others who were hurrying along the sidewalk. The young man rejoiced because no one even took notice of him. Indeed, he did fit in perfectly! Now one of the crowd, he flowed along with the mass of people until he came to a street crossing. He stood waiting on the curb for the light to change. As he did, he looked down with pride at his postoperative gift. Then he glanced across the street at the people waiting on the opposite curb. What he saw shocked him. Then he looked around at those standing beside him. Every man and woman within his field of vision was carrying a Doctors Franken and Stein free postoperative gift: a briefcase!

40

Igor sat silently in the old easy chair. I realized that his story of the young man was also my story. "Igor, that story was much like one I read long ago as a youth, a tale from Greek mythology. It believe it was called 'Procrustes' Bed,' or something like that."

"Yes," he replied. "You might call it a modern adaptation of that old story, a myth which is never old, just timeless. I take it you found it to be a mirror?"

"Yes, Igor, like a lot of men, I'm afraid I've been to that famous clinic. And as I've grown older, I've found both to my embarrassment and my delight that my tear glands *are* growing back. I hadn't thought of that as a virtue until...." As I spoke, a strange thing was happening: Igor was shrinking before my eyes! And, like in those cartoons where characters have little white balloons over their heads with words inside, one of those balloons was forming above his head. Inside it was the word *Vale*, which, if I remember my high school Latin, means "farewell." In a matter of seconds the large multilingual dragon had shrunk to the size of a garter snake, then a wiggling worm, and with a little puff of white smoke he was gone!

Igor had disappeared so quickly that I didn't have time to ask him about growing old and gloomy that Martha and I wanted to present to him. Now I had this new parable to ponder as well.

One thing struck me right off: If I'm going to travel very far on this questventure, I need to continue to recover the parts of me that the Doctors Franken and Stein of my culture have cut off or ripped out, especially my "tear gland" emotions and deep feelings. Besides the need I feel to get in touch with my intuitive side, that recovery has to help strengthen my connection with Martha and our mutual questventure. At least I might be able to understand and appreciate her approach to the journey a little more. God, grant me the grace to be fully a man and fully human.

Before I left the hermitage to have dinner with Martha, I tied not just one knot but several in the measuring cord that hangs on the wall. Truly this hermitage day in the Voyage of the Red Dragon had been very significant for me, potentially worthy of many miles of growth.

# Ship's  Log

**Vessel:** *the Hermitage*

**Officer at the Helm:** *Martha*

**Date:** *Saturday, September 16*

**Time:** *0900 Hours - 9:00 a.m.*

I slept here last night on an old army cot. I wanted—no, I needed—to get an early start on my time here. While I've done somewhat better with feeling exhausted, I'm only beginning to learn how to say "no." It's not easy for a woman. We're supposed to be giving, and doing it all the time. Yet giving all the time means soon becoming empty. I needed this time to fill my reserves so as to give freely, joyfully, and not out of obligation.

I'm still looking for some kind of group or community, even a few close friends with whom George and I can share our quest. While a lot of people are religious, not many are really interested in the spiritual quest. However since hope is now a real part of my creed, I am still hopeful, even confident, about finding a group. In the spirit of the Lucky Lux parable, I'm like Amelia Earhart, the aviator, the first woman to solo the Atlantic. I'm a flying ace in search of my own squadron of luminous ones.

I have been feeling a kind of spiritual wanderlust, a need

to spread my spiritual wings. I recently saw an ad about a pilgrimage to the Holy Land and wondered about that as a possibility. This town is so provincial; if George and I would make a pilgrimage to Rome or Jerusalem or Mount Sinai, maybe we might...

"...Spend a large hunk of money, Czarina?" said Igor, his nose pressed tightly up against the front window of the toolshed. "Martha, Czarina Alexandra also had great love of pilgrimages to Jerusalem, as did her husband Czar Nicholas. As then, so today, going on a pilgrimage isn't cheap!"

"Come in, you old Peeping Tom," I joked as I stood up and opened the door. The air of a mild September morning flooded into the hermitage.

"Thank you and good morning, madame. Indeed, I may seem to be a *voyeur*, but in reality I am a *voyageur*, as they say in Quebec—Igor Voyageur, humble guide to the wilderness of the inner desert. Martha, you're here early today! From the sleeping cot in the corner I surmise that you've spent the night here."

"You'd make a good Sherlock Holmes. Yes, I needed to fill my spirit-tank, and so I stayed overnight. May I offer you some good fresh coffee, Igor?"

"Thank you. After my sunrise flight here, I'm ready for a cup. You know, Martha, we celestial dragons read minds, and as I was landing I couldn't help but read your reflections on taking a pilgrimage to some holy city, river or mountain."

"Yes, I know that it's costly, but it seems like it'd be worth it," I said as I handed him his coffee.

"Depends," he said after a sip. "What is it you're seeking on the pilgrimage? Perhaps a parable à la Lucky Lux might help you decide. Here's an early morning flying story, reminiscent of that famous woman flier from Atchison, Kansas, Ms. Earhart. She crashed, you know, somewhere in the Pacific, all very mysteriously, in 1937, before the Second World War."

"I'm ready," I said. "I've strapped on my seat belt and I'm ready for takeoff."

After taking another sip of coffee, Igor began:

the plane began sputtering. The engine gagged and choked, and then was silent. The only sound was the whistle of wind as the pilot attempted to guide the small plane to the ground in hopes of landing safely.

Just a moment before, all that could be seen in any direction was the limitless expanse of the rocky desert; there was no village in sight. The only visible landmark was a distant mountain off to the east. The sunlight seemed to be reflecting off something halfway up the mountainside. Suddenly, the bleak desert came racing madly upward as the small single-seater biplane plunged earthward like a dead bird. In an instant, the desert and the small plane violently embraced one another in a thunderous crash and a blinding cloud of dust and sand. Then all was silent and still.

The pilot slowly climbed out of the wreckage of the plane, dazed but uninjured, except for a few bruises. "Thank God, no bones are broken and I'm still alive. But you, old friend, don't look so good," the pilot said to the plane. One wing was shattered, while the nose and fuselage were buried in the rocky sand all the way to the wings. The sun blistered down with intense heat as the pilot looked out across the barren wasteland. In every direction, there was nothing but desert, endless sand and rocks.

The chances of being rescued in such a deserted area, or even seen by some passing plane, were indeed slim, so the pilot decided to go in search of help. "I'm lucky—at least at my last refueling, I stored three canteens of water on board." The best heading to start walking seemed to be east, in the direction where just before the crash the pilot had seen that towering mountain.

Collecting the three water canteens, the pilot began the journey to the desert mountain. Overhead, the sky was an open door to a great oven. The desert wind came in sandpaper waves, as the sun blistered sand and skin. While frequently thirsty, the pilot carefully rationed the small supply of water. At long last, over the top of the sizzling rocks and sand of the horizon, a mountain peak became visible. As the hours passed, the mountain rose higher and higher out of the horizon. At the end of the day, the mountain stood halfway to the sky, watermelon colored by the fiery glow of the setting sun. While hopeful that help might be near, a fear, like the rising moon, arose in the pilot's mind: the mountain might only be a mirage.

That night, wrapped only in a leather flight jacket, the pilot slept on the desert ground. The next morning, stiff and sore from a restless, chilly night under the stars, the pilot resumed the journey to the mountain. The sun rose directly behind the peak, causing shafts of golden light to shoot out from behind the mountain like flaming arrows attacking the darkness of the dying night.

By late morning, the pilot reached the base of the mountain. Directly ahead, a crude stone hut was visible. As the pilot approached the hut, an old man in a black robe emerged from a narrow doorway. The white-haired man appeared to be a rabbi. To the pilot's surprise, he made his hoarse greeting in English: "Do you have any water?"

The pilot offered the old rabbi a drink from one of the canteens and asked, "What are you doing alone out here in this barren desert?"

"I am the rabbi guardian of this synagogue shrine. This is the Holy Mountain, stranger." The old white-bearded man pointed to a stone ledge above them. "On that very ledge—yes, that very one—the All Holy One gave to Moses the Ten Commandments!" The old man drank deeply from the canteen, wiped his mouth and continued, "And, over there—see that large rock jutting out from the mountain? That is the very rock that Moses struck so that the All Holy and Nameless One could provide water for the poor Jews wandering in the desert." His voice suddenly lost its enthusiasm. "Alas, it no longer gives water. Like the flood of holy Jewish pilgrims who once flocked here in droves, it too has dried up!" The old rabbi ran his tongue slowly and sensuously over his dry lips as he eyed the pilot's other two canteens.

The pilot did not respond to the old man's story that this was *the* holy mountain of the Ten Commandments, but asked, "If I'm to get out of this desert alive, I'll have to refill my canteen. Are there any springs of water higher up on the mountain? I've only two canteens of water left now."

"No! Why should there be? As I told you, *this* is the rock that quenched the thirst of the chosen people! I know that someday, yes, someday, this rock, like Israel, will again become a fountain. Yes, someday, the Promise will be fulfilled. Patience is needed...."

The pilot thanked the old rabbi for his kindness and began walking northeast along the base of the mountain with the intention of striking out across the desert again. Suddenly, a narrow path leading up the side of the mountain appeared. Looking up the twisting pathway, the pilot noticed for the first time that about halfway up the mountain there were several structures. The searing midday sun was reflecting off something on top of one of them. "That must be what I saw on the side of the mountain from my plane before I crashed! With luck, I may find some water up there."

After climbing for about an hour, a cluster of three small shrine-like churches appeared. On the top of two of the stone buildings were crosses that reflected the intense sunlight. As the pilot reached the first church, out came an aged, stooped priest in a faded black cassock. With open arms, he said, "Welcome, welcome, pilgrim! Do you have any water?"

"Yes, father. Here, help yourself." As the priest eagerly drank from the second canteen, the pilot asked, "Father, what is this place?"

"Child of God, this is *the* Holy Mountain! Here, at this precise spot," he said as he pointed to a large rock that formed part of the wall of the little church, "Jesus was transfigured in glory as the true Son of God before his chosen disciples. I am the priest guardian of this shrine, the Church of the Transfiguration. May I have another small sip? I'm really very thirsty!"

The old priest gulped from the canteen, wiping his lips on the sleeve of his cassock. "But I'll tell you, it's a lonely job, I mean, ah, mission. You see, these days only a handful—if that—of pilgrims like yourself come here to pray."

"I'm not a pilgrim, father. I'm a pilot. My plane crashed

out there in the desert. I've come up here looking for help and for water. Don't you have any?"

"All I have, my child, is a little holy water. I'm sorry. I've been tempted, mind you, to drink it just to slack my thirst, but...look at the time! It's time for noon prayers! I must go now and ring the bell. Thank you for the water. Are you sure you don't wish to purchase even a small bottle of holy water?"

"No, father, thanks anyway." The old, stooped priest turned and entered the little church.

Just across the road was a second church, which had a large onion-like dome on top of it. As a bell rang out from the top of the Church of the Transfiguration, from the onion-domed church came an equally aged priest with a long white beard. Dressed in the black robes of an Orthodox monk, he greeted the pilot, "Welcome. God be with you, holy pilgrim. Do you have any water?"

The monk's eyes danced with delight as he consumed what water was left in the second canteen. Wiping his lips, he added, "Come inside, pilgrim, to the Shrine of the Transfiguration." The monk led the pilot inside the small, dark church where a few skinny candles were flickering. "See there, next to the icon screen, the very rock upon which our Lord and Savior Jesus Christ stood as he was transfigured in light and glory."

"Excuse me, father, but I was told the transfiguration of Jesus happened over there, across the road where the Catholic shrine is located!"

"Oh, no, pilgrim, *this* is the holy rock. Don't listen to that beardless Roman heretic. Come, light a votive candle; light two or three. Perhaps you would like to buy an icon, as would any holy pilgrim?"

"Sorry, father, I'm not a pilgrim, only a pilot who's lost in the desert. I've come in search of help and water."

"A godless age, I swear! A faithless time, filled with godless people," muttered the old monk as he shuffled off into the darkness. The pilot made a profound bow to the icon screen and walked out of the shrine into the blinding noontime sunlight.

Directly ahead was a whitewashed building that gleamed in the desert sunlight. Unlike the other two, on the top of this church was no cross. However, next to the doorway was a sign in English that read, ROCK OF AGES CHRISTIAN CHURCH. Standing in the doorway was a woman in a clerical collar clutching a large black Bible close to her heart.

"Welcome, friend, to the true Church of Christ! Do you, by some remote chance, I hope, have any water you could spare?" The pilot handed her the last full canteen from which she drank deeply. She handed it back with a smile. "Have you been baptized in the Spirit? If not, stranger, come in and let me pray over you."

"At this moment, pastor, I'd rather be baptized in water! You don't have any of that, do you?"

"No. And, I've begun to think the Missionary Society back home has completely forgotten that I even exist! Friend, let me tell you, it's so lonely out here on this mountain. It's been years now since a Bible tour has come to visit and pray here. God in heaven, it's lonely on this mountain!"

"I can understand that your mission out here could be lonely, but may I ask, why don't you visit your neighbors, the priest or the monk who live just across the road?"

"We have nothing in common to share, except maybe our thirst. You say you're lost? You certainly look like it. But the answer is simple: Return to the Bible! Jesus alone can give you the water that will quench your thirst forever. Friend, our Savior and Lord Jesus alone is the fountain of living water. Let us bow our heads and—"

"Thank you, reverend, I would like to pray, but I must be on my way. I have to find some water, and then find my way out of this desert." As the pilot turned to leave, the minister pleaded, "Please, stranger, before you leave, could I have just one more small sip from your canteen? It's so hot today!"

As she drank deeply, the pilot saw that the path that had led to the three churches continued on up the mountainside. With the hope of finding water higher up the mountain, the pilot climbed for another hour as the path grew narrower and rockier.

As the narrow way skirted the edge of a steep cliff, from high overhead came a piercing scream that sliced through the hot midafternoon air: "Be gone, Satan!"

Handfuls of rocks came crashing down from a ledge in front of a hole in the mountain that appeared to be an entrance to a cave. On the ledge, wildly waving his arms, was a skinny, youthful man dressed only in a dirty loincloth. His eyes were sunken sockets, and his scraggly brown beard reached almost to his waist. Again he screamed, "Leave me alone, Satan!"

"I'm not the devil! I'm only a pilot whose plane has crashed out there in the desert. I'm looking for water."

"Don't you try to fool me, Prince of Lies," screamed the hermit. "I *know* who you are! You've come to tempt me with the gift of clear, cool water. I heard you mention the word water. You've come to trick me into sin. Be gone, Evil One."

"Do you want some water? Here, join the parade, have a drink!" Like a spry young mountain goat, the skinny hermit leapt down over the rocks until he was standing next to the pilot who took a deep breath. The hermit smelled as if he hadn't bathed in years! His hand quivering with delight, the hermit reached for the canteen. "You're an angel of God, sent to me in my distress. How beautiful are you, the answer to my prayers!" The hermit tilted his head back and drank in great gulps.

"What are you doing all the way up here alone on this mountain?" asked the pilot, quickly reclaiming the canteen.

"How shall I address you," asked the wide-eyed hermit, his head tilted to one side, "as the Archangel Gabriel? Uriel, perhaps? Which of God's holy angels are you? No, I should not ask such a question. You, however, Holy Angel of God, have asked me why I am here. Come, let me show you my cave." He led the pilot up the path to a gaping hole in the side of the mountain. "Come inside. Look at this holy place. *This* cave is the very spot where Jesus spent his forty days in the desert. See the rock that extends outward from the face of the cliff, that one over there? That's the very rock ledge on which Jesus stood when Satan tempted him by offering to him all the kingdoms of the earth!"

The hermit's eyes lusted after the pilot's canteen as he continued, "I have come here to find God! I've lived here in this cave for ten years in solitude, in perfect chastity, fasting and praying. I have battled the legions of demons from hell who have come to visit me in every clever form and disguise the mind can imagine."

The hermit reached out his bony hand to clutch at the pilot's arm. "Friend, come live with me here in this cave. It only takes two to make a community! We can pray together, fast together and together become saints. Come and live with me, and I will teach you all the secrets of how to find God, and more importantly," and here his face took on a sinister glow, "how to escape from the Evil One."

"Thank you for the offer of such knowledge. While I appreciate such a priceless opportunity, I have to be on my way. I must find water and then find my way out of this desert."

The hermit's eyes grew larger as he whispered, "Beware, pilot, *this* mountain is the dwelling place of the Devil, the Prince of Darkness. I know, for I've seen him daily!"

The pilot said good-bye to the hermit and continued the journey up the mountain. After another thirty minutes of climbing, the pilot saw yet another building high above on the side of the mountain. This one had both a dome and a tower. A loud voice called out from the top of the tower, "Allah akbar, God is One, and Mohammed is his prophet."

"I'm sorry to interrupt your prayers," the pilot shouted up to the man, who stood at an open window at the top of the tower, "but I'm looking for water. Do you have any?"

"Water!" shouted the mullah. "I'll be down in a minute." The Muslim holy man, his brown robe rustling in his hurried descent from the minaret, said, "Ah, welcome, child of God. Did I hear you say 'water'?"

"Here," said the pilot with a smile of resignation, "I'll bet you're thirsty." The mullah drank without pausing to take a breath before finally handing back the almost empty canteen.

"Allah be praised. Blessings on you, pilgrim. Water is the most precious gift one can give in the desert. Without doubt, you must be on your way to Mecca. How fortunate that you have stopped first at this holy shrine. Here at this very mosque is located *the* cave, the very cave where the Prophet Mohammed was visited by the angel Gabriel. It was here on this mountain that Allah gave to the prophet *the* book, the final divine revelation, the Koran! And right over there, contrary to what the others say, is the very rock from which Mohammed ascended to heaven."

"From what I've read, sir, I thought that Mohammed ascended to heaven in Jerusalem, from the rock located in the mosque at the Dome of the Rock?"

"No, no, Pilgrim, it was from here, on *this* holy mountain that the Prophet's blessed ascension took place. Those who say it was in Jerusalem are wrong. Come, pilgrim, let's go inside and I'll show you the cave."

"Thank you for your offer, but you see, I must move on. I must find water. It's been almost two days now since my plane crashed in the desert, and I have only a little water left."

"In the words of the Sufi master, Olin Sufidim, 'To find God is better than to find water,'" said the mullah, his hand resting gently on the pilot's arm. "Come, let's go and venerate the holy cave."

"I'm sure that's true," replied the pilot, "I mean, those words you quoted about God and water, but I must be on my way. Is there anyone or anything higher up on this mountain?"

"No, or at least I don't think so. I have never gone any higher. Why should I? The prophecy of Mohammed was the last and the greatest of all revelations. *Nothing* more is needed! What was good enough for the Prophet, well, friend, is good enough for me!" Having said that, the mullah hurried inside the mosque for his time of appointed prayer.

The sun had by now journeyed far into the western sky. The pilot knew that the only chance of finding water, if any existed, lay somewhere on the rocky path that led to the heights of the towering mountain. The vista was breathtaking: an endless desert spread out below, yellow and barren in every direction to the edge of the horizon. While thirsty, the temptation to drink from the canteen was resisted. What little water remained needed to be conserved. After resuming the ascent, faint, almost ghostlike clouds of mist began to form. They were devoid of moisture, more like dry wisps of cotton.

Amazingly, out of the mist-like clouds came the sound of sheep! Then the clouds parted briefly, and a lone shepherd appeared leading his flock of sheep over the rocks. The shepherd was a dark-skinned, handsome youth with jet-black hair. As quickly as they had appeared, they disappeared when the gray-mist clouds shifted.

The pilot's heart pounded with excitement, for if there were sheep on top of this mountain, then there must also be water somewhere! As suddenly as the clouds had closed in, they again parted, revealing the shepherd youth now only ten feet directly ahead. "Young man," cried the pilot, "do you know where I can find water?"

The shepherd did not speak. Again the fog and mist boiled upward like steam clouds, enclosing the pilot. "It must have been a mirage!" the pilot thought. "Or perhaps I'm hallucinating—tired, thirsty and..."

As the clouds billowed about, once again the sound of sheep could be heard. This time the sound came from behind. As the pilot turned around, the clouds parted. Standing no more than an arm's length away was the dark-skinned, youthful shepherd.

The shepherd was smiling. "Are you thirsty? Come closer and..." The pilot came face to face with the youthful shepherd as a cloud enveloped both of them. This time the cloud was wet with moisture, and the thirsty pilot breathed deeply, drinking in the moist air. At that moment, the shepherd leaned forward and kissed the pilot on the lips. His kiss too was moist, sweeter than any fruit the pilot had ever tasted.

In an instant, the mountaintop was filled with a great roaring sound. Brown clouds filled with the stinging bites of dust and sand whirled like a great tornado about the mountaintop. Lifted by several pairs of hands, the limp body of the pilot was placed on a stretcher.

As the helicopter rose off the floor of the desert, the pilot's last conscious memories before they reached the hospital were of the voices. "Still alive, but unconscious. Better start an IV." Then another voice spoke, "That's strange! Look at this: three canteens, and they're all *filled* with water!"

Igor sat smiling at me from the old easy chair. Then he reached into his tail pocket and removed a long white silk scarf. Getting up from the chair, he came over and gracefully draped the aviator's scarf around my neck. "There you are, Martha, a small sign that you are indeed an ace! You are on a flight, a voyage of discovery not into outer space but inner space, a journey to find the Source." Then he began singing, "'Off you go into the wild blue yonder, flying high into the sun.' And, Martha, I do mean the *wild* blue yonder."

"Thank you, Igor, I love this white scarf. But the story, the parable: what does it mean?"

"What does it mean? Do you mean to me or to you, Martha? What it means to you is what's important. In fact, it's critical to your questventure, as you and George call your search for the flaming pearl. Like all great quests it can be dangerous and even deadly. To see God face to face, as the ancients knew, meant to die, to be zapped, eliminated, puff—gone!"

The word "gone" was barely out of his mouth when Igor disappeared from his head to his waist! Horrified, I jumped up from my chair. "Igor, Igor!"

"Don't worry, *senora*," came Igor's voice from the direction of his navel. "A little visual education to show that a questventure is no child's play. It's more than a search to find a suitable church to attend or join. It's a venture—an old word, short for adventure—an undertaking with a doubtful outcome. What makes the quest hazardous is not just in coming very close to the Source. Where to look can also be hazardous, or it can be helpful." As he spoke, his dragon's body began to materialize slowly from the waist upward. "The true pilgrimage in search of the flaming pearl doesn't set roots along the way; it's a lifetime of climbing higher and higher. It's a spiral ascent that's hard work, and it's risky, fearful and threatening because all too easily, as old sailors say, you can 'turn turtle,' you can capsize!"

"One thing seems certain, Igor: I don't need to go on some exotic pilgrimage to make life exciting! It also occurred to me that in order to keep climbing higher and higher, the best way is not alone like the pilot in your parable, but in the company of others."

"Good insight, Martha! That's also a good way not to 'turn turtle.' Having more than one in the boat helps distribute the weight. Companions can help you keep your balance. Have you and George found a group yet?"

"No, but we're working on it. We hope to get together in the next couple of weeks with some friends who may be open to being part of a questventure."

As Igor smiled at me, another amazing thing happened. His right eye became a sun and his left eye a moon! I could have sworn that I also saw two breasts form on his dragon's chest as he blew me a kiss and cried out, "*Adieu*, Madame Martha, and anchors aweigh! See, the tide has changed, and so my day is arranged!"

Igor gave me a snappy naval salute, clicked his heels and flew up and out the door. Soaring easily above the treetops, he banked sharply to the right and circled over the top of the hermitage. Standing in the doorway, I waved good-bye with my white scarf and said aloud to myself, "I wonder if I'm the only one in this neighborhood who's witnessed a flying dragon's takeoff into the wild blue yonder?"

I returned to the desk with Igor's words echoing in my heart: "What did it mean to you, Martha?" What wisdom did Igor, or was is it Sophia, cleverly sandwich into that parable for me?

For a long time I sat in the chair and explored the story's different aspects: a search for water at numerous "wellspring" sources that were themselves thirsty; how it was sad, and funny, at times; the mysterious ending with the shepherd.

The day is now gone. Time to depart. I feel renewed, and I'm eager to share supper with George. I'm sure he'll find this tale a delight. It's like a second installment of Lucky Lux—which he loved. Before I close the cover of this logbook, I note my intention for the coming weeks.

Intention: To search beyond the various traditions, beyond the structures—each claiming to be the true one—to find the Source. May I search in the most unlikely places to find the dark-eyed, seductive Shepherd of Souls and feel his kiss on my lips.

I conclude my hermitage time with a prayer:

Blessed One,
    you who gave to your thirsty children
    flowing water from a rock
    during their desert exodus,
    make rocks flow for this your thirsty child.
Creator of fountains, pools and vast oceans,
    as I wander in my desert,
    fill my heart's jug with your elixir of life.
Come, my beloved,
    on this my solitary "desert day"
    and kiss me on the lips.
Kiss me not with a hot passionate love
    but with your moist, gentle and fertile kiss.
I pray in the name of the Good Shepherd,
    the Endless Fountain of Living Water.
Amen.

# Ship's Log

**Vessel:** THE HERMITAGE

**Officer at the Helm:** GEORGE

**Date:** SATURDAY, SEPTEMBER 23

**Time:** 0900 HOURS — 9:00 A.M.

An early morning rain has been falling, causing some of the yellow autumn leaves to fall with it. The backyard has a shiny, wet yellow-green carpet of grass and newly fallen leaves. This is a welcome rain; it's been dry now for several weeks.

While the dry, mild weather has enhanced this Indian summer, it's been too dry. My spirit, like the earth, could use a good shower. I feel dry of soul. Tried to pray this morning, but all I got was words.

*1200 HOURS — NOON*

No sign of Igor yet. The day is going well, even though, with all the work that's piling up in this busy season at the office, I feel I should be doing something constructive with my time out here. I was tempted to bring my unanswered mail with me, but I resisted. Still, it's amazing how difficult I find it to do nothing, at least nothing that's productive.

Time for lunch. I plan to make a sandwich in the small galley-kitchen which Martha and I have created here. Our ship's galley is hardly large enough for a two-man Japanese sub; it has only a small camper-style refrigerator, a microwave oven, a hot plate and a coffeemaker. But it's enough for us to have light meals here.

In the corner opposite the prayer space, we've set up a Japanese screen, behind which is a camper-style portable toilet. Our makeshift hermitage is really very comfortable; it allows us to stay inside here for an entire day, and even overnight.

Not having eaten breakfast, I'm beginning to feel a bit hungry. My lunch will consist of an apple, some juice and a sandwich. I'll create it slowly, with care, mindfully adding each element. I'll try to eat it in the same manner, leisurely and mindfully.

*1500 Hours - 3:00 P.M.*

The rains have moved on toward the east, and the sky overhead is clearing. A beautiful rainbow has appeared in the eastern sky. I was reading when Igor arrived singing, "Somewhere over the rainbow, way up high. Birds fly over the rainbow; why, then, oh why can't I?"

"Igor, welcome," I laughed. "I wish you would teach me how to fly. I'd really like to fly over the rainbow."

"If you were a bluebird and able to fly over the rainbow, George, you would discover a wonderful place. Not the land of Oz, but a land where every day there's a beautiful rainbow in the sky. Or so goes the story told to me as a child by an old and wise senior dragon."

I smiled, for I felt a soul-shower coming. The pores of my spirit opened wide as I said, "Please tell me that story, Igor, if you can remember it."

Igor sank into the old easy chair as effortlessly as a cloud sitting down on a mountaintop. Then he winked at me and began:

# Once, far from here,

yet not that far in distance since it was just over the rainbow, there was a country called the Land of the Perpetual Rainbow. Because of the rainbow's perpetual presence, those who lived on the other side of the rainbow lived contented and hopeful lives—until slowly the rainbow began to fade. Day by day it grew fainter and fainter until it completely disappeared! On that day, gloom and despair began to settle like fine gray dust on the land.

A silence, not the good kind but a strange and empty silence, filled the land. No songs were sung, not even those of birds, no laughter was heard and no one danced. Also, no lovers became engaged, no couples married and no mothers gave birth to children. Without the rainbow, who could look forward to a new tomorrow with hope?

The council of the elders, scholars and priests met, and the elders decided that an army should be sent forth to search for the rainbow and bring it back. Knights and warriors armed with swords and spears marched forth in all four directions to great fanfare and the shouts of cheering crowds. Many months later, however, they straggled sadly home without having found any sign of the lost rainbow.

The scholars then proposed that the rainbow may have suffered from fallen arches and had simply slipped below the horizon. The council ordered that an expedition of scientists be sent forth to the other side of the earth. Sadly, after many long months, they too returned to report that they had found no sign of the lost rainbow.

Next, the priests gave orders that all church bells be tolled as at a funeral, and they declared a holy fast for all the people. The highest in the realm to the lowest, even the beasts of burden, put on sackcloth and ashes. Animals and people marched in long, purple penance processions, chanting prayers that begged God to bring back the rainbow. After forty long days of itching from their sackcloth garments and stomachs aching from fasting, the people saw sadly that the sky was still without their beloved rainbow.

The gray gloom that began as a fine dust had now piled up in great drifts both outside and inside people's homes as well as public buildings. While the sun shone each day, the despair that covered the land made even daytime seem like midnight.

One dark day, a youthful man from a small village presented himself to the great council of elders. He was called the Dreamer by the people of his village, and he proposed to the council that he would go and find the lost rainbow. At his offer, the entire council chamber was filled with loud laughter.

"You, a mere dreamer!" said one elder. "Do you think that you can do what our great armies, the expeditions of scholars, and all the holy prayers and penances of the priests have failed to do?"

"Yes, venerable elders, I've come to ask your permission and blessing on my journey to bring back our rainbow." Again the chamber echoed with laughter.

Holding up his aged hand, the chief elder silenced the loud laughter and asked the Dreamer to step out of the council chambers and wait. When the door was closed, he said, "Members of the council, consider well the situation. What have we to lose by our sending forth this dreamer? Perhaps a spark of hope may be lit in the hearts of the people. While they are more docile without the rainbow and easier to govern, we must do something lest the people rebel and demand new leaders capable of finding the lost rainbow!"

Heads bobbed up and down in agreement as the elder continued, "If this young fool does find it—which I assure you is highly unlikely—we can claim credit for having sent him to search for it. If he does not find the rainbow, we are no poorer than we are today." So with their permission, the Dreamer set forth to find the lost rainbow.

He left by the Sunrise Gate and traveled eastward. After some miles, he entered the great dark forest in which legend said lived a fierce dragon and all kinds of terrible evils. The towering trees overhead swayed slightly in the wind, and he felt they were trying to tell him something. The Dreamer, however, did not know the language of trees and so could not tell what they were trying to say.

Around the trunks and branches of some of the oldest

and largest trees large green serpents were coiled, cleverly disguised as rope-like vines. The Dreamer shuddered as he sensed their powerful poison. He wished he had an umbrella to protect himself from their deadly droppings.

Although he had traveled only a short distance into the forest, he began to get weary. Yawning, he paused to lean on his staff. While forcing himself to continue, his weariness grew the farther into the forest he traveled. Again and again he was forced to stop and rest. Yet, while he longed to lie down and go to sleep, he pushed himself onward in his search for the lost rainbow, which he now felt certain was hidden somewhere in this dark forest.

Pausing again to lean on his staff, he saw through the dense thicket of trees a blue-green lake. As a banquet table draws a starving man, so the coolness of the lake drew him, and he hurried toward it. Reaching the shoreline, he sank to the ground yawning again and again.

It felt so good to finally stop and rest. Not even a whisper of wind moved in the forest and all was deadly still. As he looked at the lake, the blue-green waters swirled this way and that in beautiful slow spirals. He yawned again and hung his head between his knees, so weary was he.

Never before had he been this tired, and he yearned to slip naked into the water just as he would slip into his bed at the end of a long day. However, he struggled to remain alert, for he knew that this lake was not a bed. As he wrestled with weariness, the continuously coiling, many-colored waters of the lake silently promised rest and peace.

Then, as suddenly as a shooting star crosses the dark night sky, he realized that the lake was not really a lake! It was a giant serpent-like dragon coiled in the hollow of the earth! For some strange reason, however, it did not impress the Dreamer as evil, as had those large serpents he had seen coiled around the trees. In a short time, however, he began to doubt the reality of his discovery as once more he was overcome with great heaviness.

He again yearned to slide off the bank, sink into the peaceful waters and simply go to sleep. He longed to just let go and be at peace and have no more meetings to attend, no more people to visit or letters to write to promote the Dream of which he was the carrier. The carrying of any dream is hard work, and he was so weary of bearing his. He wished for a time when he would no longer have to prepare enthusiastic talks about the Dream to be given to people who were at best only half-interested in a more beautiful tomorrow.

He slowly leaned back and laid flat on the grassy bank. He began to close his eyes when he suddenly remembered that the lake was not a lake but a dragon pretending to be a lake. Sitting up, he shouted, "I know who you are! You're the one who stole the rainbow. Even now you're making a meal of it, and you also want to devour me. I must escape from here as quickly as possible." He forced himself to stand up and seize a huge boulder laying nearby. He struggled to lift it high overhead. Summoning all the force within him, he threw the boulder into the heart of the waters.

A towering geyser of blue-green water shot upward into the sky, and out of it came the rainbow all covered with the dragon's teeth marks. The rainbow, glorious and luminous, arched overhead in the blue sky and began healing itself of the great chunks that had been eaten from it.

A hair-raising, piercing scream erupted from the center of the lake as a violent earthquake shook the ground. What seemed to be an earthquake, however, was actually the great dragon standing erect. The menacing creature thrashed its horned tail about, causing tall trees to crash to the ground as if a hurricane had swept across the forest. Out of the great dark pit that had appeared to be a lake, came long, green, coiling tentacles grasping after the Dreamer as he ran for his life.

As he struggled to maintain the distance between himself and the dragon's reach, the Dreamer's body felt as if it were made of stone, so heavy was it with weariness. Overhead, the great vines that hung from the trees swung down and also tried to catch him. He dodged left and right to escape their grasp as he felt the hot breath and the deadly presence of the dragon ready to devour him.

Finally, emerging from the edge of the forest, the Dreamer saw the city from which he had departed on his quest. Arched high above it was the rainbow! Church bells were ringing as joyfully as at a royal wedding, and countless colored flags were waving in the wind. Exhausted, he stumbled through the city gates shouting, "Close the gates! Guard well the walls! The great dragon is coming close behind!"

Quickly a crowd gathered around him as he cried out, "Friends, I return with the rainbow—and also with precious knowledge for all of us. While our rainbow has returned, we must beware, for we can just as easily lose it again. Take care to guard your dreams."

Pointing eastward he said, "Be vigilant. The evil dragon comes not as a great serpent! It may be so cleverly disguised that you will not recognize it. But you *will* feel its presence. It will unrelentingly weave over you a wrought-iron web of weariness, seducing you to slumber and to surrender your dream. Surely each one of you, at some time in your life, has had a dream!"

Someone in the crowd shouted, "I once dreamed of being a great musician and making beautiful music, but..." Another voice cried out, "I dreamed of having a family, of living in a lovely home, but..." Still another shouted, "I once dreamed that I would be a great teacher, helping the young to..."

"Friends," said the Dreamer, "take up again those dreams that you once gave up—one by one—for it was the gradual surrender of them that caused the rainbow to fade away and finally disappear. Beware, however, you who dare to take up again your dreams, for the dragon feeds like a hungry lion on the vitality, hope and very aliveness of dreamers, who are forever youthful regardless of their age. Yet take heart. Know that as long as there are dreamers who refuse to surrender to weariness, who refuse to give up their dreams, the rainbow will remain always in our sky."

Then someone in the crowd cried out, "Then we must guard well our dreams, lest the dragon devour them!"

"Indeed, be on your guard," replied the Dreamer, "but

the dragon who stole the rainbow can't really eat your dreams! All great dreams are divine—any dream that makes you or your world more beautiful. No, your dreams will survive, for the evil dragon cannot digest divine food—and dreams are divine. Now dreamers on the other hand, dreamers are flesh and blood! The great serpent-dragon hungers like a vampire for the lifeblood and flesh of dreamers.

"Some of you here need not be afraid of the dragon. If you have given up on your dream or never had one, there is no reason to fear. Those who lack a dream are safe, for they are dead and the great serpent-dragon is no scavenger. It eats nothing dead!"

"The great serpent-dragon eats nothing dead, nothing dead!" Igor repeated, then fell silent. We both sat in silence. The first thought that struck me was the paradox that the teller of the tale sitting next to me was a cousin to the devourer of dreamers! It didn't take time, however, to recognize that just as there are good angels and bad angels, there are beneficent as well as evil dragons.

My silent reflections quickly revolved around the conversations Martha and I had had about the weariness we both have experienced, that destructive kind of exhaustion, the sense of being so tired of soul that you lack enthusiasm for—

"For prayer, for the journey, for the work of making the Dream a reality," Igor said aloud, finishing my thoughts.

"Igor, you Peeping Tom! I should have drawn the blinds

on my mind. But you're right, as usual, those were the very words I was about to say."

"George, you're not unlike so many others, especially in your work-addicted society. When you're young, you have lots of energy. As you age it becomes more difficult not only to be enthusiastic but also hopeful. Older people tend to be like the Saturday rain clouds outside; their thoughts are gray and gloomy about the condition of the world. Seeded with such thoughts, they often rain on other peoples' parades! Their conversations are usually limited to—are anchored in—gloomy stories about the growing wave of crime, the collapse of moral values and what's wrong in the world or with young people. Therefore, few are the rainbows they are able to see!"

"Why do you think that happens?" I asked.

"Custer's Last Stand, George! The slings and arrows of outrageous fortune—and those of the outrageous establishment, whether the political, cultural, business or church establishment. Too many arrows have pierced the elderly's rainbow dreams and hearts, and pierced hearts leak hope.

"As you age, your dreams and hopes lose their resiliency and more easily become victims of time and reality. It's easy to give up hoping that things will really change, that conditions in the world will essentially get better. Then you reach a certain age—it varies from person to person—and you surrender, realizing that you'll not see your hopes or dreams achieved in your lifetime! Feeling surrounded, as was General Custer, by a superior force, the aging surrender hope and become prisoners of gloom."

"Martha told me your parable about Robin Hood, who didn't surrender. He sang on despite the odds, regardless of the slings and arrows, especially the most poisonous of all arrows—the fact that so few were being changed by his song."

"Yes, that's one good example, but there are others. Among the greatest heroes are the aged who have not grown old. Remember how the dreamer in today's parable spoke about the necessity of keeping one's vitality and not giving in to the temptation of weariness. The secret to resisting that oppressive weariness of soul lies in what you're wearing now,

George—your slacks!"

"My slacks? What do they have to do with exhausted souls?"

"Ah, a bit of trivia, a tiny tidbit from my titanic treasure trove of trifles. Way back in the late 1940s, the Haggar Corporation coined the word 'slacks' for their new product. They introduced to the market a type of pants to be worn during slack time, which, in those charming laid-back days, meant the time between work and hard play."

"I see. You mean the secret is slack—that is, free—time?"

"Yep! Both of us know that you and Martha—like 85% of Americans—lack slack! Who today has free time? Who has time that's like a ship's slack sail—time with nothing to do, nothing that has to be done? With so much to do in so little time, the winds of work keep your sails full all the time. But no slack in your sails is *verboten*. It spells big trouble if a storm suddenly hits your ship."

"I'm no great sailor, Igor, but that only makes sense."

"No wonder you're weary and find it hard to be a dreamer of a better world—equal rights, justice—the big dreams. While some people are disciplined to weekly exercise and hard play, few are disciplined to weekly slack. Yet, slack not only *sounds* like snack, slack time is food for the soul. That's the quest-wisdom, George the Dreamer, of your disciplined time here in your hermitage!"

"Martha usually wears 'em here as well. They could become our hermit habits!" I laughed. "We could create an entire new religious dress as significant as the orange robe of the Hindu saddhu, the purple robe of the Tibetan monk, or the Benedictine monk's black habit. By our slacks they will know that we are slackers!"

"Aye, mate, 'by the cut of his jib' is sailor's slang for knowing someone by how he or she behaves. George, take some time to reflect on today's tale. As for me, the telltales tell this old dragon that it's time to go."

"Telltales?"

"More ship talk, lad. Telltales are short strings of yarn attached to the shrouds—which are the wires that stabilize the mast. Telltales tell you which direction the wind is blowing. I hung a few telltales off the gutter of your hermitage—see 'em? And they say the wind has shifted. It's time for me to be on that new wind. *Ate logo*—till we meet again."

A sudden gust of wind blew open the door and danced, veritably pirouetted, into the hermitage. Igor, as if he were a feather or a piece of paper, floated upward on the whirlwind, swirled round in circles and then was gone in an instant. I looked out the window, but there was no sign of him. All I saw were the telltales, those pieces of colored yarn dangling from the gutter, swaying in the afternoon wind.

I close this entry in our hermitage log, and my time at the helm, aware of the need to protect an endangered species: my dreams, especially my present dream of finding the flaming pearl. If they are to survive both the aging process and the slings and arrows of daily bad news, if my immune system is to ward off the disease of cynicism, then I must be like my slacks! I intend to share the Rainbow story and Igor's gifts with Martha tonight at supper, slacks and all!

# Ship's Log

**Vessel:** the Hermitage

**Officer at the Helm:** Martha

**Date:** Saturday, September 30

**Time:** 1200 Hours - Noon

It's a quiet morning in early autumn. Warm and sunny, at midday I pause for a bite to eat. I smile as I think about the blue slacks I'm wearing being my religious habit. Not as romantic as some medieval nun's dress, but they hold special meaning—have become symbolic clothing—for both George and me. I wonder if Igor will say anything about them.

*1500 Hours — 3:00 P. M.*

No sign of Igor yet. I took a small nap. After I awoke, I was combing my hair when I heard a familiar tune, "It's a beautiful day in this neighborhood, a beautiful day..." I laid down my mirror. "Don't tell me Mr. Rogers has come to visit me!" Smiling and still singing, Igor appeared at my open door.

"Martha, you're 'a sight for sore eyes,' to quote old Jonathan Swift. It's a beautiful day because I'm looking at a beautiful woman—whose beauty is indeed a cure for sore eyes, if mine were sore. I like your holy hermit's habit, your blue slacks!"

I was embarrassed that Igor arrived as I was combing my hair. I felt a sharp tug of guilt about vanity. Public grooming of oneself isn't proper, even if society gives women more freedom in public than it does to men. That's what powder rooms are for—

"Not originally," Igor said. "On old man-of-war sailing ships, powder rooms were compartments where they kept gunpowder in bulk. Excuse me, Martha, for listening in on your thoughts about vanity. For us Chinese celestial dragons, you see, your thoughts are no different than any of the sounds in creation, whether birdsongs or the babble of flowing water. Thoughts are like speech; they're forms of energy. Since we dragons have a keen, razor-sharp inner radar for detecting energy forms, it's possible for us to hear or, as you say, 'read' your thoughts! To be perfectly honest, this natural dragon ability can be a real problem at times. You can imagine, I'm sure, some of the awkward situations that can arise when you know what others are thinking!"

"I can imagine—especially since we humans often say something other than what we're thinking at the moment. And when we're not talking out loud, we talk to ourselves, another name for thinking.

"Since you've read—or rather, heard—my thoughts about vanity and especially a woman's concern about how she looks, what do you think, Igor? Should I feel guilty about wanting to make a good impression on you—or anyone for that matter?"

"Vanity is not a weakness only of women, Martha. Men are often just as concerned about their looks. Yet society permits them to have a more casual concern. *Ma chere*, don't be anxious, the sin of vanity means *excessive* concern; the concern itself is a human condition. Sadly, the Scripture lines, 'Vanity of vanities. All is vanity!' have been the root of guilt over even modest attempts to enhance one's appearance. Some spiritualities, past and present, even denounce makeup and other cosmetics as sinful. Zealous spiritual pilgrims of all traditions who make vanity *verboten* end up looking as drab and unattractive as an abandoned gas station in a ghost town. Enough, madame. With your permission, a dragon's humble parable-response to your question."

Seating himself comfortably in the old easy chair, Igor amazingly folded his legs into a yoga-like figure eight, then began:

# From the beginning

he knew he was an angel. In his mother's womb inside the mountain, he was aware that his name was Angelus! Coming forth from the quarry—as the stonecutters lowered him onto the great wagon—he rejoiced that soon all would see the splendor of his angelic beauty.

His excitement grew as the wagon lumbered toward the city whose new Gothic cathedral rose up like a great stone mountain out of the surrounding flat countryside. Entering the city, the great slab of granite was taken to the unfinished Cathedral of Notre Dame. After the stone was placed in a workshed next to the cathedral, the stone carver walked around it and studied its shape. "In this stone I see a marvelous angel, a creature of great beauty. I shall call this my masterpiece 'Angelus, the Redeeming Angel of Notre Dame,'" he said, and the heart of Angelus exploded with joy.

Then the stone carver was called to the far side of the cathedral for a meeting with the chief architect. Angelus couldn't hear what they were saying, but they seemed to be having a disagreement. At one point the stone carver pointed to the large portal that arched over the entrance, while the architect pointed upward toward the cathedral's bell towers.

Angelus was thrilled when the stone carver, with broad chisel strokes, began to release him from within the slab of granite. He was surprised, but honored, when the wife of the stone carver asked if she also could have a hand in chiseling his features. Next, one of the cathedral priests asked if he also might take the chisel, and he was followed by a teacher from the school. These and others wanted the joy of knowing they had a small part in the carving of this masterpiece.

As the work progressed, lacking a mirror, Angelus wondered what he looked like. He was excited by the praise of onlookers who expressed their awe at the craft of the master stone carver. From his position, Angelus could see the great beauty of the statues that stood over the cathedral's center doors. There in splendor was the Christ and, next to him, the Virgin Mary, for whom the cathedral was named. Mary was surrounded by saints, Old Testament prophets and countless angels. He noticed the angels' graceful upswept wings and how the folds in their robes flowed like streams of water. It was their faces, however, that were the most stunning. No saint's face, not even the Madonna's, expressed such ethereal beauty, divinity and peace.

After many months of carving, finally thick ropes were wrapped around Angelus as workers hauled him to the front of the cathedral. He could see in the portal over the front doors an unfilled space next to the statue of the prophet Elijah. "What an honor," he thought. "Think of the pilgrims who shall see me standing there and be inspired to holiness as they enter the cathedral."

The great pulleys and ropes creaked as they began to raise him up, up and up. To his surprise they did not stop at the entrance portal, but creaking and groaning with the great weight of the stone, the ropes continued to raise him higher and higher. Then, without warning, halfway up the cathedral, they stopped! From high above came shouts from the workers that something had gone wrong with the ropes and the winch raising him.

The ropes that held Angelus began slowly to twist around. To his delight he saw that he was stalled directly in front of what would be the cathedral's great rose window, but which at this point in the construction held only clear glass.

"Wonderful!" he exclaimed. "Now I can see inside the cathedral." When he looked in the window, however, Angelus screamed in terror at what he beheld. For what he saw looking out at him from inside the Cathedral of Notre Dame was a horrible monster with an ugly, almost demonic, deformed face and a beast-like body. Terrified at the beast, he tightly closed his eyes.

Then, from high above came the workers' shouts, "The ropes are tangled, we can't pull up the gargoyle!"

"Gargoyle!" screamed Angelus, as he slowly twisted in the air like a man hanged from the gallows. He realized then that the ugly image in the window was his own reflection! "My God, I've been carved into a gargoyle! What have they done to me? I'm an angel, not a waterspout carved like some grotesque bird or beast, a gutter to throw dirty rainwater away from the building!" Tears flooded from his eyes, as high overhead came the shout, "It's free again, up he comes."

He was placed on a ledge next to the bell tower and cemented into place, this half-bird, half-beast that crouched on its haunches with bat-like wings sweeping behind it. The mouth of Angelus, which he thought had been carved wide-open to sing God's praises, was instead the spout out of which he would vomit rainwater. Each day his pain-filled eyes looked down on the medieval city far below. Each day at sunrise, from his open mouth came the cry, "God, I hate who I am. And I hate You, You who let them, all of them, deform me and make me so ugly! I hate You!"

Angelus was consumed by rage. Indeed he was stone, but he was less granite than petrified poison. It was no wonder that he prayed to die. He prayed that he might be struck by lightning; his mortar loosened, he would fall from his perch to his destruction at the base of the cathedral.

One day a flock of sparrows came, saying that God had heard his plea and had sent them as divine messengers. They were to peck away at the cement that held him in place so that he might fall to his death. They pecked and pecked away for weeks until Angelus screamed in anger, "Leave me alone! It will take centuries for you to free me!"

He also prayed for darkness, for an eclipse, whenever pilgrims would come up to the top of the bell tower to look out over the city. "Look," they would cry out—since he had become legendary—"there is the Monster of Notre Dame! Have you ever seen anything so ugly?"

One day a group of orphan children, led by a nun, came to the bell tower. The ugliness of Angelus was more attractive to them than the view. A spring storm was forming overhead, and the nun began to gather up her charges like an anxious mother hen. Off in the distance, long jagged fingers of lightning stabbed downward, and thunder rumbled loudly. As the children quickly scampered down from the tower, one little girl lingered behind, fascinated by Angelus.

A sudden gust of wind blew her bonnet off and sent it out of the tower onto the slanted roof. Fearfully, she reached over the parapet to get it. "Sister will be angry if I lose my bonnet," she cried. However, she leaned too far and fell out of the tower onto the slanted roof, sliding down to the very edge. Fortunately, the ledge stopped her slide, and she was able to regain her balance and stand up.

Meanwhile, the top of the cathedral's steeple was now covered with a swirling dark cloud. From the center of the cloud came a blinding bolt of lighting which struck the cross on the spire. Blue-white tongues licked down the steeple, running instantly like liquid fire down the sides of the towers.

"My prayers have been answered," screamed Angelus, "now I shall die!"

The little girl, terrified by the lightning and high winds, began to teeter as the serpent-like blue tongues of lightning licked quickly along the stone ledge. Noticing her great danger, compassion suddenly filled Angelus like a flood as the girl swayed back and forth in the wind on the edge of death. To his surprise Angelus found the rage and anger inside him reversing direction. Like a transformer, he now willed to be something other than what he had become. He radically redirected the dark energy locked inside him and turned it into light. Dramatically empowered by this transformation, with great effort he pulled up one stone claw, jerking it free from the ledge. Astonishingly, it was transfigured into a graceful angelic hand that quickly reached out and cradled the little girl.

Soon afterwards the rain stopped and the wind ceased. When the nun and one of the bell ringers appeared in the tower, they gasped, and quickly traced over themselves the sign of the cross. The little girl was safe! In one hand she clutched her bonnet, while both arms were wrapped around the neck of the gargoyle, the Monster of Notre Dame. The bell ringer climbed out and onto to the roof and led her back, announcing, "She's safe, Sister, but look at the gargoyle! It was struck by the lighting."

Indeed, lightning had badly disfigured Angelus with a great crack. His mouth was even wider now; gone were the jagged fang-like teeth. The crack's upward slant had changed his expression into a perpetual smile. Something else had changed too. Angelus became the most famous of all the cathedral's gargoyles, becoming known as "the Smiling Monster, the Redeeming Angel of Notre Dame."

Igor was silent. I did not open my eyes. I kept them closed because they were filled with tears. Beautiful in itself, Igor's parable had awaken the past for me. There was a flood of memories of my childhood and my teenage years, memories of how concerned I have always been about how I appear to others.

Transformation is not an achievement of cosmetics or high fashion. It's breaking through to your true face. It's knowing who you are from the beginning—in the womb of the mystical mountain—that counts. Regardless of society's standards for beauty, the styles that change so radically from age to age, if only you can remember who you are most deeply inside, then...

I opened my eyes to see that I was alone. I wiped a tear from my eye, grateful that Igor, with great sensitivity, had left me alone with my private thoughts. It's almost time for me to leave. Before I do, I close my entry in the ship's log with my usual intention and prayer.

Intention: In these coming days, while still concerned about my external appearance, I will not forget who I am inside. While properly caring for my face and body, I'll not neglect to inspect my spirit as well. May I remind myself of the unique

77

beauty of God that I bring to my world, simply by being me.
I conclude the day with my prayer:

O Wondrous One,
  whose beauty fills heaven and earth,
  remind me that I am your mirror.
Continue, O God,
  to fuel my desire for these slack times
  so that in this solitude
  I can hear your voice calling me,
  "My beloved, my beautiful one."
I rejoice at the end of this day
  that I am indeed both of those in your sight.
Grant me the grace
  to see myself as you, my Lovely One, see me.
Amen.

# Ship's Log

**Vessel:** THE HERMITAGE

**Officer at the Helm:** GEORGE

**Date:** SATURDAY, OCTOBER 7

**Time:** 0800 HOURS - 8:00 A.M.

Igor has just left, after having awakened me before sunrise. I'd decided to spend the night here on the cot, and was in a deep sleep when I felt a hot wind, rich with the smell of carnations, blowing in my face. I awoke to find Igor leaning over me. With a wide grin he was gently blowing his dragon's breath over my face.

"Igor," I said, sitting up in surprise, "you're here really early today!"

"*Requiescat in pace,*" Igor said in a mock priestly solemn tone. "May he rest in peace! A rest—siesta, nap, couple of winks, a night in the feathers—whose peaceful slumber I've now interrupted.

"Alas, comrade George, I have a full day ahead of me—which is a polite way to say that this Saturday I'm really busy! I was afraid that unless I came before the day got going I might miss seeing you. I didn't startle you, did I?"

"Surprised, yes, but not startled. Carnations are among my favorite flowers. As I awoke I had the sense that I was floating in a field of them, surrounded by their scent, only to find that it was just an old dragon's breath! Thanks for that aromatic awakening."

"It's good at times to be awakened by a sense other than sound."

"Igor, I'm curious about the change I see in you. I don't recall, when you guided me on the quest several years ago, you being so playful, so whimsical. Did something happen, or is it a sign of age?"

"True, age does grant certain freedoms. But you know, Sent George, it's more that *you* have changed! My dragon radar sensed that you needed a more level approach before, seeing as how you were operating under the illusion that religion is a serious business. And who takes a joker, a *jongleur*, seriously?"

"A what?"

"A *jongleur*, a wandering medieval minstrel, a free-spirited entertainer found on the roads—and, I might add, hanging around certain hermit toolsheds—in France and Norman England. Alas, fair George, it's a shame that all ministers are not minstrels."

"I agree, Igor *Jongleur*, you wise old gypsy dragon."

"Bah! *Old* dragon, my foot! George, I could use a cup of good coffee. Let me fix some for both of us while you get dressed.

"*L'chaim*—to life, George," Igor toasted with his coffee cup.

I returned his toast, "*A vuestra salud*—to your health, Igor!"

"And *a vuestra salud* to your small group of companions, George! Have you given it a name?"

"Yes and no; we want to keep it simple and for now are just calling it 'the group.' Thanks for your suggestion about forming it. The first gathering went well, I guess. At least we had a lively discussion—in fact, it centered on your parable about Angelus."

"I'm glad that it provided a round table for some soul talk. It's not easy to open the gate to that secret garden of the soul. A parable can be a great way to begin the process. At the same time, I hope that your times together include more than just talk."

"It does! We've decided to start with a time of prayer, silent prayer—at least for now. For a group with such a variety of spiritual tastes, it's a form of prayer that everyone feels comfortable with."

"George, maybe we should begin this morning with a little of that silent sunlight that opens the pores of the soul." We sipped our morning coffee together in silence, watching the eastern sky grow orange before the sun appeared. The sunrise ushered in a crisp October morning, full of life and beauty.

Igor then proposed that we do our morning meditation together. So we sat silently in the prayer corner for about twenty minutes. I was impressed that such a large dragon could so easily sit in the lotus position.

After meditation, we prayed a psalm together and finished with some Tibetan chanting. I've always enjoyed praying with Igor, and as he sat down in the easy chair I said, "Igor, your presence added a wonderful sense of depth to my prayer this morning. It was like I was praying with the past, with the ancient ones, as well as with all creatures wild and tame."

Igor added, "And insane!"

"Well, yes, my beloved and insane dragon master! As my personal MOO, Master of the Occasion, what did you bring in your tail pocket to enlighten Sent George this morning?"

Pretending he was digging deeply in his back tail pocket, Igor shortly held out two closefisted claws, saying, "Choose, George! Which shall it be, where lies the mysterious parable, in the right or the left?"

"Left," I said, tapping it with my finger.

"*Magnifico!* Wise choice, George, a wise and challenging one," Igor said, slowly unfolding his five-clawed dragon's fist. With no further fanfare, my mentor began to weave this tale:

# In the special place

where all stories begin, there was a large neighborhood. All the other houses in the neighborhood called it the "big house." The great dwelling stood high atop a hill, making it look even larger and more impressive. Soundly constructed out of stone and wood, the big house was three stories high and had many rooms.

One day an old man came walking up to the big house, his cane tap-tap-tapping along the walk that led up to the front door. He paused for a moment to catch his breath and then rang the doorbell. No one answered. He rang it again and waited. No response.

Trying the doorknob, he found that the door wasn't locked. He pushed open the door with his cane and asked, "Anyone home?" There was a long silence, at the end of which the old man gave the door a whack with his cane. A small voice answered, "Who's there?"

"Just an old Jew," the old man said.

"What do you want?" returned the small voice which seemed to come from somewhere within the walls of the big house.

"I'm interested in living here; I would like to move in. You see, my house is the large one at the end of the street, but I want to live somewhere else."

"You mean the grand stone house with all the marble? But why would you want to move?" asked the small voice. "Does the roof leak? Is the plumbing broken?"

"No, I'm lonely," answered the old Jew. "Oh, my children do come to visit me, true. Not as often as before, but a few are faithful in coming by. Yet they rarely speak to me! Oh, they speak about me, like one would speak about the wallpaper—but hardly ever to me."

"I'm sorry to hear that," replied the small voice. "I see how you could be lonely."

"Yes, of course," said the gray-haired Jew as he eyed the elegant carpets and comfortable-looking furniture. "I have a few questions, please, if you don't mind. May I ask: Who lives in this house? Are they nice people?"

"No one lives here!" replied the small voice. "While a

family does call this home, they live elsewhere."

"You mean," asked the old man with childlike delight, "they have a winter home in Florida?"

"No, what I mean is...well, it's confusing...they don't really live here—they...stay here," answered the small voice. "You see, the Mr. and Mrs. live at work! The Mrs., you know, has a grand profession and has really made something of her life, and the Mr. is what you'd call up-and-coming. The three children live at school, or the gym or in their cars."

The old Jew stood shaking his head, his eyebrows knitted together in puzzlement. Then, raising his head slightly, he began to sniff. "Smells to me like someone lives here!"

"Well, yes," answered the small voice, "*they* still do! This is still home to some old, retired memories. Please come, I'll introduce you to them." Slowly from out of the walls there appeared faded, gray, ghostlike memories. The living room was the first to speak of the memories that it held. It told of family gatherings and games played together, of hours filled with reading books and newspapers, of the family discussing what they had read and of people conversing in the warmth of the crackling fireplace.

Next, the dining room shared memories of long, leisurely meals rich with conversation, of feast day dinners with the family gathered around the long table. Like treasures were the memories it revealed about shared prayers of gratitude on special occasions and blessings pronounced on birthdays and anniversaries.

While wearing a white apron that was old and faded, kitchen was nonetheless plump and happy. Its voice was rich with wondrous smells and shared memories of meals cooked with love. It stirred up again times of dreams, troubles and fears shared as food was being prepared or dishes washed.

The doorway chimed in with fond memories of hospitality extended and welcomes received.

Upstairs, old, wrinkled bedroom warmly greeted the old Jew with memories of times full of romance and love, of prayers said on bended knees, of quiet times of rest and peace, each of them so full of love and life that they brought tears to

84

the old man's eyes. "Beautiful, beautiful," said the old Jew to the house as he slowly came down the staircase. "But aren't there any young memories in the house?"

"No, I'm sorry, only old, faded ones from the good old days," said the small voice.

"Thanks for the tour," the old man said, "but I'm not interested in moving in. The large house I'm living in now is also full of memories! I want to live with more than memories. Thank you, I'm going back home."

Several years later, there was great excitement in the neighborhood. All the houses were rejoicing because the big house had given birth to a little house. Now it wasn't really a little house, and it really wanted to measure up to the big house. But, sadly, economics and world events had determined that it would never be as large and grand as the big house, its parent. So, although it was two stories high with nearly as many rooms, the new house was named "Les," short for the "less big house."

A few years after its birth, on a bitter winter day, the old Jew who lived in the grand house at the end of the block came walking down the street. The December wind tugged at his long white beard and sent the long white hair which stuck out from his black hat trailing behind him like the mane of a galloping horse. "Tap-tap-tap" came the sound of his cane as he walked up the sidewalk to the front door of the less big house. He poked the doorbell with his cane, causing the sound of chimes to playfully ring forth. No answer. This time he pressed the doorbell long and hard, leaning full force on his cane. Still no answer.

"Anyone home?" he shouted as he used his cane to nudge open the front door of the less big house. "Hello, hello, anyone home?"

"Who's there?" asked a small, youthful voice.

"Just an old Jew looking for a home," came his reply as he stepped inside. He saw the tastefully arranged living room: the comfortable leather furniture, the oil paintings on the walls, the richly colored Persian carpets. "May I ask, please, who lives here?"

"No one!" answered the small voice. "They only *stay* here; they live elsewhere. One is really successful, up-and-coming, and the other is active full-time in the Movement."

The old Jew tapped his ear with his cane, "Is there an echo in this house? No mind, just a little personal joke. I am, however, disappointed. I'm looking for a house to move into—in fact, I've been looking for years now. It's so lonely where I live, and it gets lonelier all the time.

"The kids are busy, and if they come to visit, they're more interested in visiting with one another than talking to this old Jew! As full as their lives are, they usually leave as quickly as possible when the visiting hour is over."

Then, fixing his cane firmly to the floor, he leaned his head back and sniffed in every direction. Again, he sniffed deeply. "Sad to say, age takes its toll. I don't smell anything in this house, not even memories! The old nose just doesn't work like it once did."

"While you are old, sir," said the less big house, "your sense of smell hasn't left you. You see, no memories live in this house!"

"What?" demanded the old Jew. "Look at this gorgeous living room and this spacious dining room. Surely—"

"Never lived in!" said the small voice.

"But, house, at least some memories must be starting to form here in the living room!"

"If so, they belong not to a living room but a courtroom! There is only confrontation here: arguments, accusations and judgments passed."

Pointing his cane at the lovely dining room, the old Jew said, "Look at this marvelous walnut dining table and chairs, and this beautiful china. Surely, some memories must be forming here!"

"No different from those found in a restaurant where strangers dine."

The old Jew turned and began to climb the stairs. "Certainly, if we would go up to the bedroom—yes, let's go up—"

"No use, sir, a waste of energy climbing the stairs,"

moaned the less big house. "Any memories up there are no different from those you would find in a brothel! I told you, *no one* lives here!"

"How sad, how sad, how sad," repeated the old Jew as he regretfully retreated from the newest house on the block. "Tap-tap-tap" his cane chimed in, like the tune of a hammer driving nails into a coffin—"tap-tap-tap" it echoed as he slowly walked back up the street to his grand house at the end of block.

Many years later, all the houses on the block were again joyful, so joyful that their shouts were heard as far as the grand house at the end of the block. "A child is born! Everyone come and see, the less big house has had a little house." Indeed, the less big house did have a little house! While it came forth fully formed from its parent house, it was nothing like its parent or its grandparent. Since it was only one-and-a-half stories high and had only a handful of rooms, it was called "little house."

After a while all the big houses in the neighborhood began to look down on the little house. They gossiped about it over their back fences: "She's only one-and-a-half stories high! She's so small and insignificant; she cheapens the neighborhood. Just you wait and see, the next thing you know they'll be putting in mobile homes!"

Some years after the birth of the little house, "tap-tap-tap" came the old Jew down the street to visit the newest house on the block. Nodding to both the big house and the less big house as he passed them, he paused to catch his breath at the front door of the little house. As he was about to ring the doorbell, he was caught by surprise when the front door swung open. "Come in, sir. You look tired; let me have your coat and hat," said the hall tree cheerfully. "Welcome, sir," chimed in a strong voice from within the walls, "welcome and God's blessings on you."

A cozy fire popped and crackled in the small fireplace in the corner. With delight, the old Jew's eyes swept through the little house. The pieces of furniture—none of which matched—

were dotted with food stains. The few paintings were simple—some of them homemade—there were as many family photos on the walls. Magazines, papers and half-opened books carpeted the floor. This house would never appear in *Better Homes and Gardens*. Cocking his head to one side, the old Jew could hear piano music coming from one of the rooms—not from a CD but from a real piano! The house was also filled with wonderful smells from the small kitchen in the back of the house. Its sink was full of dirty dishes and pans.

The old man smiled. Leaning his head back, he sniffed this way and that. "Wonderful! I smell young memories and more! I smell ritual and prayer. I smell feasting and family. I smell hospitality, holding and being held. I smell sorrows shared and problems creatively resolved. I smell anger and disagreement, but they're saturated with peace and pardon. Oh, wonder of wonders, I smell conversation, laughter and loving. I want to live here! Little house, would you consider taking in this old Jew who longs to live in a house that's truly lived in?"

All the houses in the neighborhood were amazed; it was the talk of the block on that cold winter night. The old Jew never went back to live in his grand house at the end of the block. "Imagine," they said, "leaving all that marble, the solid oak furniture and the gold candlesticks! Makes no sense at all!"

But what followed on that night when the old Jew moved into the little house struck the other houses speechless. That night, there was a spectacular display of light inside the little house that not only illuminated every window and door but poured forth from the house like giant searchlights.

The light from the little house could be seen for miles and miles. It became a beacon light for travelers lost in the night. It was a beacon of hope for those living in loneliness, a beacon of promise for those who had resigned themselves to living in empty and dark houses. From the moment the old Jew came to live in the little house, no one ever again referred to it by that name. It was now simply called the "Lighthouse."

"Igor, that's a wonderful parable, but wouldn't it have been a more appropriate one for Martha since it's about home and family rituals?"

"Well, George, remember that you chose it! I just held out my fists, and you selected the left one!"

"OK, I'm no match for your draconic logic. While it seems to be a story more suited for Martha, I'm sure you had a purpose in telling it to me."

"Indeed I did. Making room for the Divine Mystery to live in your home is not exclusively a woman's or a man's work. Taking in God as a roomer is the primal vocation of *all* who live under the same roof: man and woman, woman and woman, man and man, or adults and children. The 'Guest who came to dinner and stayed'—be that Guest an old Jew, an old Hindu, an old Muslim or any old Spirit—the meaning is the same, *amigo.*"

"Martha and I have filled our house with memories. And while I've never thought about us having a Mystical Boarder living with us, I guess we do. Also, Igor, since we began to use this old toolshed as a mutual hermitage, we've found that we do more living at home. We do less eating out, and our home has become our playground, our holiday resort for leisure and relaxation."

"Perhaps, George, some Saturday I should come to your home for supper!" he said, removing a large Russian Army pocket watch. With a theatrical gasp, he added, "*Mon Dieu,* look at the time! It's later than I thought, *Monsieur* George. Time to pipe me down the gangplank of the USS Hermitage."

"I wish you didn't have to leave. I've got a number of

questions about your sunrise story, Igor. I guess they'll have to wait—or I'll have to come up with some answers myself."

"You might also ask Martha. I'll wager that she can put an interesting spin on that story, and on any questions you might have." Igor rose from the chair, and, with a flick of the wrist, he sailed his coffee cup and saucer across the room toward the desktop. Wide eyed, I followed their smooth flight across the room and was astonished as the cup, still in the saucer, circled my desk and then made a perfect landing on it, sliding slowly up next to the log. I turned around from my desk, applauding Igor's feat, only to find that I was the only one in the room!

*1600 Hours - 4:00 P.M.*

I conclude my hermitage day more aware than ever of one truth. I am never alone, here or anywhere, even when I am physically in solitude. Part of my reflection on Igor's parable is that my "slack time" here is a day spent with the Divine Mystery who loves the smell of coffee, the trails of little rituals and that "lived-in" look in a home. I pocketed my unanswered questions about the Lighthouse to share with Martha. I look forward to being with Martha and to making some Saturday night memories of our own—the kind that will make God enjoy living with us.

# Ship's Log

**Vessel:** *the Hermitage*

**Officer at the Helm:** *Martha*

**Date:** *Saturday, October 14*

**Time:** *1400 Hours - 2:00 P.M.*

Earlier this afternoon I heard a sound at the door and thought it was Igor, but it was only our cat. George must have left her outside, and she came here looking for me. This is the first time she's joined me here at the hermitage. I've enjoyed her presence. As I write, she's sleeping in the old easy chair. Part of me wants to look up and see Igor sitting there.

The day has passed slowly, and I realize how important Igor's visits have become as part of my solitude time. I should more correctly call my Saturdays in the hermitage days of solitude and story! I hope he's not as busy as he was last week when he had to visit George before dawn.

*1600 Hours - 4:00 P.M.*

I'm beginning the dogwatch, as they say aboard ships, referring to deck watch from 4 P.M. to 8 P.M. Keeping watch with me, and no longer napping, is our cat, Friday. The children gave her that name when she first appeared at our back door as a skinny stray on a Friday the 13th. The children begged to keep her. They're now grown and have left home, but Friday remains part of the family.

As I was journaling in the log, her tail suddenly began to swing back and forth, her ears became as alert as satellite dishes scanning for extraterrestrial life. Then I heard what Friday had sensed long before the "tap-tap-tap" on the hermitage door frame.

"Come in, come in, you old dragon," I called out with delight, "I've been expecting you!" Friday jumped down from the easy chair to inspect this new arrival in the hermitage. Igor leaned down and stroked her back, then picked her up and carried her to the easy chair.

"*Ciao*, Martha. Sorry I'm late, but this has been another full day," he said as he settled down into the old chair. "What's your cat's name?"

"Friday—her full handle is Friday the Thirteenth," I said.

"Friday XIII, sounds like the name of a pope! It would have made a good name for a couple of them, from what I know of Church history. Then again, the Church is for sinners and not saints—at least that was the original vision of Jesus. So perhaps a good sinner at the head of the Church makes all the rest of the Church more honest."

"And, Igor, I would think, more humble. You know, your playing around with Friday's name as a name for popes is really insightful. I carried something out here to the hermitage with me today: the question of law—particularly church laws—and the spiritual quest. Every religion has its own list of 'Thou Shalt Nots' for everything from diet to dress."

"Close quarters, Martha, as they said on eighteenth century sailing ships! Close quarters was the space defined by wooden barriers protecting a ship's deck as the crew fought off enemies boarding the ship. Religious laws help to give identification to a religion's 'deck,' providing protection to its members: no meat on Fridays, no women's faces unveiled in public, no ham, no this, no that—close quarters."

"Close quarters is what I find so suffocating about religion, Igor. It's that sensation of being trapped, feeling fenced in on every side by a constricting papal statement or religious law. We've got enough civil laws to fence us in, you would hope for a little freedom when it comes to religion."

"Friday," Igor said to our cat, "I think a mini-parable might be of profit here." Then he held out his two closed fists. "Martha, choose one."

"I'll choose your right fist," I said playfully. "I know it holds just the right story for me, you old MOO."

"Well, well, well, what have we here?" Igor said, looking at his opened right hand. "Look, Friday, it's the tale of Fred, the fire truck driver—taken straight from the morning newspaper." Out of the center of his dragon's hand a tiny technicolor whirlwind began to spin around as he imitated the sound of a fire alarm bell ringing.

On Friday afternoon,

according to a report issued by the city fire department, fire station #24 received a 911 call to respond to a fire at 12th and St. Peter Avenue. As firehouse bells sounded the alarm, firefighters slid down the twin brass poles and climbed aboard the big fire truck.

The driver, Fred, whose last name is being withheld at this time pending an investigation, raced out of the station at full speed, with the other firefighters still pulling on their coats and helmets. Cars along 5th Street quickly pulled to the curb as Fred sped by with sirens blaring and red lights flashing.

At the intersection of 7th and Spruce, the traffic light turned to red. Fred slammed on the brakes, waiting until the light changed. Then the fire truck roared off once more, but only for another three blocks. At that intersection a funeral procession was crossing. Fred stopped, waiting for the long line of cars with headlights aglow that followed the black hearse.

When the last car had passed, Fred put the pedal to the floor and was off again for the fire. He drove at top speed until he saw a yellow sign: **School Zone, 20 M.P.H.** Fred hit the brakes and crept through the block-long school zone. Then he headed for the interstate, a short cut to 12th and St. Peter Avenue. With all his red lights flashing and sirens wailing, Fred raced up the ramp that led onto the four-lane expressway.

At the end of the ramp was a sign: **Stop and Merge with Traffic**. Fred stopped, but merging was another matter since it was rush hour. All four lanes of the expressway were bumper-to-bumper. After a long wait, a friendly driver waved him out, and he slowly edged his way into a crowded lane of traffic.

Exiting three slow miles later, Fred hurried the remaining three blocks to 12th and St. Peter Avenue. They arrived at the address an hour and a half after the 911 call had been received at the fire station. All that was left at the site of the fire was a great pile of smoking ashes. This case is presently under investigation by fire department authorities.

"Quiz time, Martha! Should Fred be congratulated or corrected?" Friday looked up at Igor and then at me.

I winked at my cat and said, "Friday, old MOO has done it again. Great parable, Igor, even if it is a little bizarre. I mean, the image of that fire truck, sirens blaring, red lights flashing—and waiting for a traffic light to change!"

"I admit it was a tad ridiculous, Martha, but it does bring into focus how different laws can be in seeming conflict. You asked me about religious laws, church laws and their place in the quest. Well, just as traffic laws protect everyone's safety, so, too, religious laws are important. They help to set boundaries for human behavior based on Scripture. They're necessary until people grow up and become true lovers. Love knows no laws, or rather, has no need of laws."

"Igor, I'd like to believe that we could love enough to have no need for laws. But, you have to admit, it's literally a jungle out there—violence, immorality, greed and corruption!"

"True, Martha, but no matter how bad it is—and it's always been bad—laws are the last resort to control behavior. They are signs of failure, not progress. But since evolution toward maturity is so slow—*à la* snail speed—laws are necessary. Yet would it be necessary to have traffic laws requiring people to reduce their speed in school zones if *all* drivers were fully conscious of the potential danger in such areas?"

"Maybe we wouldn't have to have laws that threaten to punish such speeders if every driver treated school zones as the play areas of his or her own children! I see what you mean about love not needing laws."

"That's equally true, Martha, for religious laws. Among religious founders, Jesus is most unusual for his astonishing failure to decree laws. While he challenged his disciples to greatness about nonviolence, simplicity of life and married love, he didn't make laws about them. In fact, he criticized those who let their holy laws become a straitjacket. While he honored the spirit of the law, he cleverly rolled the over 600 laws of his own religion into only two—really one! That one law is summed up in a single word: love, *amour, amore.*"

"And Fred, the fire trucker driver, loved law instead of

having love be his law—is that what you're saying, Igor?"

"Yes, law-abiding Fred. While even the most romantic followers of Jesus would admit that laws are necessary at this stage of human evolution, there were exceptions that allowed Fred to be 'outside the law.' Of course, all emergency vehicles —fire, police, ambulances—are exempt to traffic laws that everyone else must observe. They have the right-of-way. Likewise, there are certain emergency occasions in daily life when religious laws are suspended, giving the right-of-way to conscience! The key, of course, is determining when something is an emergency. But your conscience is the highest law, and no authority on earth has the power or right to force you to act contrary to what your conscience says is right or wrong."

"You're speaking of freedom of conscience?"

"Yes, it's called that, and when properly exercised over narrowly confining laws it truly is an act of liberation. The reason there's a long list of traffic laws for those traveling Lover's Lane is that the majority are *not* mature people. Holy freedom, that glorious freedom of the children of God, paradoxically requires *adult* maturity. It requires prayer, wise guidance and careful self-examination for selfishness. For without full spiritual maturity, we speed down Lover's Lane endangering self and others, doing grave harm even while claiming that our conscience said it was all right."

"Thank you, Igor, for reflecting on the parable with me. You know, at one point I wondered if the building located at 12th and St. Peter might be the Church!"

"Interesting thought, Martha! That's what makes parables so delightful; they have countless possibilities."

"Can you suggest any good books to help me do more reflecting on my own?"

Pointing to Friday, Igor said, "No, but I can suggest a good symbol for your reflection—your lovely cat, Friday. Cats are good symbols of freedom. While being loyal and faithful— if not lovable—unlike dogs they remain free creatures. They were held as sacred by the Egyptians where they were first domesticated 2000 years before the Christian era. The Swiss and Burgundians of old had cats on their coats of arms as signs of liberty!"

"Hear that, Friday?" I asked. "I may just have to paint my own coat of arms and include you as my symbol of liberty."

Removing his large silver pocket watch, Igor said, "Speaking of liberty, this old salt's liberty—that is, shore leave—is about over. Must be on my way, Martha. I've enjoyed the visit. Give my best to George." Gently setting Friday down on the floor, Igor made a grand European bow to me and said, "*Senora*, with your permission." Then he jumped out the door shouting, "*Liberte, egalite, fraternite*—liberty, equality, fraternity—and in your case, sorority!" In a flash of red, white and blue, Igor was gone.

I conclude this day in the hermitage with an intention:

Intention: With God's grace, I desire to live in the glorious freedom of the children of God in the coming days. When challenged by some legalism that doesn't seem to fit, I will, by prayer, mature reflection and meditation on Scripture, listen to what my conscience says. Yet before failing to observe any law, however small, I will carefully look first to see if my exemption is based on a selfish desire or if it is truly a loving and caring aim.

My prayer to close this log entry:

O God, whose middle name is freedom,
    you who led your children Israel out of slavery,
    be the clear, sharp voice of my conscience.
May I hear your voice whenever I'm challenged by legalism.
Daily guide me along the path of my quest
    as one who is fully committed to observe
    the single law of Jesus with passionate fidelity.
Grant to me as I do so the conviction of your son, Jesus,
    who was no law-breaker—but an out-law.
May I follow him in choosing to live outside
    restrictive religious laws
    in order to more fully live out your one great Law of Love,
    even to death on the cross.
Amen.

# Ship's Log

**Vessel:** THE HERMITAGE

**Officer at the Helm:** GEORGE

**Date:** SATURDAY, OCTOBER 21

**Time:** 0945 HOURS - 9:45 A.M.

As I sit here writing in our hermitage, the view from the desk window looks like sunset, even though it's only midmorning! The trees ringing our backyard appear to be great orange-yellow clouds floating over the lawn in a Franciscan-like habit of brown autumn death. Nature, with the craft of a medieval glass artist, has created a stained glass window before me to rival any Gothic cathedral masterpiece. This toolshed window has been transformed into a compelling meditation on the trinity of dying, death and burial.

I usually tend to look away from death, but I know that the voyage of this vessel, the Hermitage, as with any *real* pilgrimage-quest, must pass through the Dead Sea. I'm not referring to that saltwater sea in southern Israel, infamous for its seashore sin-cities of Sodom and Gomorrah, but rather the soul's Sea of Death.

I once read that the Dead Sea in Israel is formed by the Jordan river and several streams flowing into it mostly from the east. None of these inlets, however, has an outlet; the sea swallows them up! Usually covered by a haze caused by heavy evaporation, you can only rarely see across to the sea's far shore. No fish swim in its salt waters, and those who enter it from the Jordan die instantly.

The Dead Sea—no outlet! It's natural for us creatures who can ponder our death to wonder whether the Sea of Death we must sail also has no outlet! None of those who have sailed across it, at least none whom I've known personally, have ever returned to port to report what, if anything, lies on its furthest shore. Spending this amber autumn day at the helm of the USS Hermitage makes me feel like a captain of a feared and dark ship. From its mast flies the Jolly Roger, a black flag bearing the emblem of a white human skull with crossed bones. The flag is not a sign that this is a pirate vessel, but rather a ship of the dead! Also, am I the helmsman, or part of its cargo? Since I can't see the other end of this Sea of Death either, I'm eager to drop anchor as soon as possible.

"Dropping your anchor, George? Would that entitle you to be called an anchorite?" asked Igor. Without my hearing him, my mentor had arrived at the hermitage door.

"Welcome, Igor, old Master of the Occasion and navigator of the good ship Hermitage. I guess I am an anchorite, even if only a weekend recluse, my maritime *maharishi*."

"Not a *maharishi*, more a *mahout*, which is Hindi for an elephant driver! Today I ride one into your hermitage."

"An elephant? I don't understand!"

"Patience, *sahib*. I'll come to that in a minute. First, let me say something about anchorites. While being Chinese, I know a little Greek, and anchorite in Greek means 'one who has withdrawn from the world.' Yet you and everyone else in this world is an anchorite at one time or another. Death makes us all anchorites—withdrawers from the world! The best count to date is that 99% become anchorites against their wills.... But am I invited in today, or am I supposed to play a traveling salesman who gives his pitch at the threshold?"

"*Scusa*—see, I know a little Italian. Excuse me, come in and have a seat."

"Thanks, George." Igor sat down in the old easy chair as

if it were a royal throne and picked up where he had stopped. "Blessed are those who die to being busy and so become amateur—from amare—anchorites, lovers of solitude."

"I agree, Igor. Being a weekend anchorite probably makes it easier to be an amateur one. But my patience is weak. I'm curious, Igor the Mahout, what kind of elephant did you bring in here today?"

"Elephants, George, to most of us are just big animals in the circus or zoo. Ah, but once they were signs of royalty since it was mainly kings who rode on them. Also, a white elephant announced the birth of Buddha, and in India, Ganesha, the god of writing and wisdom, has an elephant head."

"Ganesha would make a good patron spirit for writers and authors, Igor, even the kind of writing Martha and I do in this log!"

"In ancient China elephants were symbols of strength, logic and intelligence. In the West they've had strong exotic, even erotic, associations. The trunk, you know! The elephant of wisdom is the one I bring you. To paraphrase the old Sufi proverb, 'Happy are those who die before they die'; wise and happy are those who choose to be anchorites before they become anchorites!"

"Great play on words, Igor, that anchorites beat death by withdrawing from this world. Knowing your powers to read the energy of my thoughts, you know that this morning I was reflecting on this questventure as a voyage into the Dead Sea."

"Yes, I can't help hearing-reading-scanning those fields of energy you call 'thoughts.' But, you know, this autumn season is a golden sacrament of awakening, a prayerful preface to the approach of death, for elephantine—that is, wise—pilgrims. Many are blind and fail to see this season's hidden treasure. Youth is blind: when you're young, autumn only means football and homecoming dances."

"When you're middle-aged, it means raking leaves!"

"Another sacrament for the elephantine! When you age, you begin to see what you wrote about in the log, the famous stained-glass window of the great cathedral of creation. Meditating on creation's golden death helps a voyager to hear clearly the call, 'Anchors aweigh.' It's a call, George, that says it's time to check on whether you might be aground, hung up on the shore or stuck on the bottom. Are you?"

"Not that I'm aware of—at least since you came on deck in August. But, you old wise dragon mentor, knowing you, I suspect that your question means I should take a look to see if something has me hung up."

"Easy it is, mate, for a ship to be aground and not know it. It's easier still to be dragging an anchor and fail to know that it's the reason your voyage is so slow. Easy, that is, unless you check your wall log to count your knots," Igor said, pointing to the old ship's log and knotted cord that hangs on the wall of the hermitage. "To make progress on the quest requires that you be free of those anchors with the big flukes!"

"Flukes?" I asked. "You mean those arrow-like endings on ship's anchors?"

"Right, the function of flukes is to catch the ground and hold the vessel, even in a strong wind. A captain can pray for a good wind to set sail on a voyage, and the prayer may be answered. Yet what good is a strong wind if the ship's anchor is deeply fluked to the bottom of the sea?"

"Give it to me naked, Igor! Let's have a strip tease of all this elephant and anchor talk. I know you talk in pictures, but what is it that you're trying to say?"

"A grudge, George! How's that for coming to the point, *au naturel*? A resentment anchored in the past, whether due to an injustice done to you, an infidelity, abuse or neglect. It can be a real or sometimes even an imagined offense. Any grudge easily can become a heavy yet invisible iron anchor with large barbed flukes. It's a great deadweight connected to you by the heaviest of anchor chains."

"Well, I'm not aware—"

"George, grudges are sometimes deeply buried in your memory. If you have such an anchor, you may make some headway—with a good wind. But progress is slow, and you can actually be sailing in circles if the chain is long enough. Now, if you desire to sail with the tide, to ride the waves, then it's all 'Anchors Aweigh'!" Igor began singing the famous

U.S. Navy song with great gusto.

"Join me, George, *vivacissimo*; lively, lad, very lively now."

"Igor, you and I both know I can't sing. I also know I don't have any grudges that I'm aware of. But if I wanted to inspect my vessel for hidden grudges, how would I go about it?"

"Several ways. And it may even be possible that your past is free of being hurt by others."

"Hardly, Igor. I expect that everyone at one time in life has been offended and has suffered some injustice. To my knowledge, Igor, I've forgiven those who hurt me. Could I be hanging on to some grudge, though, and not really have forgiven someone?"

"Well, this dragon's advice would be to send a diver down to check what's below your vessel. Be like a diver so far down in dark waters that you have to feel your way. After all, resentment comes from *sentire*, meaning 'to feel.' Grudges are such heavily deadweighted memories of past injuries that they're sensuously sentimental—you still feel them! Yet even if you cut yourself off from your pain, all their emotional fallout continues to play itself out in your life."

"You mean grudges are barbed memories that can cause you to feel shame, guilt, anger, jealousy...?"

"Yes, and if, as you said, George, you've forgiven those who have hurt you, if you've truly forgiven them, then you will feel none of those emotions when you recall the original event! You're free, and it's anchors aweigh. Now if, on the other hand, you still feel anger at being offended, feel the sting of infidelity, the jabbing love-hate of jealousy, the pang of guilt—well, then you're hung up, you're aground."

"I want to send a diver all the way down!" I said with determination. "And I'd like to do it today. I'll spend the rest of this hermitage day, this anchorite day, diving to see if anything is hidden below. Could you come back, Igor, if only for a half an hour, to help me with what I find down there?"

"In dreams, elephants often symbolize some earthly reality that is not clearly worked out, but must be. In medieval bestiaries, elephants are celebrated for their chastity. If today you find some hidden anchor and can become free of it, you will have worked out a specific earthy problem that must be resolved before your death. Great is the chastity of those pilgrims who are pure, who are really clean of grudges. In short, George, yes. I will help you examine whatever is hidden in the deep waters inside you. I'll return late this afternoon, and I am willing to help however I can. Be careful as you descend, George, and be forewarned! Those you love most deeply—spouse, friends, parents, and even God—might be attached to a grudge!"

Igor left the hermitage, and I closed my eyes and prayed. I prayed to God to give me light, for dark and murky are those subterranean waters of the sunken past. I prayed for the light of love to accept whatever I might see down there since the ocean is the world's greatest junkyard and burial ground. I wanted to embrace with love whatever dark, hideous reality I might find to be holding me back.

Breathing deeply, again and again, like a deep-sea diver I slowly descended beneath the surface.

*1610 Hours - 4:10 P.M.*

Two hours have passed since I surfaced with *it*. It did indeed have huge flukes, ugly barbs long and sharp. As Igor had implied, it was buried miles beneath the surface. I have long felt it, but denied that it was a source of resentment. Cleverly and adroitly I have habitually attributed to some rudeness, offhand remark or slight of the day the pain and other emotional fallout that belongs to my grudge-anchor.

While I had—with difficulty—raised *it* up here to the deck of the Hermitage, I was now at a loss about what to do with it.

"Let's have a funeral!" Igor had suddenly appeared, standing at the doorway with a bouquet of flowers. "I couldn't find a wreath, but I did round up this bouquet of white and red carnations."

"A funeral?"

"Yes, George. Take a full piece of paper and write *it* out, describe your grudge as fully as possible. I'll go to the garage and get a shovel."

104

*It* resisted being placed on paper, but I forced it onto the page, all the gory details, word by word. Elephants are famed for long memories, and this elephantine grudge certainly had a long, rootlike memory-tail. Furthermore, it was a dead elephant, a deceased event. As I wrote it down, each sentence embalmed in ink, the work became easier, and soon I was finished. I laid down the pen, sat back and looked at *it*.

"Kiss *it*, George! Kiss it good-bye with both grief and relief!" Igor had returned and was standing with a shovel at the door. "Now we need a coffin," he said, looking around the toolshed. "Up there, on that shelf behind you, that old cigar box will be perfect." Leaning the shovel against the wall, he walked over and took down the cigar box, emptying its contents. As he returned to the desk, he said, "With loving care and reverence, fold *it* neatly until it fits inside."

I folded the paper, placed it in the cigar box and started to close the lid when Igor said, "Wait, George! We must observe the proper ceremonies. First, a wake!"

Igor picked up the cigar box and carried it to the prayer corner along with the bouquet of carnations. We both sat in silence in front of the box. Soon I heard electronic organ music! I turned my head and saw that it was coming from Igor. His fingers were playing an imaginary organ keyboard while out of the left side of his mouth came the pious funeral-home music.

Several large crocodile tears appeared in Igor's eyes and dripped their way down his dragon's cheeks, while out of the right side of his mouth, without losing a single note of his organ imitation, he said, "Good grief, George! Show a little grief! *It* is dead, and we both know it's been dead for a long time. It's been deadweight, but soon it will truly be D & G: dead and gone!"

"I'm glad to see it go! Why should I grieve?"

"But, George, how well it's served you! What a loss! No more warm showers of self-pity: it's gone! Soon the hidden source of those warm, juicy feelings of having been abused, mistreated, overlooked, bypassed, kicked around will be buried! Dead is the soul-weeping delight of having been a doormat for others to clean their feet on; gone is your heartthrob, your broken heart's broken record: 'Poor me, poor me, why me, why me...?' Soon the source of anger and guilt that has fueled your making your way in the world will be entombed forever!"

More fake organ music filled the hermitage, blending with the heavy aromas of carnations, embalming fluid and canned pine-forest spray (or was it disinfectant?). I pondered Igor's insightful invitation for me to grieve, to let go of all *it*'s secret rewards. In the midst of this mock wake, I confess that there were slight pangs of regret at *its* demise. Igor intoned in a dark-suited mortician's somber voice, "Friends, it is time to close the casket, to say farewell to the deceased and depart for the burial rites."

After ceremonially closing the lid, which bore a Spanish coat of arms and the words "Don Tomas, Finest Handmade Honduras Cigars," Igor handed the box to me to carry as a pallbearer. He walked in front with solemnity, carrying the flowers and shovel to the far end of our backyard. Somewhere a church bell began to toll—I guessed it was actually from Igor! When we arrived at the burial site, Igor dug a deep hole and then placed the shovel against the fence. With folded hands, in a preacher's pious voice, he began:

> Friends and family, we have gathered here today
>> to bury *it*.
> Alas, *it* has been dead for a very long time,
>> yet it's been an old and faithful friend.
> We bury it deeply into the earth
>> with the joyful promise of *No* Resurrection—
>> not in three days, not in three thousand days!
> Old *it*, you are gone forever.
> We bury you, old faithful, clinging *it*.
> We plant you deeply in the rich, juicy soil of the earth.
> May her hungry worms
>> consume you for breakfast, lunch and supper,
>> all of you,
>> every piece and memory of your ragtag tale.
> Down to the last crumb,
>> may they devour your names and faces,

all your pains and clever hooks,
chains and barbed wire flukes.

"Tum-ta-tum, tum-ta-tum, tum-ta-tum..." Igor began imitating a bugler playing taps as he saluted the cigar box. Then he lowered it into the earth and handed me the shovel, saying, "Next of kin has the honor."

I shoveled dirt on top of the cigar box while Igor began a singsong litany, "Old *it*: *Adieu, adeus, addio, au revior, Auf Wiedersehen, ave atque vale, ate' logo, sayonara, adios,* so long, bye-bye, see you later—NOT!"

I covered the little grave, and Igor placed a large rock on top of the mound of dirt as the sun dipped below the luminous golden treetops. Our backyard was filled with warm golden light as the two of us walked back to the hermitage.

When we reached the door, Igor smiled and winked at me. "Time to close up this anchorite's anchorage for the day, and tonight to make some new memories with Martha. George, you're a free man—for now! There may be more than one grudge-anchor down there; time will tell—as will future dives into the deep. For now, rejoice in what you've accomplished. You were brave to go in search of that old grudge. It took courage to dive so deep and to face *it*—courage to bring it up to the surface and then to cut yourself free of your goiter grudge since it had grown into a part of you. I'm proud of you!"

"Thanks, Igor. Having discovered and buried one grudge, it should be easier to do it to another. I'd guess that grudge-anchors can come in all shapes and sizes."

"And, George, they can also be brand new! Easy it is, mate, to tie a knot around some offense or slight and drag it behind you. Your time of silent sitting offers you a good opportunity to explore for any as-yet-undiscovered anchors and to become aware of new ones before they submerge and become deadweight."

"I promise I'll be vigilant. Thanks again for handling the burial rites, Igor. They were impressive—and sufficiently humorous!"

He slipped an arm around my shoulder and kissed me on the cheek. "Now, mate, at least at this moment in your questventure for the flaming pearl, your great voyage of the spirit, you can say with all your heart: Anchors aweigh!"

After Igor left the hermitage, I was left with much to ponder. His insights helped me to see how easily the questventure can be stalled or slowed by some resentment that anchors you in the past. The quest for the flaming pearl involves a daily search for that pearl of great price. It requires living in the present; resentment and regret anchor you in the past. And the more anger or guilt, the more you're hooked into the past.

This day's final log entry takes the form of a prayer-wish:

Each time I begin my anchorite time
    in this hermitage vessel,
        may I do it by singing "Anchors Aweigh"!
Merciful God, help me to be free
    of all resentments, grudges and regrets.
Help me find a way to say "Anchors aweigh" every day.

# Ship's Log

**Vessel:** *the Hermitage*

**Officer at the Helm:** *Martha*

**Date:** *Saturday, October 28*

**Time:** *1300 Hours - 1:00 P.M.*

Igor was humming the old Civil War song "John Brown's Body Lies a Mould'ring in the Grave" when he appeared today. As I looked up, he sang out loudly, "Glory, glory, hallelujah! Glory, glory, hallelujah! Glory, glory, hallelujah! His truth is marching on."

"Hi, *Memsahib* Martha! Happy Halloween! And happy burials!"

"Hi to you, Igor. You're right, 'tis the time of year when skeletons and graves, tombstones and graveyards are the decor of homes and stores. George told me about the funeral you two celebrated last week. He and I visited about *it*. The discussion was painful at first, but it was like labor pain—it helped me dredge up an anchor or two myself!"

"Does that mean we need another funeral this morning? I could go and get some flowers and—"

"No need, Igor. We had a burial at sea, so to speak. George and I symbolically washed some personal and mutual resentments down the drain. But for now I'd rather not talk about my anchors."

"Don't worry, Martha, I'm not one to use screwdriver questions...." Igor's voice trailed off as if his sentence, so smoothly rolling along, had dropped off a cliff. After a few moments, Igor began again, "Woe to those who pry, who ask too many questions, those damnable screwdriver ones!"

I nodded my head in agreement. I've also been ambushed by bearers of screwdriver questions, immodest invaders who have wanted to force open what was none of their business.

"Instead, Igor, I'd like our agenda today to deal with my desire to be new, to change! I not only feel freed of old anchors, but I know that the quest involves drinking from the fountain of youth. So I'm eager to be enchanted by the new and the renewed. Yet, while I find new clothing styles and new recipes to be exciting, I hate to let go of the old and familiar in other areas, like my religious practices."

"I'm not sure what the fountain of youth tastes like, Martha, but I recall Jesus saying something about no one being eager to drink new wine."

"But wasn't it new wine that Jesus was offering?"

"Yes, radically new wine! But as someone once said, the revolution—all that the *new* implies—comes one funeral at a time! So, Martha, let me wish you a Happy Halloween! It's a great feast for those sailing the Dead Sea. It should rank as one of the high holy days on the calendar of all good hermits and all serious seekers of the Sacred."

"Why would Halloween rank so high? I ask that like an idiot, since I know you're leading me on, you old rascal—I should call you 'old mystic *mahout.*' Are you about to take me for an elephant ride?"

"Ah, yes, the elephant. May I be seated, Martha?"

I nodded to him as he not only sat in the old easy chair but seemed to become part of it. His features faded into its fabric; seemingly from inside the chair came his melodic voice. "Martha, whether at Halloween or Easter time, we've all heard those terrible school-bus horror stories—the ones in which a sleeping child is accidentally left inside a locked bus at the end of the day. This is one such sad tale. *Rien ne va plus,* as the croupiers at Monte Carlo say when the roulette wheel is about to be spun and no more wagers may be placed, *Rien ne va plus*.

# Once upon a time,

yet on time in every time zone, in the big white house on the hill, preparations were taking place for the glorious feast of Easter. A few days before Easter, Cook had set aside a carton of eggs to be dyed for Sunday's celebration. The joyful uproar inside that egg carton was so great you'd have thought that instead of containing plain old white eggs, it had been filled with Mexican jumping beans!

The egg carton was more rambunctious than a school bus filled with homeward-bound third-graders on the last day of school before summer vacation. The eggs jabbered loudly to one another about being painted in all the colors of the rainbow for the coming feast.

Their minds were whirling round like merry-go-rounds with visions of their anticipated psychedelic, multicolored appearance in the great Easter egg hunt. Yet their visions were but pale black-and-white versions compared to what *really* happened on Easter Sunday morning. Little girls in bright pink Easter dresses and white hats, and little boys in new Easter suits screamed with joy as they discovered each hidden gloriously colored egg. Electric was the excitement as the children were given their various prizes.

Yet like all high holy days, before you could say, "God bless you one and all," Easter Sunday was over and gone. As with Christmas, but even faster, Easter was quickly boxed away for another year.

The family that lived in the big white house on the hill, since they had to attend to matters of grave importance, soon forgot all about Easter. No one in the house, not even Cook, paid a moment's notice to what was left on the top shelf in the pantry: an abandoned, empty gray egg carton, on which was printed in large red letters, GRADE A EXTRA LARGE EGGS.

However, unknown to everyone who lived in the house, the abandoned egg carton wasn't really empty! Alas, in the last seat, in the very last row, sat one frightened, very lonely egg. As the days and nights passed in quick succession, the lonely Grade A egg in the last seat worried if anyone would ever come and find it. The egg, realizing its life span was short, chewed its fingernails in anxiety, fearing that it had missed its big chance in life.

One bright moonlit night, Dr. Tooth Fairy rushed to make a house call at the big white house on the hill. Dr. Tooth Fairy was in a particular hurry since she had several house calls to make that night. Black bag in hand, she quietly slipped in the back door and crept through the kitchen on her way to the upstairs bedroom of seven-year-old Tommy who that very afternoon had lost a front tooth. Tommy was now sound asleep, having said his night prayers and piously performed the ancient ritual of putting his lost tooth under his pillow.

Dr. T. Fairy, as she was known, was a skilled physician, even though she was not recognized by the AMA because she practiced magic! As she hurried past the pantry door, out of the corner of her eye, she noticed the abandoned egg carton on the top shelf. Tiptoeing into the pantry, she carefully opened the lid of the egg carton and peeked inside.

"Well, well, well! What have we here?" said Dr. T. Fairy, introducing herself to the egg. "I'm glad that I followed my intuition. I had a hunch that if I took a peek inside I might find something interesting. Why, may I ask, are you sitting all alone in this empty egg carton?"

"It's all my fault," wept the lonely, frightened egg. "I hesitated, and now I've missed my chance in life! I froze when Cook called, 'Everyone out! Time for dying!'"

"You hesitated?" asked Dr. T. Fairy, as she used a kleenex to wipe away the tears that were streaming down the oval face of the egg.

"I was frightened! I didn't want to die!" sobbed the egg. "After all the other eggs had jumped out of the carton, Cook came to me and asked if I'd like to join them. I told Cook I needed time to think about it, to ponder such a major decision. Well, Cook never came back—which is not all that bad since, you see, I still haven't made up my mind about what to do, even though it's been days—well, actually two weeks—since Easter."

"Oh, I'm sorry," said Dr. T. Fairy, "but I'm afraid you misunderstood Cook! Oh, dear, English can be such a confusing language. Cook, you see, wasn't inviting you to die, but to *be* dyed, to be made colorful by being dipped in brightly colored dyes."

"Really? I thought for sure that Cook meant to *die!*" said the egg, who wasn't young and fresh anymore but by this time had become a middle-aged Grade A egg, and even had a few gray hairs. "I wasn't ready to march off to some execution. But even now that I know what she meant, I don't think it makes any difference. I think that dyeing might be dangerous and quite painful too. And over these past two weeks I've already examined the question of pain and dying from every angle, and I'm not sure that in the end taking such a risk in life would have been worth it after all. Oh, I don't know what to do! Please, Dr. T. Fairy, you're a competent doctor; don't you have a solution to my problem?"

With a flourish, Dr. T. Fairy suddenly unfolded her luminous, multicolored wings, as elegantly as if they were a Japanese silk fan. As she did, clouds of kaleidoscopic colors swirled around the walls of the pantry. Then she began humming Irving Berlin's *Easter Parade*, "Dee da dee da dee da, da dee da dee...," while doing an imitation of Fred Astaire's soft-shoe routine. This was Dr. T. Fairy's practice whenever she was concentrating on a problem, and the problem of the lost vocation of the indecisive Easter egg required her utmost attention. Egg, for its part, waited patiently, as is expected of a good patient.

After some moments, Dr. T. Fairy stopped dancing and looked the troubled egg straight in the eye. "I'm sorry, but your affliction is outside the realm of my medical expertise. I'm a specialist in extraction and implants. I extract an old tooth from under the pillow of a sleeping patient, and instantly, without awakening the patient, I make an implant of a gift of money, or some small treasure. It's a very intricate operation, but I'm very good, being a graduate of the Harvard Medical School! Yet I'm sorry, *your* affliction is outside my field.

"I would refer you to an egg specialist, but I don't know any. You have a very serious problem; you see, Easter is over, finished, lost, gone, *kaputt*, as the Germans say. Easter was weeks ago, so I'm afraid you'll just have to face reality! At this late date, no one is the least bit interested in a colored Easter egg!"

Egg groaned and began to cry again. "I've missed my big chance in life. Please, doctor, don't you have one little bit of magic for me in your black bag?"

"Wipe away your tears and don't cry. Perhaps together we can find a solution," Dr. T. Fairy's voice softened and became soothing. "Tell me, what do you *feel* like doing?"

"Well, doctor, as you know, I've had a lot of time to think about it, and I've looked at it from various perspectives. I think the most prudent thing would be—"

"I didn't ask you what you *thought*!" said Dr. T. Fairy. "I asked you what you *felt*! I'm no egg expert, but let's face it, you've become an egghead, if you'll pardon the expression. You've analyzed your decision to the edge of death. Tell me, what does your *heart* tell you to do?"

"That doesn't sound very logical, to rely on 'heart' feelings. Shouldn't one proceed logically and methodically? Now, since Easter is over, I should logically wait till next year, and then..."

"Next year?" snapped Dr. T. Fairy. "By next Easter you'll be a rotten egg, you'll stink to high heaven! Trust that if you open your heart to the problem, your heart will guide you. Trust that your first heart impulse is usually the right one, then follow it."

"But, doctor, that's foolhardy! We must approach life decisions prudently and make mature, logical choices by taking the time to analyze each of the—"

"Logically? Logic is what has made you a Lone Ranger egg! You can be *too* systematic in an age of rapid and radical change. Logic and careful deliberation made good sense for the old Greeks, and even for those who lived in the Middle Ages, when significant social change took a hundred years to come about. Today, my egghead friend, with change so rapid, so radical, who has time to logically ponder even important decisions? No, trust your heart, your gut feelings— that little voice that nudges you from deep inside. Too much

115

thinking is the reason why you've been left to die in this old abandoned egg carton."

"I don't know," the egg said. "I'm so worried. I don't want to die, and I'm also afraid I'll make a mistake."

"Isn't being the last one left in this dull, gray egg carton a mistake? Who can live without making mistakes? Trust that deep down inside you dwells the Great Mystery, who's more eager than you are for you to be happy. Listen to messages from *that* voice. Egg, no more thinking about it! Put an end to this fantasy of being able to find a perfectly logical and foolproof solution. You *know* what to do!"

The next morning shortly after sunrise, a scream echoed through the big white house on the hill, causing poor Cook to drop a plate of toast on the kitchen floor. At the top of the stairs, screaming for joy, stood Tommy holding something in his hand. "Everyone, come quickly and look at what I found under my pillow! Look at this wonderful gift from the Easter Bunny!"

As I said when he began his tale, Igor and the chair seemed to have fused as one. Now that the story had ended, well, it was just me and the chair. Even as Igor was telling the parable of the hesitant egg, I had to strain my eyes to focus, for at times all I could see was a talking old, worn easy chair. It's almost as if he had exited from the hermitage via the bottom of the chair. Then I saw a small folded piece of paper on the chair. I picked it up and opened it. Written in red ink was one word: *Sayonara*.

Dear log-journal,

He really is a clever dragon! I'm like the last egg. I too am afraid to die—or is that dye? To be new and renewed requires the risk of dying to what is well known and valued. Death to old ways of prayer—or even doing the laundry in a certain way—is part of keeping life fresh. That implies finding a balance between keeping some familiar daily rituals that make life easier or more pleasant and changing or adding new ways—whether to spice up life or when a real change is needed—even when that means dying to the old.

I've certainly come to know over these past months how necessary is some sort of inner death for real spiritual rebirth to take place. Yet to be perfectly honest, I have to admit that death scares me. This season of autumn is a constant reminder of death as creation dies all around me, is being dyed orange and yellow and brown in the colors of dying. This dyeing of creation is both beautiful and frightening.

Since I've never died, I doubt that I can regret dying. What I really dread is leaving those I love. My dread is not to die but to say good-bye. Yes, it's saying good-bye to George, to the children, to my friends, relatives—everyone I love.

Love is both the reason for regret and the dogma of no-regret. After all, perfect love casts out fear—even the fear of death. Yet it's easy to proclaim a glib dogma of life after death when you're young, when death seems no nearer than the next ice age...but when... My pen wants to lift itself from the page of the log as if some invisible force were elevating it. My mind wants to shut down, my brain's brakes lock, the sentence sits like a train on a siding.

I noticed in the last log entry how old multilingual Igor created for George a funny psalm-litany out of famous good-byes: *Adios, adieu, ate logo*...in a string of languages. As long as good-bye is only for a day or a week, it's OK. But the final good-bye—what's good about that?

Alone—and at peace—during the last hours of daylight in my hermitage, I close my entry as officer at the helm with this intention:

<u>Intention</u>: I desire, in the coming days, to invest with respect and reverence my good-byes—to George and everyone else I love. I will be vigilant not to treat those expressions in a casual way, but will take them as significant reminders of how I must let go, with love and with trust, those I love. May each departure be a statement of my faith: "Good" is our farewell, all farewells, till we meet again.

This is my prayer:

O Blessed One, you who are the invisible presence
    at all entrances and exits,
    you, the Divine Doorway,
    give to this priestly daughter who fears life's exits
    your grace of faith.
Grace me with the touch of your embrace
    so that I can trust
    that it was you who artistically created death
    as the doorway to you.
Help me who fears to come and knock at your door,
    fearful lest you open it.
Help me, daily, to open all of death's little doors,
    those *Alice in Wonderland* little doors,
    that lead to your wonderland
    hidden here in my daily life.
Grant to me, your pilgrim daughter,
    gifts of faith and loyalty.
Gift me with the same fidelity you gave to Jesus.
Gift me with that Gethsemani grace,
    whenever I am tempted to flee from dying.
Amen.

# Ship's  Log

**Vessel:** THE HERMITAGE

**Officer at the Helm:** GEORGE

**Date:** SATURDAY, NOVEMBER 4

**Time:** 0900 HOURS - 9:00 A.M.

As I make this log entry, I'm very conscious of how the daylight is slowly being drained away. Each morning it is darker longer, and each night the sunset comes more quickly. The gifts of this season include a greater awareness that things are always changing and a heightened sensitivity to time's passage in one's life.

Thank you, Late Autumn, for making me more mindful of the passage of time. Lately, however, I often feel myself caught between the sense of time passing quickly and time being suspended. As I was reflecting on this, I glanced at the clock on the desk here in the hermitage, and the hands were turning backwards! Startled, I squinted again at the clock, but no question about it: the hands on the clock were moving swiftly in a counterclockwise direction.

Regaining my wits, I shouted, "Up periscope! Our ship's either sailed into the Bermuda Triangle or there's a playful dragon busy with his own rapid version of daylight saving time!"

"Daylight saving time? Whether day or night, I'm always experimenting, George, in timesaving devices," came a voice from on top of the roof. In the minute it took the clock's hands to spin backwards an hour, Igor had flipped himself over the edge of the roof, dropped down and entered the hermitage. He stood by my desk as the clock read 0300 hours. Igor waved a long finger at the clock and the hands stopped their rapid retreat. "Engines, full speed ahead!" he cried out, and in a flash the clock read 9:10.

"Whether measured by sand hourglasses, sundials, time candles, sticks of incense or clocks of various kinds, time is important onboard ship. Time is important on any questventure—waste anything but time." Tapping the log-book, Igor added, "You can jot that bit of dragon wisdom down, George, just in case you might forget it."

"I doubt I'd ever forget that one! But don't worry, wise one, I'll enter it later. Congratulations on that clock trick! Want to show me how to do that?"

"Sorry, it's a trade secret among us fourth-degree dragons, but I will share a story if you're interested? No need to answer since my radar has already read your reply."

Igor perched himself on the edge of the desk as if he were a small child and spread apart his arms. I took his sitting on the desk instead of in the easy chair to be a sign that this was going to be a brief visit. I said to myself, "Time will tell."

"The question, Sent George, is: Time will tell what? And as your faithful MOO, this occasion calls for..." With a wave of his hand, he began:

One day,
not far from here,

but still not quite within reach, a patient went to a physician complaining of a painful rash. The rash had caused severe irritation, and the patient felt that the source was an allergy of some sort.

The doctor ordered a long list of tests to determine what had caused the rash. Various foods and fabrics were tested, but none was found to be the source of the problem. The patient continued to complain of bouts of random irritation. Next, the patient was tested for a sensitivity to dust, mildew, ragweed and various household chemicals, none of which proved to be the source of the irritation.

Having had no success, the physician called in a folk healer. The healer carefully reviewed all the tests and asked various questions about the patient's family history. Then the healer announced, "I believe the source of your rash and your irritation is your wristwatch!"

"My wristwatch?" said the startled patient. "Am I allergic to its leather band or its metal case?"

The healer smiled and said, "Neither! It's not even the actual watch you're wearing that's causing the problem. It's the one you're wearing underneath it!"

The patient looked puzzled, so the healer continued, "There on your wrist underneath your wristwatch you—and, I might add, even those who don't wear wristwatches—wear a childhood watch. This toddler timepiece is the most unique of all clocks since it shows no hours, minutes or seconds. It's a watch that reads only one time: *now*! Your irritation is caused by your need to have your wants met right now, at this very moment, as does any three- or four-year-old child. And I would guess that your childhood watch causes you not only pain and distress but also is an irritation to those with whom you work and live."

After a long, thoughtful silence the patient asked, "Is there a cure for this affliction?"

The healer handed the patient a pair of glasses and a pocket calendar. "With these glasses," the healer said, "first look to see how busy people are before asking them to deal with your pressing needs. With the pocket calendar, practice patience and learn to postpone for hours—even days or weeks—having your 'pressing' toddler needs met. Be willing, and learn to be able, to write them in your calendar as needs with almost unlimited deadlines."

"Before you ask a question, George, close your eyes and think about what you're going to say. Let's not be in a hurry to open the suitcase-story, even if it's only an overnight bag. Patience, George, patience." Igor's voice floated to me slowly, softly, hypnotically, and I obeyed.

"At regular intervals, George," he began after a period of silence, "any serious pilgrims on the quest, such as you and Martha, must have inspections. Ships once flew a yellow flag as a sign that the plague was on board; in that tradition let's have all hands on deck for a health inspection. All hands, hold out your hands so the captain can check to see if on your wrists—or even hidden in your pockets—there are any toddler's timepieces!"

I held out my hands in front of Igor as he continued, "My old yin-yang Chinese sea clock has this wise inscription written on its face: 'No time to waste, and no time in haste.' Blessed are those pilgrims with a balance of those natural urges: the ability to master the moment, to get what you want right now—because now is the only time there is—and the ability to delay your needs, since you've got all the time in the world."

"'No time to waste,' I understand," I replied, "especially since I'm part of that 85% of Americans who say they don't have any free time. For instance, finding some night when everyone in our group is free has been a real problem. While we value the energy and support of the group—and really enjoy getting together—it's really hard to find time for it. A couple of members of the group have dropped out because of that. If I could get you drunk, Igor, and pry out of you the secret of your timesaving device that can make clocks run backwards, I'd be a millionaire—no, make that a billionaire."

"But also, George, you, like everyone, start every day as a millionaire. You've got as much time as anyone else—and as much as you *really* need. How you spend it, how you invest it, is the secret key to wealth. I agree that the older you grow the less time you have, or so it seems. Wise investors of time use the same cleverness as Wall Street brokers who invest money. They are aware that the toddler's timepiece that reads only *now* is the enemy of all who wish to be wealthy. Why, you ask? Because that timepiece is a bank robber that steals contentment, and it's contentment that makes us truly rich."

"I hate to wait; it's such a waste of time," I replied. "Like now, let's just get to the bottom line: What's the point of the parable?"

"The point or *points*? There are more than one, for sure. For example, George, I'd wager that you've been eager to form community with the group you and Martha have started. I'd give three to five odds that you've even had a discussion about how to do it. Would I be right?"

"Well, yes—"

"Perhaps you can create a political group overnight, but a spiritual group must age like fine wine. Most people are too impatient to allow deep feelings about soul matters to slowly rise to the surface, and in that impatience they end up performing autopsies on the living! They overanalyze and suffocate the embryo before it has a chance to grow. Prayer, spiritual communities, love and good wine all take time."

"I still hate to wait."

"Hate to wait, wait to hate!" Igor said grinning, his eyes changing color from green to yellow, then to flashing red. "If you don't know the art of waiting, then you are only waiting to hate, to be upset, angry, vexed—the old churn-up-stomach-acid time. The art of waiting is another form of investing. Patience pays dividends, and learning how to use 'wasted' time is like playing with interest. You say you lack time to think, pray and dream? The next time you have to wait, don't agitate—meditate!"

Removing a large silver watch from his pocket, he glanced at it and then began in a singsong voice, "'I'm late, I'm late, for a very important date. No time to say hello, good-bye, no time, no time...' *Adieu*, George, much *adieu* about nothing...." And he was gone—disappearing faster than the white rabbit in *Alice in Wonderland*.

*1705 Hours — 5:05 P.M.*

As I close the logbook for this Saturday, I'm pleased to report that I feel time-rich. Today I've used the desktop clock as my spiritual icon. For the first time I've seen it as a mandala, one of those round Tibetan images used for meditation. I've meditated by looking prayerfully at the clock, looking beyond the twelve numbers on its face, beyond its endless windmill-whirling hands. My clock has been my reflection on time and my quest. I've resolved to embrace the discipline of frequently "checking" the time—not simply checking the time of day, but what kind of timepiece I'm using, and what time zone I'm in.

I prayed today that I would have the courage to wear a prophet's watch. That's a special timepiece set two or three hundred years ahead of actual time. Those who wear one are brave enough to act as if the future had already arrived. Their behavior blows the whistle on those who drag their feet on reforms, who delay bringing about an age of full justice for all. Wearing a prophet's watch can make a person seem sort of timeless and harmless at times, and very dangerous at other times since he or she seriously challenges the status quo.

I asked for the grace to never wear a toddler's watch here in the hermitage or when consciously traveling the Way. I need not be impatient when it comes to becoming godlike;

that's one process in which God alone is in charge. Nor can I become impatient when social justice, when God's age of peace and equality, seems stalled. Laws can change overnight, hearts take a long time to truly change.

I leave here today richer with the knowledge that I must invest every hour wisely by first enjoying the moment, and then by exploring it for little pockets of wealth. I resolve to not hate to wait! I resolve rather to invest all "dead" times with life and enjoyment. I resolve also to continue to "make" time, like some clever attic inventor, especially to make time in my day and life for what's important. Yes, I want to see the difference between what's important and what simply *seems* urgent, that which comes racing into my day with a loud siren and flashing red lights!

I believe my time today alone with God—and Igor's visit—has helped me to know the difference between those emergencies that are real and those that are created by people, including myself, who are wearing toddler's wristwatches. What's important to me is my time with God, with Martha, with myself, time for healthy work, for exercise, good reading, fun and time for my friends.

Like those who long ago set sail on ships across the ocean to find gold in the New World, today, aboard this ship, I've found real gold. And I've found it in the strangest of all places: in our hermitage desk clock.

# Ship's Log

**Vessel:** *the Hermitage*
**Officer at the Helm:** *Martha*
**Date:** *Saturday, November 11*
**Time:** *0930 Hours – 9:30 a.m.*

Yesterday George and I attended the funeral of our friend Michael. It was a sad service. Not yet middle-aged, he died of AIDS. Though not unexpected—he's suffered terribly and wasted away over the past year—his death is a loss to both of us. He had been such a vibrant man; he so enjoyed life.

Part of my church ministry has been in a hospice program, being with seriously ill people as they prepare to die. The last year with Michael, as well as my hermitage time here with Igor, has renewed and deepened that ministry—I've even had a taste of real compassion. It's felt, for the first time, as though I've really been of service in simply being present to the dying. I dedicate this hermitage day of prayer to Michael. God grant him peace and life.

Death as chilly as this November day has become my pervasive companion today. I've reflected on death so much since Igor's Last Easter Egg parable, and now with Michael's passing it's again inserted its bony question mark into my solitude. By a holy coincidence, this Saturday is also the traditional commemoration of Veterans Day. It's a secular feast which like many sacred feasts is not celebrated with gusto by everyone. Some people don't even acknowledge it. I'd like to have my meditation time on today's anniversary of the end of the First World War include a remembrance of the millions who have died in wars.

The gray November clouds hang low over the garage and hint of an early snowfall. On this day of parading soldiers and old veterans, a sharp north wind marches detachments of brown leaves across our backyard.

I stopped writing and placed my pen on the desk to watch the fallen leaves drifting across the yard like ghost soldiers going over the tops of their trenches and racing toward enemy lines. As I reflected on them, there was a knock at the door of the hermitage. "Come in, Igor. *Como le va*? How's it going?"

"*Chin-chin*," he said, opening the door. He entered along with a gust of wind and a squad of rushing dead leaves that dropped at once to the floor when he closed the door. "*Chin-chin* is a Chinese toast, but it's also a polite greeting and farewell."

"What does *Chin-chin* mean?"

"'Please, please.' Rather nice, isn't it? I mean for a formal greeting. Please, please, may I bother you," he said, picking up a large brown oak leaf. "Eternal rest grant unto you, fallen leaf, who's given your life for us." He gave me a big smile as he placed the dead leaf on my open logbook.

"Cheery entrance," I said. "You're right in step with the drummer of today's veteran's holiday. Your entrance also fits my somber mood on this gray November day, with its bare branches and crowds of dead leaves blowing across our yard."

Slowly reclining in the old easy chair, Igor nodded. "November, August or March, any month or day—especially when a friend has just died—is a good time to reflect about the ultimate experience, eh? It's like the story a friend of mine told me about the surprise he found in his mailbox."

"A surprise?" I asked. "I'll bet the surprise is today's lesson."

"I just dropped by to say hello, Martha. But, perhaps that tale may hold insights worth a reflection or two. It just might open a door in your soul. Let me warn you in advance that this is a strange and complex story—also a *megillah*, a scroll, as the Jews call a long story."

Ozone day a friend of mine

went to his mailbox. As usual it was crowded. As he sorted through the customary handful of letters, bills, catalogs and junk mail, one envelope stood out as unique. It was an invitation-size envelope, edged on all four sides in black. My friend's curiosity was so great that he felt impelled to open it right away. The black-edged invitation card that he removed from the envelope read:

You are invited to attend my Deathday Party
on March 15th at 7:30 P.M.
at 3535 Woodbine Ave.
All guests are asked to wear a skeleton costume
and to bring flowers.
RSVP

The card was unsigned, but he recognized the address immediately: "Steve...that's Steve's house number!" Holding the card in his hand, he sat down and read it again with a puzzled look. "A deathday party? What kind of joke is Steve pulling? Or is it a joke?"

Later that day in another part of town the bell on the door of a costume shop jangled as a woman entered the small shop filled with unusual outfits. The owner came out of the back room and asked, "Can I help you?"

"I hope so," said the woman. "I'm in need of a skeleton costume. Do you have one?"

"You're very lucky; I do, but it's the last one! It's really strange—you're the fifth customer in two days to come in and ask for that particular costume. I mean, it's weeks since Halloween, and that's the only time we usually have a run on skeleton costumes."

"Yes, I know it's a bit unusual. But I need it for a costume party that I'm attending. I hope that your last suit will fit me."

The owner looked at her with his head slightly canted and said, "Hmm, I believe it should do nicely since it's a Small and you have a slight build. I haven't questioned any of the others, but may I ask: Is this some special kind of costume party, with guests all in skeleton suits?"

"A good friend of mine is having a deathday party, or at least that's how the invitation reads. We're all supposed to wear skeleton costumes and bring flowers. I know it sounds a bit weird, but he's really a unique and creative person."

"Can't say I've ever heard of a deathday party before," said the owner, disappearing into the back room. In a moment he returned with a skeleton costume, complete with a skull hood. "Is your friend sick? I mean, with some..."

She held the costume up against herself and said, "Not that I know of. He looked in perfect health the last time I saw him. I think it's just some kind of gag, at least I hope so! This will fit fine; I don't think I even need to try it on."

Several streets away from the costume store, a man in a skeleton costume was stepping out of his car and entering a flower shop. A couple of passersby, doing a double take, shook their heads and continued walking down the street. Inside the flower shop, the clerk looked up from behind the counter with surprise.

"I need a bouquet of flowers," the costumed customer said, "something appropriate for a deathday party a good friend of mine is having—perhaps a funeral arrangement."

"Carnations would be nice," replied the clerk. "I take it this is some sort of joke, so why not add a silk ribbon with the words 'Rest in Peace' on it?"

"That sounds excellent—including the ribbon. I don't know what Steve is up to, but I might as well play it to the hilt. I'm glad you're open until 8 P.M. I was late leaving work tonight, and if you hadn't been open I'd have had to go empty-handed."

Collecting the flowers from the cooler, the clerk said, "We had another guest for your party in here just twenty minutes ago. If it weren't for your humorous costumes, I'd think this was something serious—I mean, gathering around a friend who announces that he's dying. Your friend isn't ill, is he?"

"He's in perfect health—at least to my knowledge. We were out to dinner a month ago, and he looked fine. Didn't say a word about anything being wrong. I guess it's just one of his crazy, creative parties. Only this one is costing me a bit more than usual since I had to rent this costume and buy these flowers."

He paid for the flowers and drove away through the dusk-covered streets of an old neighborhood, until he arrived at a house with the porch lights aglow. Parked in front was a large black hearse. Another skeleton-costumed guest carrying a bouquet of flowers had just walked up the sidewalk and entered the house. Taking his own bouquet from the front seat, he walked up to the front door. A large black ribbon was draped across the door, and from inside he could hear what sounded like circus music!

When the door opened, he was greeted by the smiling host, also in a skeleton costume, but without a skull hood. "Welcome, good friend. I'm so pleased that you could come. The flowers are beautiful. Carnations are my favorite, you know! Come in, but I ask that you leave on your skull hood; your identity is to be a secret."

The entire house was decorated with black silk ribbon. The walls were covered with cardboard skeletons and on tables were placed skulls with glowing candles inside. In the living room, four other persons in skeleton suits with hoods were visiting around a large coffee table.

"Can I fix you your usual?" asked Steve. "The others all have their drinks."

"Sure, Steve, looks like some, ah, party—weird, maybe, but it should be fun! Who are the other guests?"

"Ah, my friend, that's part of the mystery, but they're all among my closest friends. Who else would you invite to your deathday party?" Motioning to the next room, he added, "You can put your flowers in the dining room if you'd like."

As Steve went to fix the drink, the last guest walked into the dining room. In place of the usual dining table was a large casket mounted on a stand. Around this "table" were seven chairs. After placing his bouquet along the wall with the other funeral arrangements, the final guest went into the living room. The other guests were laughing as they flipped through catalogs of tombstones and caskets.

Steve returned, handing the most recent arrival a mixed drink. Then he addressed all his guests, "Well, we're all here now. Thank you, good friends, for coming tonight. Each one of you is very close to my heart. I ask you, for the time being, not to remove your skull hoods. It'll be part of the mystery to see if you can guess each others' identities. I know that this isn't your usual sort of party...(strained laughter trickled out from the guests)...but why not have a party that makes fun of death—mine and yours?" Steve reached over and shook the foot of a life-size plastic skeleton hanging on the wall. "Right, Old Bones?"

Looking at the guests one by one, he continued, "I hope that none of you here is superstitious! You know the Irish saying—they would rather die than talk about death! So for them throwing a party to celebrate one's death would be the ultimate threat, wouldn't it?"

"Are you...," asked one of the guests, "in good health, Steve? You haven't called us here to tell us some bad news, have you?"

"What's health got to do with it?" he replied with a big grin, taking a knife from the cheese board. "Death can, at any moment, make love with you or me! A drunken driver runs a red light, and *zap*!" For emphasis he used the cheese knife to puncture with a bang one of the black balloons that had been hanging in a cluster on the wall. "Or the airliner on which you are traveling crashes on takeoff, and *zap*! So I decided, along with a yearly birthday party, why not also have a deathday party?"

Raising his glass, he continued, "A toast, good friends, to death: whether today or tomorrow, on the road or at home, at sunrise or in the dark of night, but never alone—may we die surrounded by those who love us."

"I'll drink to that," said one of the guests, and they all took a drink from their glasses.

"Party time, then, friends," said Steve. "Please follow me to the dining room for the funeral feast." Everyone stood up and walked to the dining room doorway. "A little ritual of entrance. Before coming into the dining room, we each have to kiss our friend here who guards the doorway," he said, motioning toward a realistic-looking skeleton leaning against the wall. With mock reverence Steve placed a large kiss on its lipless skull. Laughing, the others did likewise as they entered the dining room. Each guest took a chair at the casket-table in the middle of the room. The table was draped in black silk; on it were two large candlesticks with glowing tapers.

"We need a little dinner music," Steve said, inserting a cassette into the recorder on the sideboard. Funeral home organ music filled the room. Smiling, he returned to the coffin-table. "I've saved a bottle of wine for just such an occasion as this. It's a 1976 Saint Julien Bordeaux—at one's deathday party it should be all stops out, shouldn't it?" After pouring wine in each of their glasses, he set the bottle in front of his place and sat down at the head of the table.

"Are we missing anyone, Steve?" asked one of the guests. "There are seven chairs—but only six of us."

"The seventh chair is reserved for a distinguished, most disgusting guest of honor, a guest whom no one in his or her right mind ever invites to a party. Tonight, as host of my own deathday party, I propose that we poke fun at our greatest and most feared enemy. Since childhood, each of us has been cautioned in countless ways to fear death: 'Be careful when you go swimming! Take care when crossing the street! Drive defensively!' I realize that a party like this may seem like madness after such ingrained training. But because of each one of you, I trust that it will be a real celebration, a night to remember.

"I'd like to begin by proposing a toast to my good friend on my right. You were my first real friend. I remember so clearly the initial fire of our friendship. It was the first time I felt that incredible experience of oneness with anyone other than my parents. You and I did everything together; we were constantly with each other. While the passing of time has quieted the intensity, my affection for you has deepened over the years. Nor have new loves lessened the depth of ours. I know tonight that even Old Bony Death can't break the bond between us." Raising his glass, Steve continued, "Thank you for your friendship; thank you for the memories of all the adventures we shared as we stood on the doorstep of adulthood. Thank you for stealing death's power over me. To Life!" All the guests at the table toasted and drank from their glasses.

"Good wine, eh? As I said, it's a 1976 vintage, a good year. Now, my second toast," Steve said, looking at the guest in the next chair, "is to you, my good friend, whom I have also loved. Ah, but yours was a very different kind of love. Rich as ripe fruit was the passion we shared. For my part I realize now that much of it was only my being in love with...being in love! What we call 'love' is often the rare intoxication of being loved by someone in a way that makes you feel lovable. You and I, old friend, had some good times together! Tonight I thank you for the love you gave me which made me want to give myself away in gifts and tokens—and, yes, in the center of that furnace of being in love, a willingness even to give away my life for you."

The guest in the second chair nodded in agreement as Steve continued, "Thank you for that gift by which the loss of life is no longer the greatest of all tragedies!" Raising his glass high, Steve was about to toast, when the second guest said, "To you, Steve, and to all of us! To Life!" Again everyone joined in the toast and drank.

Steve echoed a previous sentiment, "My, but this is good wine! As I said, I've kept this bottle of Saint Julien Bordeaux all these years for some grand occasion, even if I didn't know it would be as special as tonight's party." Muted voices from within the skull hoods all agreed.

"Now, for the third toast. To my next mystery friend—I especially want to thank you for coming to my party tonight. Of all my guests, you had to travel the longest distance. Know that I deeply appreciate all the trouble you went through to come here. Tonight's deathday party would be incomplete without you!"

The guest in the third chair stood up and took a playful bow as the others at the table applauded.

"Friends, my third guest is a unique friend, and perhaps the one who most makes tonight's party possible. Like most of us, I was infected early in life with the disease of rugged individualism. Our heroes and heroines in life are mainly soloists. They fearlessly flew across oceans alone, amassed great fortunes by their own abilities or discovered great wonders in their solitary laboratories. For all its benefits, that solo disease warps the brain, implanting the idea that only weaklings need help from others. Most of us have launched ourselves into life as Lone Rangers, convinced of our ability to reach the top alone.

"I admired you, my good friend, for your strength and courage. You taught me about determination, about the hard work and tenacity necessary to be successful in life. But the greatest gift you gave me was one you probably were quite unaware of.

"Remember when we went mountain climbing together many years ago? I recall, with a little shame now, how much I was in competition with you at the time. More than wanting to share in the struggle and adventure of mountain climbing, I wanted to be better than you! I guess I thought that if I were better, you would admire me—yes, even love me—for it. It's strange how silly that sounds tonight as I confess it to you in the presence of my other good friends."

The third guest responded, "I remember well that camping trip, Steve. But don't feel ashamed; no doubt both of us were in competition. It's symptomatic of that disease you were talking about, always having to prove to ourselves or others that we are more than we really are. We'd rather die than appear less than—"

"That was your great gift, my friend. You gave it to me as I hung on the side of that mountain, clinging there for my life. You freed me from that fear-motivated need. You freed me from the prison of my solitary confinement. Do you recall that moment frozen in time?"

The guest in the third chair slowly nodded his hooded head as Steve continued, "I had lost my footing and slipped over the edge, hanging on only by my fingertips. Below me death was waiting at the bottom of the canyon. I was terrified. You climbed down and extended your hand. Oh, how I wanted to take it, but I realized that I could so easily also take you with me! I could see us both plunging to our deaths. And you must have seen that fear in my eyes, for you said to me, 'Here, take my hand. Don't worry, together you and I will cheat death.'

"Because you were physically so strong, you single-handedly pulled me up and over the edge to safety. The feel of your hand around my wrist is as powerful tonight as it was those many years ago." With his left hand Steve slowly rubbed his right wrist.

"Thank you not just for saving my life, but for awakening me to a great truth. Life is lived in its fullness only when we live it with and for others. That day, long ago, on the mountain side, you taught me that to need others isn't a weakness; it's actually a doorway to greater life. To you, good and faithful friend, I propose a toast."

Moved by the depth of Steve's story, all the guests stood and raised their glasses.

"By your love and your willingness to give your life for me, I can make fun of death tonight: To Life!" Everyone drank to the toast and sat down again.

"Steve, I have a strange feeling," said the fourth guest, "that you're going to announce something to us this evening that will make this more than just another one of your crazy parties."

"Ah, my good friend, you always were one to race ahead in a plot to figure out the ending. You too are a most important guest. Over the years we have enjoyed some great movies together. As we would watch a film, you always were ahead of the plot, excited by the mystery. I could have guessed that your mind was leaping ahead this evening as well. You deserve a toast at this deathday party. Thank you, for by your love of the great classics you have helped me learn not to fear death. You were always quoting from Dostoevsky or Shakespeare, or comparing our life situations to something you had read in Dante or a play by Tennessee Williams."

Following the previous guest's lead, the fourth mystery guest also stood and took a bow—but with a curtain-call gusto.

The party was gathering steam. After a burst of applause and a couple of cheers, Steve continued, "What wonderfully engrossing times we had sharing the insights of the great thinkers, drinking the rare wine of their ideas about life and forming our own great thoughts. Those evenings when we discussed philosophy, politics and history taught me a great truth: that ideas don't die! In a very real way, gifted writers are more alive today than when they walked this earth. Death can claim the body, but it has no mortgage to collect on our dreams and ideas. And it's not just true for the Aristotles and Einsteins but even for us ordinary people. And so, for your great gifts, my friend, I propose this toast: To Life!" Everyone at the table chanted "To Life" and drank deeply.

"The final toast, friends, could also have been the first. Each of you has given me a priceless gift. My fifth mystery guest, and my good friend, I am grateful tonight to you for your special gift. Time and again during our long years of friendship, you showed a willingness to love me in spite of my shortcomings. I confess that I always wondered why you did—what it was that you found attractive about me—but know that I have greatly valued your friendship. Your greatest gift, however, was unique, and I doubt you even knew that you gave it to me!"

The guest in the fifth chair comically began to scratch his skull hood as a sign of ignorance. The guest seated next to him patted him on the back.

"For my part," Steve continued, "I was drawn to you by your great zest for life. You possessed so much that I myself would have loved to have. You are one of those who seems to be graced with an overabundance of gifts. As we moved through life, I wasn't surprised at your financial success and your high position in the business community and the larger community. I was proud to be known as your friend, to be close to someone so successful."

"You mean, Steve," said the guest on his right, "birds of

a feather flock..." and everyone added in a singsong chant, "together."

"Perhaps, only I wasn't in the same class—or flock—of successful people. But, my friend, then came your defeat—I mean the bankruptcy of your company! The creditors were like wolves all over you. You lost everything: business, home, money and name. Yet in the course of it all, you didn't change. Your zest for life was as electric as before; in fact, you became even more dynamic. I thank you tonight for the gift of freedom from fearing the death of my good name! Yes, my friend, even freedom from the fear of death by disgrace and shame. You've taught me that there is something beyond all the rewards that we seek from early childhood on. You've gifted me with the knowledge that even death itself can't bankrupt us of what's really important. For this I toast you with gratitude, good and dear friend: To Life!"

"We'll need more wine if you've got any more toasts up your sleeve, Steve," said the fourth guest, "or are we ready for dinner?"

"Yes. The toasts are over. Now, let the feast begin! As with any birthday party, it's time for the cake." He rang a small bell, and someone in formal dress, wearing a skull hood, carried in a large black cake covered with lighted candles.

"The difference between a birthday and a deathday party is that here everyone makes a wish before the candles are blown out! Take a moment, friends, to think of a wish, a special wish, and then together we'll blow out all the candles—those on the cake and the others in the room."

After a long silence, Steve leaned forward, as did all the guests, and with much laughing they blew out all the candles. The room was thrown into complete darkness but still filled with laughter and applause.

Finally, one of the guests said, "Will someone please turn on the lights!" Another guest fumbled in the dark and then found a switch. As the lights came on, they saw that the host's chair at the head of the table was empty! It was empty, that is, except for a piece of paper on which was written, "Till we meet again, in paradise."

*1645 Hours - 4:45 P.M.*

Igor left after his *megillah*, his long story about the deathday party, was finished. I'd guessed in advance that at the end of the story, when the lights came on, the host wasn't going to be there!

While, unlike most of Igor's tales, you could see what was coming, it was still a powerful story. I jotted down, as an exercise, the persons I'd invite if I had such a deathday party. Like Steve's Last Supper in Igor's story, I found that those with whom I have shared love had indeed stolen the poison out of death's arrow. It could still pierce, but it couldn't kill!

I'll be leaving within minutes to share dinner with George. I resolve not to take him, or our time together, for granted. I'm really struck by how silly it seems to waste precious time being concerned about matters of little importance. Today I'm keenly aware of how I allow George's moods and little quirks to blind me to the reality of his loving presence in my life and to his complete loyalty to me and our marriage. I resolve to relate to him differently than I have in the past.

An intuition is growing inside me as if it were a child. Igor's Deathday Party parable makes me suspicious that one day soon he'll exit from our lives, as Steve left his friends. One day we may find a note with the same message. He's reminded both George and me that a good mentor has a short life span. George said that he had told Igor that we'd both be eager for the mentorship to grow into a friendship. I would hate for Igor to leave having only been his/her disciple. I say 'her' because at times I've had the intuition that Igor could quite easily be both male and female.

My hermitage time is over. Time to make my resolution for these coming days.

Intention: I resolve to let these last gray weeks of autumn, exotic with the perfume of death, awaken me to a better way to die. May the fading light enlighten me to invest myself deeply in life. May I spend these days, and all days, relishing each gift each day holds, especially my gifts of love and friendship. My closing prayer:

> O God of the Living, you who have taken
>     your son and our friend Michael home to you,
>     hear my prayer.
> I thank you for the gifts of life that he gave to us.
> I thank you even for the sacrament of Michael's death,
>     rich with the promise
>     of awakening me, and all who loved him,
>     to the nearness of death.
> I pray for the gift of a happy death for George and me.
> May death not find us drugged by worry and anxieties,
>     asleep to the delicious joys of life.
> Even if we die in our sleep,
>     may we die happy and awake to life.
> I pray that we may have a happy death,
>     surrounded by those we love,
>     those who have added so much to our time on this earth
>     by their friendship.
> May they stand about our deathbeds
>     both physically and in spirit.
> Grant us the gift of a happy death,
>     to die in deep love and communion with you,
>     our beloved God.
> May our deaths be a party whose hidden guests
>     will be Christ, his holy Mother, all the saints of heaven
>     as well as all those we have loved on earth.
> Amen. Amen. Amen.

# Ship's Log

**Vessel:** THE HERMITAGE

**Officer at the Helm:** GEORGE

**Date:** SATURDAY, NOVEMBER 18

**Time:** 1145 HOURS - 11:45 A.M.

I began my day by reading from the New Testament. I flipped it open at random and landed at Luke's Gospel, chapter 12. My eyes fell on verse 16 where Jesus, like Igor, told his disciples a parable about a rich man who wasn't so rich. Instead of sharing what he had with others, he kept building bigger and bigger barns to store his surplus. Jesus' parable ends with the rich man being the poorest of the poor. Death came and stole his life, and the man found that he had failed to become rich in God's sight.

I pondered on the reading for some time. It fed into the prayer and discussion Martha and I have recently had about death—and about how to live in the face of death. It also seemed especially appropriate since we're only a few days away from Thanksgiving. In the middle of my reflections I heard a strangely beautiful stringed instrument and someone singing in Russian. I looked up to see Igor dancing on the lawn, playing a three-stringed triangular guitar.

I opened the door and called out, "What is that?"

"It's a *balalaika*, and I'm dancing the *kazachok*. It's a Slavic dance performed by men. Care to join me? To dance, George, is to make perhaps the greatest statement about being alive! So, comrade, let's dance!"

"Thanks, Igor, but I'm a little shy when it comes to dancing."

"OK, OK, but am I in time for lunch? I hope so! Nothing elaborate, mind you. Perhaps a glass of chardonnay and some simple fare, like filet of sole on a bed of wild rice...."

"How about a peanut butter sandwich?" I cut in. "For a dragon, I must say, you've got expensive, high-class tastes!"

"George," Igor moaned in mock offense, "the muses aren't drawn to peanut butter! No, they're magnetized by good food and drink, the kind that tickles the tongue and makes your taste buds tingle. Believe me, I know! But being wealthy is more than dining on filet of sole for lunch. Old Isabella knew that!"

"Isabella, the Queen of Spain who gave Columbus seed money for his voyage? Or, can I guess that you have another Isabella in mind?"

"George, you're becoming a mind reader. Your skills never cease to amaze an old dragon like myself. Yes, I was referring to an old friend, Isabella Veracruz. If you fix me that peanut butter sandwich, with a little frost of mayonnaise on it and perhaps a wedge of cheese, I'll tell you the story of Isabella Veracruz." As we munched on our sandwiches, Igor began:

Isabella Veracruz

was a garment worker in her late fifties. She had worked for the shirt factory for close to fifteen years sewing men's dress shirts. Isabella and her husband, who was unable to work because of poor health, lived in a small four-room house in the poor part of town. Daily, since they didn't own a car, Isabella took the bus to work at the shirt factory.

The Bow and Arrow Shirt Company, one of the largest shirtmakers in the country, had just ended a series of fierce negotiations with the Garment Workers Union. Like other companies, it was in the process of transferring most of its production to Korea and China since the Asian countries were offering cheap labor. The battle between management and labor over benefits and a salary increase had lasted for months. The compromise that averted a strike was a salary increase, but also a reduction in long-term benefits. The threat of a strike resolved, it was "business as usual" at the Bow and Arrow factory.

On the last day of the month, Isabella Veracruz, with a determined step, walked away from her sewing machine to speak to her foreman. As she made her way through the maze of the whirring sewing machines, the women said to each other, "Looks like Izzy's in a tizzy. What's wrong now?" Isabella was famous for her strong opinions, and she had been a fighter on the front lines in the recent union conflict.

Because of the noise from all the sewing machines, her coworkers couldn't hear what she was saying to the foreman, but from the look on his face it wasn't good. He tried to argue her out of her position, but without success. At the mid-afternoon break when the machines shut down, the foreman was overheard saying, "God, Izzy, things have just quieted down. Why can't you be satisfied like the other girls. This is out of my area. I've got to call the plant supervisor."

He picked up the phone and dialed. "Jim, we've got a problem down here in the Oxford button-down department. It's Izzy again. Yeah....I know....No, I can't explain on the phone. We're on our way up to see you."

The word that Isabella was on her way to the plant supervisor's office leapt from sewing machine to sewing machine. "Izzy's in a tizzy. She's on her way to the Super." Ten minutes after that meeting, another message sprinted along the lines of sewing machines: "Izzy's goin' all the way to the top. She and the Super are on their way to see the Pres—must be *big* trouble this time."

The president's secretary told the supervisor that they had come at a good time. The president had an appointment in ten minutes with a Chinese businessman to negotiate a new contract, but was free now. She escorted them into the president's walnut-paneled office. "Ah, Mrs. Veracruz, how nice to see you again," the president's voice echoed through a plastic smile, his fingers nervously tapping on his desktop.

Isabella stated her demand again, repeating what she had told her foreman and the supervisor. "Mrs. Veracruz, don't you realize the difficulties of your demand...ah...request. Really, think of the other workers. And, God, what will the union say? We don't have any provisions for this kind of an arrangement; we've *never* had to deal with this issue. Really, why can't you be like the other girls?"

A determined Isabella flatly refused every compromise offer made by management. In the end, she won out, and the company, frustrated and fearful of the consequences, agreed to her demand. As she and her supervisor were leaving, the Chinese businessman was ushered into the president's office.

"Ah, Mr. Wong, how nice to see you again," the president managed to utter.

"Ah, yes, pleasure to see you. Excuse me for interfering, but you look distressed. Having labor problems again?"

"No, Mr. Wong, woman problems, and just when the shop was peaceful again. The woman you saw as you entered the office, do you know what she was demanding? She refuses to take her new 8% pay raise! Can you imagine that? Said she didn't need the money! She, living in some shack with a sick husband, told me that they had all they needed! She refused to take more money!"

"Most unusual! Ah, yes, not common for shirt factories to employ women who are millionaires!"

"Millionaires? What do you mean, Mr. Wong?"

146

"In China, we have a wise and holy book, the *Tao Te Ching*. In chapter 33 it says, 'If you realize that you have enough, you are truly rich.'"

"Isabella's refusal to take a pay raise, Igor, makes your story a fantasy! I don't know of anyone who's ever refused a pay raise! I'd bet if you asked even those who are well-off, most would respond, 'I deserve a raise. I can salt it away in an IRA for the future.'"

"True, George, I admit that that's the case."

"Who would say, 'I have all the money I need?' Even millionaires always look for ways to make more money."

"George, the parable of Jesus about the farmer who had a bumper crop is easily brushed aside as outdated or irrelevant to modern industrial societies. But shouldn't you ask why Jesus called the successful farmer a fool? What's foolish about building bigger storage bins for a record harvest? What's foolish about enjoying the security of a great harvest?

"Jesus' parable, however, is a moral lesson that made sense to his listeners. Unlike American culture, where people place great value on the future, first century Mediterranean culture valued the present—not unlike many third-world countries today. The farmer who wanted to build bigger bins for his surplus grain was judged a fool and criticized sharply by Jesus for acting so American!"

"American, Igor? You say that like it's some kind of a disease or affliction."

"In a way, George, it is. American culture has turned Jesus' message about the rich farmer upside down. Generally in preindustrial cultures it was understood that you had an obligation to share the surplus of a bumper crop with your friends and neighbors. What you did not need at the present moment was given away to neighbors or those in need, not 'squirreled away' for personal enjoyment.

"Yet the message of the parable of Isabella is transcultural! Americans have perfected the need for more, but it's not just an American problem or a Western problem or a modern industrial problem. It's a global heart problem, George, and all heart problems must be taken seriously. Your heart, since childhood, has been trained to constantly desire more! Every heart on this planet, I fear, has a congenital defect, a natural inclination to be greedy."

"I try to share my wealth with the needy, Igor. I give to various causes, the United Fund, to my church. I—"

"Sharing is important, George, but the issue goes deeper. Greed is part of the old Adam and Eve syndrome. It's that great itch, the itch of not being satisfied, even if you're living in the lap of luxury—as they were in the Garden of Eden. It's an itch that we believe will be relieved by more, but it never is. That birth defect, passed from parent to child, has been enlarged by America's cultural tenet that more is better.

"George, to realize that you have enough is a gift. Yet that realization comes only with practice. Daily you have to practice being contented. As a heart patient must exercise to recover, so too this heart problem requires exercise along the road to health and true wealth. It can be painful to become contented since you have to say 'No' to your addiction, the narcotic craving for more, more, more. It's especially difficult and painful since you live in a culture where you see and hear endless advertisements urging you in the cleverest ways to feed your addiction. As for all addicts, who invariably find it painful to surrender their addictions, the question is, 'Why give up your addiction?' The answer is simple: This one is so hard on your heart! In fact, it makes you hardhearted."

As Igor spoke, I had this feeling that my heart was made of marble. Various images of hearts of stone, a term I've found often in Scripture, floated through my mind like boats.

"Have you ever noticed, George, how people who are not content, who are always dissatisfied, are also usually hardhearted, lacking in compassion? But hardening of the heart prevents the sufferer from enjoying life, and those who suffer from that affliction are easily recognized because they tend to frown much more often than they smile. Lacking in compassion, they even find joy in other people's disasters and problems. Perhaps this strange twist is caused by the fact that in competitive societies we often profit by others' disasters. And when we don't actually gain by those difficulties, then at least they make us feel fortunate because we don't have such problems ourselves."

"I can't argue with what you say, Igor. It all makes good sense, but how does one learn contentment?"

"George, the practice of contentment is made easier if you recall the parable of Jesus. Old hollow-eyed death, all dressed up in the blueprints of new grain bins, comes to the rich farmer. Death puts an end to his future and all his plans. Death cancels the farmer's opportunity to be rich in the only wealth that really counts.

"Being content is made amazingly easy if you can but remember death, your own death. A new beatitude is needed today: Blessed are those who daily are conscious of death, for they shall be millionaires."

"Igor, with your help I'll try to practice that beatitude in the coming days. You're right; I am a millionaire. Who needs to win a lottery or inherit a fortune from an unknown relative?"

"Well, J.P. Morgan—or are you one of the Rockefellers?— with that insightful realization, it's time for this poor thread-bare dragon to say good night, *adios* and *addio*. Enjoy your new fortune, George."

With Igor gone, I close this entry in the log with a note of thanks. Because of Igor's visit today, I feel that I am truly a wealthy man—may I let death remind me of that. O God, give me the grace to live in this state of perpetual gratitude— and also the grace to enjoy my wealth to the max.

# Ship's Log

**Vessel:** *THE HERMITAGE*

**Officer at the Helm:** *GEORGE*

**Date:** *WEDNESDAY, NOVEMBER 22*

**Time:** *1930 HOURS - 7:30 P.M.*

"*Cataclysmos*, Armageddon, the end of the world!" Igor shouted to me from high up in the tree by our garage. "The end, George, is at hand! At least if you listen to many people today."

I'm writing all this down shortly after Igor's departure. He appeared about 5:30 P.M. on this Wednesday, just as I was walking from my car to our back door. It surprised me since his pattern has always been to visit on Saturdays. I had come home knowing that Martha was away for the evening because of a meeting at church. It had been a long day at work and I was tired. Igor's greeting, however, suddenly energized me.

"Welcome, Igor! You surprised me! What's all this about Armageddon? And what's a *Cataclysmos*?"

"Do you mind, George? I'm not a bird, you know! How about inviting me to come down from this branch?"

"By my pocket watch it's tea time—or, better yet—happy hour! Let's go to your hermitage and have a cup of tea or a glass of good scotch. If you have any, I'll take Johnny Walker

150

Black Label."

"Expensive taste for a simple-living, threadbare dragon! OK, come down from that tree and go to the hermitage, and I'll go to the house and get the scotch. Don't go away. I'll be there as soon as I get out of these clothes and into something more comfortable."

I returned in my old gray sweatpants and shirt, carrying an ice bucket and a bottle of scotch. I found Igor camped out in the old easy chair in the hermitage, playing his *balalaika*. He had set out two glasses on the desk. As I entered, he began to sing out with full gusto, "A round of grog for all hands on deck!"

"I enjoy hearing you play that Russian guitar—a *balalaika*, you said?"

"Yes, it's like a violin for me. I use it often when I'm asked questions with difficult answers."

"When you're asked questions? What do you mean?"

"I understand, George, that once Albert Einstein was asked a very complex question, like: What is the ultimate unifying principle of the world about us and its connection to the universe? Einstein thought for a moment and said, 'I can't explain it in words, but I can play it for you on my violin!'"

Igor began playing his balalaika with great passion, as he would say, with *abbandonatamente*. "There, George, is an answer to all your questions about life. But let's come back to this later," he said, placing his instrument on the floor. Then he lifted his glass with a toast, "George, to *Cataclysmos*! Cheers!"

As we sipped our scotch he began, "I know you're familiar with cataclysms, but *Cataclysmos* is a feast held on the island of Cyprus. It commemorates the time when Zeus, king of the gods, sent a flood, a *cataclysmos*—an old Greek-Latin word meaning 'deluge'! So Zeus sent the flood to destroy all humans on the earth for their wickedness. Zeus, it seems, was angry about the technological advances of the Bronze Age! All were destroyed but the good king Deucalion and his wife Pyrrha. They built an ark and took with them

151

pairs of animals and birds, which in the flood came to rest safely on the Mount Parnassus. Any of this beginning to sound familiar, George?

"Anyway, to celebrate the end of the flood, King Deucalion held a feast. In Cyprus they repeat the feast of this Greek Noah each year, celebrating it on June 8th. I propose that, even though it's November, we make it a movable feast and celebrate it tonight. Let's you and I celebrate the end— the *Cataclysmos*!"

"You mean an end of the world party?" I asked as I took a sip of scotch. "Martha told me about your Deathday Party parable. Igor, you're really into dark and deadly occasions for partying."

"George, life is to be celebrated—all of it! Besides, it provides the opportunity to reflect on the end. And that, my friend, is indeed a timely activity. With the sands in history's hourglass quickly running out with the approach of a new millennium, tell me the truth, George. Don't you hear deep inside a voice calling you to escape from the coming disaster? Don't you hear a voice, like the one that old Noah or King Deucalion heard, that inner and divine voice calling you to build an ark—in your case, a spaceship, or maybe a concrete bomb shelter stocked with food—so as to escape the end days?"

"Igor, you've been reading too many grocery-store tabloids! No, I don't hear any voice like that. However, lately I have heard a growing chorus of other fearful voices crying, 'Armageddon is at hand.' If you're a betting dragon, I'll wager you that in these coming years "*God's Great Cataclysmos*" will be a best-seller."

Slowly sipping his scotch, Igor licked his large lips. "Ah, George, 'tis indeed, as the old Scots were fond of saying, 'the water of life'! Not to change the subject, but did you hear about the big whale that came ashore recently in California?"

"Another gray whale whose radar had gone amuck?"

"More than that, it seems." Setting his glass down, Igor started into this tale:

According to the news reports,

a very large gray whale was found by some tourists aground along the California coast at a place called Nineveh Beach. Environmentalists, members of Save the Whale groups and nature lovers began to gather there. Marine biology experts brought in tow trucks with large cranes and tried to lift the whale and swing it out into deeper water, but they failed.

All the while, volunteers from various nature groups worked around the clock wetting down the whale. Next, the marine experts wrapped the whale in large nets, a kind of harness, and connected it to several motor boats. They were able to pull the whale off the beach and out toward the ocean, which caused rejoicing among the crowd on the shore. However, as soon as they released the nets, the whale swam right back up onto the beach—only this time, it came even higher aground on the shore!

The experts from the San Diego Aquamarine Institute were not hopeful that they could save the poor beast. They used stethoscopes to check the whale's heart, and, to their surprise, they could hear voices coming from inside the large whale! Sometimes they were very faint, and then at other times slightly more audible. As best the experts could tell, there were several different voices.

The reaction was mixed when this news was announced to the large crowd of the curious and concerned gathered about the beached whale. One tourist on the beach, a redheaded man clutching a Bible and wearing running shorts and a T-shirt with the message "Jesus Saves" inscribed on it, cried out, "Possession! This poor whale is possessed by demons, by the Devil himself. We must have an exorcism at once." Some of the crowd laughed, shaking their heads, but several began talking about calling for a priest. One tourist even offered to sprinkle holy water on the beached whale, saying she had a bottle of it in her camper trailer. Someone in the crowd shouted, "Go get it, lady; let's see what happens."

"I propose a more scientific and rational answer," came a voice from the back of the crowd. As people moved aside, a distinguished looking gray-haired man walked forward. "My name is Dr. Koenig. I'm a psychiatrist. It is my professional opinion that what we have here is a classical case of a schizophrenic whale. Schizophrenia," he smiled at the crowd as one does when talking to children, "is a psychotic reaction characterized by withdrawal from reality, *dementia praecox*. As you can see, this poor whale has withdrawn herself from the ocean, her base of reality. Lacking time for extensive therapy, I propose the use of drugs!"

Several heads in the crowd bobbed up and down, since they respected the doctor's voice of authority and were also aware that hearing voices is common for schizophrenics. However, one of the marine experts replied, "You're the ones who are crazy! Whales can't be possessed by the Devil, and they don't suffer from psychotic disorders. This is a simple case of—"

"Yeah?" shouted the redheaded man with the Bible. "Then how come you experts can't get it back in the ocean?" Another voice shouted, "How do you explain the voices from inside the whale? Do you think it swallowed a radio?" A wave of laughter rose from the crowd until the whale gave a sad groan, silencing everyone.

After much discussion, the marine experts decided they needed to have a better idea of what was going on inside the whale. X-ray equipment was out of the question on the beach, so they sent for some high-tech audio equipment to better monitor what was happening inside the whale.

Someone had called in the story of the possessed or schizophrenic whale to the news media. Whereas earlier they had given passing coverage to the whale's predicament, now it had become an "item." Like a report of a sex scandal in the Vatican, the story spread like fire in a rain-thirsty forest. Within hours, Nineveh Beach became crowded with TV news mobile units, camera crews and ever growing hordes of the curious. State highway troopers were busy directing traffic, as high overhead TV helicopters circled the scene. Off shore, a large flotilla of various-sized pleasure and fishing boats had gathered. The entire scene was boisterous and bizarre. In the center of the beach the redheaded man in shorts had organized a prayer service to pray for the whale's deliverance from the Devil. As they shouted and sang for God's help, ice cream vending trucks with blaring rock music busily hawked their cool treats among the people on the beach.

Finally, complete with a police escort, a truck with the mobile audio equipment arrived. The large crowd grew hushed as a technician wearing earphones held a cone-shaped device to the side of the whale. Lines of large, twisted cables connected the cone to the massive equipment inside the truck.

"I count four, maybe five, different voices," shouted the audio man. "Turn up the volume," he shouted back to the truck crew, "so I can hear what it is they're saying." The crowd grew tensely quiet during these pregnant moments. Then, removing his earphones, the technician called the marine experts to join him. One by one they put on the earphones as voices in the crowd began to shout, "Who are they? What are they saying?"

After some discussion, the head of the marine life experts stepped up to a bank of microphones encircled by TV cameras. "I have an announcement to make. We've made a breakthrough. We believe that the whale has swallowed a batch of...ah...religious fanatics or prophets. How or where this happened, we don't know, but we can now hear clearly a variety of voices inside the poor whale. Some are shouting, 'Doom! Doomsday,' and 'God is about to destroy the world for its wickedness.' Others are shouting, 'Doomsday! Repent! Repent!' One thing is for sure: It *is* the end for this poor whale! It's dead unless we can get it off this beach and back into the ocean where it belongs!"

"What are you going to do?" asked one of the many TV reporters. "You've tried just about everything, haven't you?"

"Yes, we've used every known method to unbeach a whale, and each has failed. However," and the expert held up a long finger, creating a palpable sense of the dramatic, "we've never had to rescue a whale from divine possession!"

Just then, all heads turned away from the circle of bright media lights back to the whale, which had begun to gag loudly. It choked in waves of great dry heaves. Then, after a series of gasps, it went into spasms. From its large mouth it vomited one, then a second, then a third, and finally all five prophets of doom out onto the beach.

Those four men and a woman hit the beach like the first wave of troops on D Day at Omaha Beach. They ran up the beach and into the crowd with loaded Bibles, and at point-blank range they screamed, "Repent, you evil sinners. Woe to you perverts, Armageddon has come! Every one of you ugly sinners is doomed to hell!" One of them, screaming "Hallelujah!" carried a placard as if it were a flag. On the placard, printed in red, was THE END! "At last God's justice will come upon all of you, unless you repent," screamed one of the beached prophets wearing only a large gunnysack as he ran wildly through the crowd throwing ashes on peoples' heads.

So wild and chaotic was the beach scene that no one noticed that the great gray whale was slowly edging herself off the beach. Once in deeper water, she turned and began swimming for the open sea. "Look," several people began shouting, "she's free! Look, she's heading out for the deep!"

"Ladies and gentlemen," spoke a news reporter into the cameras, "it's good news tonight from Nineveh Beach, California. The beached whale that has been among the top news stories for days has freed herself! She's now heading out to the ocean! The crowd of thousands which has gathered here is now headed home, pleased with the happy ending to this story. We now return you to our main studio for the rest of the news and tonight's weather." In the background, still audible over the reporter's voice, could be heard another weather report: "Doom! Doomsday's here! Tomorrow God's fire and brimstone will rain down like hell from the sky!"

"If your glass of scotch was the source of that story, I'll get you a whole bottle of Johnny Walker Black Label."

"It's not a story, George! It's a parable. I will, however, take you up on your gift of a bottle of scotch. Parables are special stories, secret stories, since inside them are hidden messages. They're like Chinese fortune cookies. Parables are not for nibbling! They are meant to be broken open so that you can find the hidden messages.

"Like buildings, parables can have several stories—no pun intended, George—and even basements. That's why old dragons like myself prefer to use parables as teaching tools. They're a close second to playing answers to life's great questions on a violin or *balalaika*."

"Igor MOO, what about your Nineveh Beach Whale tale— I mean, parable? It's most timely at this season of the year, but I must confess that I'm still not clear about its meaning. How can I break it open to get to the fortune?"

"Well, George, you won't need a sledgehammer. I might add, not only is late November a good time to ponder such a parable, these years on either side of the awesome year of 2000, when millenarianism is ripe, make for prime time! But what do you think about the parable?"

"It was like the Jonah story in the Bible, and yet it was different. In the original Jonah story the whale vomited an *unwilling* prophet on the shore, yet he *did* convert the people."

"You've touched on the Sign of Jonah paradox. On one level the Old Testament story is about Jewish exclusivity and narrow religious bias. On another level, Jonah's three days in the belly of the whale is seen as a sign of the three days Jesus would spend in the tomb. When Jesus told his critics that the only sign he'd give them is the sign of Jonah, what did he mean? But first, take a sharp-hooked question mark and pick away at the prophets inside the Nineveh Beach whale. What did you think about them?"

"Personally, I found them very unattractive! Actually, I found them to be ugly in their self-righteousness! They came ashore like invading troops, and my feeling was that they were angry—their call to repentance seemed to almost drip with deadly venom!"

"Good cracking-open, George! The same is true of the prophet Jonah. After preaching in old Nineveh City, the original Big Apple of the Middle East, the entire city repented. They dressed in sackcloth and ashes, repented and changed their ways. So God did not destroy them. It angered Jonah that God had spared them since the Assyrians who lived in Nineveh were his enemies. They were a bloody, aggressive, plundering imperial power. See the point? Jonah wanted God to punish them, wipe them off the face of the earth, destroy their city and every man, woman and child. With so much vile contempt inside him, it's no wonder that the fish who swallowed him vomited him up. We do the same when we vomit up what is offensive to our system."

"Did the beached whale in your parable represent the Church? Or was it a metaphor for our society?"

"Which do you think? Angry, hate-filled prophets of doom and destruction, be they authors or preachers, always find an audience of like-minded, angry, even vicious, people. Such so-called reformers mask their discriminations as godly hate, while despising the very persons whom they're calling to repentance. You asked if the whale was the Church—could it not also be yourself? Only when we love what we wish to reform can that work of change be the work of God. Great love is essential for any truly successful reformation."

Igor stood up, and I knew what that meant. Once he's in motion, there's no stopping him, even if I still had a batch of unanswered questions. "Why don't you take the bottle of scotch with you, Igor?"

"Well, thanks, George. That's mighty thoughtful of you. I may just have a little nightcap before retiring tonight. See you soon, mate, and as they once said on the U-boats, *Auf Wiedersehen*!" Then he was gone, having completely disappeared from sight in the middle of the doorway!

I conclude this surprise entry in the log and prepare to leave. A few minutes ago I heard Martha's car in the drive. It's late, and I've been here in the hermitage for several hours. As I go back to the house, I take with me a pocketful of questions.

# Ship's Log

**Vessel:** the Hermitage

**Officer at the Helm:** Martha

**Date:** Saturday, November 25

**Time:** 1520 Hours - 3:20 P.M.

Today's first entry in the logbook comes at midafternoon. It's been a quiet day for me. I wrote some poetry about gratitude—the smell of Thanksgiving Day, while two days past, is still in the air.

I also did some embroidery on a Christmas gift for a friend. I like to do needlework on my hermitage days; my fingers move without needing instruction as my mind drifts across the open seas. For me embroidery is a kind of needle-and-thread meditation.

I had put away the poetry and embroidery when of all things—I mean for this time of the year—I heard what sounded like an old crop duster flying overhead. I stood up and went to the window just as Igor came sailing over the treetops and made a graceful landing in the backyard. I shook my head and wondered aloud, "What in the world do the neighbors think when Igor makes his grand entrances? When he's not appearing out of nowhere, he arrives singing or making a commotion. They've never said anything, but surely they must hear him!"

I opened the door, and Igor walked in with a white silk scarf flamboyantly draped around his neck. "No, Martha, they don't!" he said. "They haven't heard any of the other things either, but that's because their ears are full, clogged with inner noise."

I closed the door as he motioned for me to take his usual place in the easy chair while he sat down at the desk.

"Martha, did George share with you the Nineveh Beach parable?"

"Yes. We both found it, ah, interesting—and cause for reflection. I don't know how I feel about those prophecies that deal with the end of the world, with the sun and moon turning into dripping globs, stars falling to earth like an April shower."

"Martha, you're lucky. You know, the world ends every day. The sun turns to blood and the moon goes out like an old light bulb every day for thousands of people. They lose their jobs, lose their lovers, their health, reputation, life's savings, children, even their lives! So woe to those who are not prepared! You and George have seen a world end, haven't you? Look at all the dramatic changes that have taken place in business, education, politics, religion and everywhere else. As for the final end—"

"Yes, Igor, let's talk about the Second Coming—talk, not play the violin! A woman with whom I work is always talking about it. I don't know what to say to her. I guess I've never thought about it enough to really form an opinion—or perhaps I should say a belief."

"With your permission, *memsahib*, let us indeed talk about it. As I flew in here today, about twenty miles from the city I flew over an abandoned airstrip named the Second Coming Landing Strip. Nothing there now but weeds, but once it was the site of an incredible series of occurrences. I first heard the story from an old man I visited in a retirement home. He was just a kid when the Emmanuelites arrived. This was the story he told me:

# One day

a traveling preacher came to town. Oh, we had preachers pass through here before, but none like this one. He wore a white shirt, tie and suit. He had this amazing gift for preaching sermons so fiery that folks passed out from pure heat exhaustion! His name was Preacher Plumberg, and he preached about the imminent return of Jesus Christ. It was in the days when flying was in its infancy, and he was convinced that Jesus was going to fly into town. So he urged the faithful to build a landing strip for Christ's glorious return.

The faithful who belonged to his church were called Emmanuelites. They got that name because they began every one of their services by singing the same hymn: "O Come, O Come, Emmanuel." The faithful gathered in the small church several nights a week and on Sundays for what they called P & P, prayer and preparation. Once they had completed the construction on the Second Coming Landing Strip, they met out there on Sunday morning before sunrise.

I was just a little kid then, and my folks became Emmanuelites. So I was part of the crowd that gathered out at the landing strip on Sunday mornings. If you go out there now, all that's left is a battered, gray, weatherworn wooden arch over the entrance. Still readable on it are the faded words, The Glorious Second Coming Landing Strip. The air strip now is a sea of weeds in the middle of which is a dilapidated wooden platform. In the glory days of the Emmanuelites, that's where Preacher Plumberg and the faithful would gather before dawn on Sunday mornings.

What caused them to abandon the place wasn't that they lost patience or faith in the Second Coming. Nope, in fact, it was just the opposite! The reason the place is abandoned and overgrown with weeds is that Jesus *did* come! It was long ago, but I'll never forget that cold December Sunday morning. Being a child, I wasn't interested in going to church, especially since we had to go before sunrise. There was no choice, however, since Pastor Plumberg insisted that everyone had to be there, kids included. He reasoned that since we never knew when Jesus was returning, if *now* was the hour, well you wouldn't want to leave your children behind!

On one December Sunday in the late 1930s, we were all out at the Second Coming Landing Strip praying and singing up a storm, mostly to keep warm—when it came! It came right out of the rising sun. First, we heard the sound of an engine. Then we saw it. It was a biplane, a pure white two-winger, trimmed in silver! It swept low over the landing strip, then circled wide around the field. As it circled overhead we could read the letters painted on the bottom of the lower wing: Great Power and Glory.

Folks went crazy, women fainted, men jumped up and down waving their hats and Pastor Plumberg kept shouting, "Hallelujah, He's come!" Then as the white plane zoomed straight over everyone standing on the platform, it dropped a small white parachute. Attached to the parachute, slowly floating down to the earth, was a silver canister. The plane meanwhile had turned and flown straight back to the east, disappearing into the rising sun.

Pastor Plumberg and his deacon, Mr. Goodfell, ran to where the windblown parachute landed and got the canister. Everyone crowded around when he opened it. The only thing inside it was a piece of paper on which was written: Next Sunday at Sunrise.

The news of the white two-winged plane spread around town and the surrounding area like peanut butter on warm toast. By Wednesday night the little church was so crowded there was hardly any room left for the Emmanuelites. By the end of the week, at the Friday-night prayer service, the crowd had grown so large they had to hold church in the high school gym. Even it was packed to overflowing since all the towns-folk, as well as the citizens of most of the surrounding little towns, were there. Pastor Plumberg was beside himself with the joy of victory. Folks from the other churches, even the Roman Catholics and Lutherans, were elbow to elbow with the Emmanuelites. Everyone was eager to know how to get ready for the Second Coming.

Pastor Plumberg preached on the end of the world, when everything would be swept away by the wrath of God, and how Jesus would come to take with him all the redeemed.

He waved his big black Bible and quoted from Luke about how Jesus had promised that the Son of Man would return "on the clouds in great power and glory." "The very words," he said, "the very words painted on the wings of the airplane of God that descended from heaven last Sunday. Plain as day they were: *Great Power and Glory.*" Shouts of "Hallelujah" and "Amen," louder than any basketball cheers, echoed like thunder, almost lifting off the roof of the high school gym.

At the end of his sermon, Pastor Plumberg asked if there were any questions. At first, only a heavy silence hung over the gym, as lead-weighted as a brooding August thunderstorm about to break loose. Then, a man stood up and asked, "Does that mean, pastor, that on this Sunday morning the world will end?" A rolling wave of mumbling rose and fell in the packed gym, for the man who had asked the question was the town's agnostic.

"Yes it does, friend," answered Pastor Plumberg, "the end of the world and the beginning of the reign of God's chosen ones. Hallelujah! Then the rewards promised to the good and righteous will be granted." Loud applause came in tidal waves in response to the pastor's words.

Then the man who had asked the question asked another one, "If it's *the* end, doesn't that also mean, pastor, that it's the time of the Judgment, the vindication of God?"

Plumberg smiled as if he'd just made the winning touchdown in the Super Bowl. "Yes, indeedy, yes it does. All those faggots, heathens, violators of the Sabbath, those who worship false gods, and members of false religions will—"

Plumberg was cut off midstream by another question from the same man, "And will that not also, according to Scripture, be the day when all that has been spoken and done in secret will be shouted from the housetops, will be judged in the light of God?"

At that question, from the church choir, a faintly audible gasp came out of the mouth of Nellie Jean, a high school senior who sang in the church choir. She looked straight at Pastor Plumberg with terror-filled eyes. He must have seen her frightened look of confusion, for he dropped his Bible!

165

Bending over to pick it up, he didn't see Mrs. Plumberg cast a fearful glance over at Stan Larson, the high school football coach.

Some folks began loudly shouting, "Praise the Lord! O Come, O Come, Emmanuel. Come, we're ready!" But then the man who had questioned Pastor Plumberg shouted in a loud voice so all could hear, "Neighbors, good townspeople, think for a moment. Besides being Judgment Day, doesn't next Sunday mean that it's the end, the end of everything you love in this world? No more Thanksgiving Day dinners with your families, no more Christmas trees and giving gifts. It's the end of pleasant summer evenings on the front porch swing, of playing with your grandkids, the end of making love, if it *is* the end! For the reward of the faithful is God, and *only* God—isn't that right, pastor?"

Deacon Goodfell, whom everyone in town knew was the secret Grand Dragon of the local Ku Klux Klan, shouted, "Pastor Plumberg, are we sure about this? Do we know for sure that it was the real Jesus in the white plane? Maybe it was the Antichrist! I propose we call a meeting of the church board tonight to discuss next Sunday's coming of Emmanuel."

That night everyone went home, talking to each other about whether they really wanted Christ to come. As the hours passed, a steady stream of the town's most important people came and went from the church board crisis meeting.

On Sunday morning an hour before sunrise, the road leading east out of town was one long parade of cars and trucks. They were filled with Emmanuelites as well as people from all the other churches in town, all headed for the Second Coming Landing Strip. When they arrived, not a sound could be heard in all those cars as everyone waited for the coming of Emmanuel.

As the sun slowly crested the horizon in the east, they heard it, coming, it seemed, right out of the center of the sun. As the white plane swooped down low, its wheels almost touching the ground, the quiet of the morning was shattered by a deafening thunderous roar! Rifles, shotguns, pistols, weapons of every size and shape, blasted away from the windows, rooftops and running boards of the assembled cars. A continuous barrage of gunfire riddled the white biplane as it flew down the length of the runway.

In a blinding flash of white and silver the plane zoomed straight upward. As it soared upward, trailing behind it was a thin stream of white smoke. The plane climbed higher and higher as if it were going to disappear through some hole in the top of the sky.

Suddenly it stalled, flipped over and began plunging downward, twisting and turning as it spiraled earthward. Long, thin tongues of fire licked backward from the engine along the fuselage, and thick black clouds of smoke trailed behind. Ever downward it plunged until it crashed in a field several miles away. Someone in the crowd began singing faintly, "O Come, O Come, Emmanuel..."

" *Salaam*, peace, Martha." Igor stood up, leaving me sunk in the easy chair with the parable.

"Thank you, Igor. You've given me more than enough to fill my day. Come again soon, please. Chin-chin, we students in search of the flaming pearl need your help."

"I wonder how much you need *my* help!" he replied with a playful nod of his head. "Remember, Martha, that the best way to learn anything is to teach it! Teaching *forces* you to look at and be open to the whole of the reality of what you're teaching, at least if you want to communicate it well and with integrity. Teaching and sharing what you love, perhaps in your group, is the royal road to wisdom. By the way, how is your small band of friends on the questventure coming?"

"We're still together, even if that has meant that we've had to become thieves!"

"Stolen time, eh? Such time *is* precious, far more valuable than what most people consider to be valuable. But, while we are eager for Emmanuel to come, it's time for Igor to go—in more ways than one. Chin-chin to you, Martha." He then did a little jig, turned with a snap of his long dragon's tail and was gone.

Intention: The next time I join with the others at church to sing "O Come, O Come, Emmanuel" I shall either sing with, as Igor would say, *affetuoso*, feminine warmth, or I shall be as closed-lipped as a spy caught behind enemy lines.

I must examine in these beginning days of the Advent season whether I truly want the world to end. I'll wear this question like a necklace: "Am I really ready and eager for Emmanuel to come?"

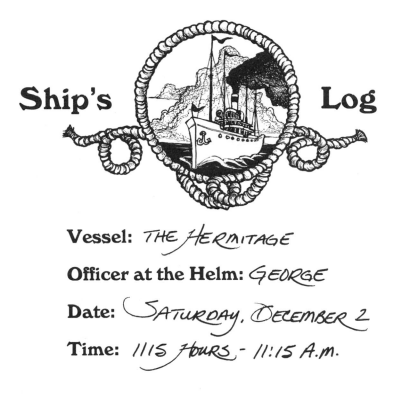

# Ship's Log

**Vessel:** *THE HERMITAGE*

**Officer at the Helm:** *GEORGE*

**Date:** *SATURDAY, DECEMBER 2*

**Time:** *1115 HOURS - 11:15 A.M.*

I had fallen asleep in the easy chair while reading when I was awakened by a soft humming. I opened my eyes to see Igor bent over me. "*Shalom*, George! Sorry to interrupt your prayers! Nice and cozy-warm here in your hermitage, and you *were* praying the siesta prayer, eh? Except that's an afternoon nap rather than a late-morning one! But don't misunderstand me, George, I really consider sleep to be good prayer. Who knows, you might have a small dream or two. These December days are ripe for dreams; it's the season of sugarplum fairies, chestnuts roasting on an open fire and the famous 'I'm dreaming of a White Christmas, just like the ones—'"

"Have a seat, Igor. I'll add to those dreams an ancient one: Israel's dream of an Emmanuel, a God-Savior who would rescue the world from evil. Even today that continues to be our dream as well. Why else would we sing 'O Come, O Come, Emmanuel,' come, God among us? Why that plaintive prayer unless we need some light in our darkness? I'm sorry to lay it on so heavily, but as you can tell, Igor, Martha and I have been reflecting on your Emmanuelite parable. It's really gotten us into this pre-Christmas Advent season!"

"No apology needed, George the Awakened. Any and every season, for pilgrims on the quest, should be an Advent, an ad-venture of God a-birthing inside them, as well as coming into the world. This a-birthing season is also the season of growing night, as the hours of darkness increase."

"Yes, Igor, and into that season of darkness come all the lights. I find them wonderful—Advent candles, Hanukkah candles and all those Christmas lights flickering in the darkness of approaching winter. It all helps me focus and deepen my personal Lucky Lux dream. That parable has also really been alive for me in these early Advent days."

"I can see that, George. Let's not forget that it's a season of other great spiritual lights: luminarias like Buddha—whose enlightenment anniversary feast is December 8, the same day as Mary's feast of preparedness for bringing to birth the Light of the World. Then there's the Prophet of Dawn, Isaiah, who lived in darkness yet was able to live out of a dream-vision of a hope-filled future. And that blazing Torch of the Torah, old John the Baptizer of Jordan River fame! Now, there's a wild, psychedelic light in the night who called Israel to become a smooth roadway for Emmanuel's entrance into the world."

"It's a road, Igor, that for Israel and for us today needs to have a lot of potholes filled and humps removed. Before I fell asleep this afternoon, I was reading an author who quoted G.K. Chesterton: 'A society is converted best by the person who contradicts it most!'"

"Well, George, Baptizer John certainly contradicted his! First, there was his 'uncityfied' dress, his camel's hair cloak and leather belt and his desert starvation diet of grasshoppers and honey. And to the religious leaders of his day, I'll bet John was more a nightmare than a dream! A nightmare to the pious establishment, and a pain in the neck nightmare to all those who felt they had no need to repent or to confess their sins to anyone. Jordan John is either a case of great madness or great holiness—or perhaps divine madness!"

"You've spoken to me before, Igor, about reform. You said

that constant reform, constant personal revolution, is *the* path."

"I have indeed, George. It's not only the beginning, but the ongoing work of every quest. It's also a most difficult work because we usually like to feel it's only others who need reform and change. Reform is for structures, institutions, churches—not you or me."

"You know, all this talk about reform and this season of dreams has made me remember that I had a dream last night, Igor. It's funny that I didn't recall it until now, but suddenly it's very clear in my consciousness—I expect your presence has something to do with my sudden remembering. Maybe the dream was due to some lost thought about Advent reform drifting in my subconscious sea. It sure was a strange dream!"

"Of sugarplum fairies or chestnuts roasting on an open fire?"

"I wish! No, this was not a sweet dream. If I had to give it a name, I'd call it "A Christmas Nightmare.""

My dream began

with me going to Wal-Mart, the large discount store, to purchase a string of Christmas tree lights. We like our tree up and decorated as soon after Thanksgiving as possible.

As I approached Wal-Mart's front door, I saw the kindly Salvation Army bell ringer smiling at me. Even with the crowds of shoppers coming and going, I spotted—lurking behind the Salvation Army woman—a wild-looking man dressed in a camel's hair nightshirt. He was barefoot, had a long scraggly beard and unkempt hair. He looked like old icon paintings of John the Baptist, only he was carrying an ax. I quickly looked the other way, but suddenly he began to scream, "Repent, you vipers, before it's too late!" I hurried into the store, dropping a little loose change in the Salvation Army pot as I did. His eyes fastened on me like two blue lasers.

I was passing the One Hour Photo counter just inside the door when I heard a shrill voice behind me, "Repent, sinner—you—now, while you still have time!" Shoppers and clerks began to stare at me, wondering what this crazy man knew about me that they didn't. Embarrassed, I looked for a security guard. Not seeing one, I hurried on. The wild man followed me and continued to hurl accusations at me. I tried to lose him by darting down a side aisle in the shoe department.

Like a bloodhound, old John, if that's who he was, came after me, swinging his ax, hot on my trail as he continued shouting accusations at me. I walked at a fast clip through the women's underwear department, took a sharp right into children's wear, then cut across to the hardware department and darted into the sports department. The aisles were crowded with shoppers, whom I artfully dodged left and right with apologies. A quick look over my shoulder assured me that I'd lost the crazy man.

The Christmas music playing on the store's loudspeakers suddenly stopped with a jerk. After a pause, a frantic voice boomed out, "Code Black and Blue...Code Black and Blue. Mr. Joplins, Mr. Joplins, pick up a service phone at once." As alarms began ringing, holiday shoppers stopped and looked anxiously around, fearing that it might be a fire or some other disaster. By now I was running for the exit after making a detour through the Christmas decorations aisle. Suddenly all the lights went out; the store was thrown into total blackness.

Blinded by the darkness, I stopped. Then I felt a hot breath on the back of my neck. It was strong with the smell of bugs and honey. "Repent before it's too late, you viper!" A pair of strong bony hands gripped my shoulders and shook me. "Wake up, you fool! Wake up and change your life!" I could feel the steel blade of his ax sliding up and down my right leg.

By now people were screaming. In the pitch-black cavern of the giant store flashlights appeared here and there like slender ribbons of light waving in the darkness. Suddenly, with a loud pop, all the lights came on again! Incredibly, the lights revealed some shoppers stuffing merchandise under their coats. Yet no one paid any attention to them! Instead, all eyes were on me! I was so embarrassed, but I had no idea why everyone was staring at me.

A firm hand grabbed me by the shoulders. "All right, sir, no fuss, please, no more commotion. Come calmly outside with us." I turned around to see two policemen, one with his hand on my shoulder. Next to him was a man whom I took to be Mr. Joplins, the store manager. Then I looked down, and to my horror I saw that I was barefoot and wearing a camel's hair sack-like nightshirt that reached to my knees. "The ax, sir! Hand it over calmly, please," said one of the officers while the other began snapping handcuffs on my wrists.

As the police escorted me to the exit of the store, crowds of people were gathering along the way. As I passed, some stared, some giggled. Others pointed at me with recognition. Infants were crying and small children were hiding behind their mothers as I went by. I burned with shame as I was ushered into the backseat of the waiting police car.

"Igor, retelling the dream, I feel like I just awoke in a sweat. Exiting that Christmas nightmare was like coming out of a sauna. I wonder what Dr. Freud would have thought of my dream. It was frightening to look into that wild man's eyes in the beginning of the dream, and then to be the target of his cries to repent. But it was really strange at the end to find myself in the prophet's clothes!

"It also made me think about your Nineveh Beach parable and the angry prophets who were vomited out of the whale. In my dream, not only was I accosted by a fierce prophet, I actually became that prophet! Is there any difference between the anger of the Nineveh Beach prophets and the Baptist-like prophet of my dream?"

"If you remember, George, like Jonah, those hateful prophets wanted vindication more than reform. The fire of a John the Baptist was intended to *wake people up*, to make them earnest about reform."

"You know, though, Igor, I have, in the past, kind of wished to be a prophet; at least I've wanted to convert society. I've wanted to change it, especially when it's so blind to the plight of the poor. Recently, I've felt a need to really do something about changing things, to get on with it. Maybe that's why I became the prophet in my dream. Yet I've always felt uncomfortable identifying with reformers or reform groups."

"There, George, lies the other difference between real and false prophets. Most reform groups are made up of people eager to reform others or the government rather than themselves!

"Yet the song on the wind these December days *is* reform! While lips in church sing 'O Come, O Come, Emmanuel,' its call to reform rarely reaches to hearts. That's partly because lips at home and at work are usually singing 'I'm dreaming of a White Christmas.' Attention isn't focused on personal reform; it's fixed on buying gifts, decorating, parties and dinners."

"I thought, Igor, that you're a party animal. You've always looked for any occasion to party. What's wrong with parties in these preparation days before Christmas?"

"Nothing. Actually, it might be a good idea for you and Martha to have an Advent reform party! For the true pilgrim, any season is a season for reform—in fact, *now* is always the best time for reform!"

"Igor, the call to reform is at the heart of my dream, and we've talked *around* my dream—or should I say, nightmare—but could you be like Joseph in Egypt and unravel it for me?"

"George, recall John the Baptist's charge to the pious leaders: 'Give some evidence that you are serious about reforming!' These days can be a nightmare if you let old hairy John catch you in the dark some night and scream, 'Give some evidence that *you* mean to reform!' Yes, these days are evidence time. If you can't provide any good evidence, then—like a Christmas Tree—you'll be chopped down, not to be decorated but to be thrown into the fire!"

Igor had built up a full head of steam, and I wasn't about to stop him as he heated up the hermitage with the fire and zeal of a boiler-room preacher.

"'The ax is already laid at the root of the tree,' to quote hairy John," Igor said as he waved an ax that had appeared out of nowhere. "George, take your New Testament. Open it to Philippians, chapter 4, verse 4, if you're looking for some evidence to save your skin. Read it aloud to me."

I read: "Everyone should see how unselfish you are." Closing the book, I asked myself if I was unselfish. Was I generous with my money? Yes, I told myself. If you want evidence, look at my long list of gifts for friends and family! Yes, I submit that gift list as my evidence.

"What kind of evidence is that?" said Igor, reading my thoughts. "You'd have real, solid evidence if you intended to give gifts to *all* your family. Not just to your children, parents and friends, but also to the other members of your family: the poor and homeless. If, to stay the executioner's ax, you want to give real evidence of your intention to reform, how about 50-50? That's right, give as much to the poor in Christmas charity as you do in Christmas gifts to family and good friends!"

"Equal amounts, 50-50? Do you want to bankrupt me?"

"But money's not all that you have to share with your whole family. How about your time, energy and service? You said that you wanted to get on with the work of changing the plight of the poor. How about getting earnest about your own reform so that you can really get on with that work?"

"Have mercy on me, Igor. My head is spinning! And stop waving that ax!" With a loud clump, Igor dropped the ax on the desk. "I'm leaving you and Martha this Advent Ax! You can keep it here in your hermitage. You can lean it against your Christmas Tree—now that would be a real conversation piece—or you can keep it in your bedroom."

"Thanks for the gift, I guess."

"Don't give me the old *malocchio*, the evil eye. Why have a spiritual guide if you're not interested in changing? Well, George, time to go. *Do svidanya*, see you later—oh, yes—and pleasant dreams!"

After Igor left, I sat for a long time holding his woodsman's ax and reflecting. I found myself singing, or praying, or both:

Lay down your Advent Ax, wild-eyed prophet of the desert,
    I'll give you evidence in these coming days
    that I'm serious about my reform!
I promise I'll be generous with my time and talents.
I promise I'll be generous doing little things for others
    as often as possible and in hidden ways.
Lay down your Advent Ax, crazy son of old Elizabeth,
    I'll make time for prayer,
    so as to enlarge my heart for Emmanuel's coming
    now, today, here.
I'll fill my potholes, level myself into a roadway
    for God to enter my world.
Lay down your Advent Ax, crazy cousin of Jesus,
    I promise I'll work for the conversion of the world
    first and foremost by converting myself.
My evidence, and this isn't easy, will be that
    my behavior and lifestyle will contradict convention.
Then I can call myself by that most beautiful of names:
    a true convert.

I sign this page in the logbook with my new name.

*George the Convert*

# Ship's Log

**Vessel:** *the Hermitage*

**Officer at the Helm:** *Martha*

**Date:** *Saturday, December 9*

**Time:** *1400 Hours - 2:00 P.m.*

This December Saturday I had decided to use the time here to write some of my Christmas cards. I hadn't intended to enter anything in the log, but because of my unusual visit from Igor, I'm writing down what happened.

I was addressing and writing Christmas cards, since George, like many husbands, leaves that task to me. While I usually come here to the garage-hermitage without bringing any work, today was to be different. I had prayed:

Help me, O God, to make into a prayer
    this work of writing Christmas cards to our friends.
Let me regard these greetings as holy epistles,
    especially since, with many of our friends, Christmas
    is the only time in the year we exchange letters.
Amen.

I had to make it into prayer; I had no choice. I had to use my hermitage time for writing Christmas cards, not having any other time! These days before Christmas are as packed for me as a department store revolving door jammed with shoppers. That image makes me aware of how I feel as if I'm whirling around as well!

Halfway through writing a Christmas card, there was a familiar voice. "*Shanti*, peace. Well, well, well, if it isn't Sent Martha, one of Santa's helpers!" Igor said as he stood in the hermitage doorway.

"Welcome to you, Igor! I didn't hear you coming. You're the one who's like Santa's helpers; when you're not entering and exiting with dramatic fanfare, you come and go in an elfish wisp. And *shanti, shalom,* to you too. Care for a cup of hot tea? There's some chocolate cookies in that tin; I baked them myself."

"You've even had time to bake cookies?" Igor asked, chomping on one. Crumbs fell like brown snow on his wisp of a white beard. "Baking cookies, along with writing Christmas cards, decorating the house, buying presents, wrapping—"

"Don't remind me!" I answered playfully. "I had to diet from all that today simply to have time to come here. I was tempted to bypass my hermitage time today because I'm so busy."

I filled two cups with hot tea and handed one to Igor. As he raised his cup in the air, he toasted, "*Banzai!*"

"*Bonsai* to you!" I said, lifting my cup.

"No, Martha, *bonsai* is a dwarf tree, usually a cedar. I said *banzai* which means 'ten thousand years.' It's a toast, and also a Japanese battle cry wishing long life to the emperor."

"*Banzai-Banzai!*" I laughed.

"Early December is an especially busy time, and so it seems logical that old P & P would be the first to go. P & P? Prayer and Play, or Play and Prayer," said Igor as he sipped his tea. "One goes first and the other follows. It's deadly to leave either out of your life, so I'm proud of you, Martha. Even if you're piggybacking your time here to write Christmas cards, I'm proud of you."

"Writing Christmas cards can be prayer," I answered a bit defensively. "We're called to pray always, aren't we, Igor?

Sending cards and decorating the house during this pre-Christmas season can be as much a part of the spiritual preparation for the feast as going on retreat or going to church, right?"

"Ah, yes, Martha, you're becoming a priest in the order of Melchizedek. Writing cards and decorating the house can be a form of ritual celebration, a way for you to exercise your priesthood by creating an environment for prayer and worship to become incarnate in your home. Just as the ancient Druidic priests considered holly and mistletoe to be sacred, so in your hands they can be more than decorations, they can be little sacraments."

"Thanks, Igor, for your vote of confidence, but I'm not sure I always do it in a priestly manner. I wish I knew how to make it sacred work."

"It isn't easy, Martha. Christmas cards and decorating can just as easily be busy work that gets in the way of what really matters. It all depends on how you go about decorating and all the other countless chores of Christmas preparation. The question at hand is: What makes any so-called 'secular' activity into a sacred one?"

"Good autopsy of my problem, Igor, but what's the answer?"

"Instead of a direct answer, Martha, perhaps a parable might be a better response to your question about prayer and these hectic days before Christmas."

While it was
only ten days

till Christmas, you wouldn't have known it. Hell looked the same as it did on any other day. There were no decorations or bright colored lights, no tinseled Christmas trees anywhere to be seen—only great clouds of steam and fiery smoke. An army of condemned sinners, wet with sweat, labored like boiler room attendants on some great ocean liner as they shoveled coal into the huge blast furnaces of hell.

High above the noisy chaos stood Satan's glass-walled office. It looked down upon great roaring blast furnaces and fiery pits as large as the mouths of volcanoes. Suddenly the door to Satan's office flew open, and in came two large demons clad in black armor dragging a frightened, guilty-looking demon by the hair.

"What in hell is the meaning of this rude interruption?" demanded the Devil. "Didn't your mothers teach you to knock before entering someone's room?"

"A thousand pardons, O Great Master of Malice, but this is a grave emergency," replied one of the guard demons. "By pure accident on our usual security rounds we discovered this useless excuse for a devilsciple secretly involved in an enemy activity. Here, see for yourself!" The guard demon dumped a bundle of Christmas cards on the Devil's desk. Then they threw the accused demon at the feet of Satan.

"What is this?" sneered Satan. "How dare you give aid and comfort to the Enemy. What is the meaning of these cheap expressions of joy over the birthday of my little brother? Surely, even a dumb demon like you knows that this sort of thing is against our religion!"

"Have pity on me, Lord of Darkness," wept the captured demon who was laying face down, rug-like, on the hot, steaming floor, "but I thought they were so...pretty...and...ah, Your Evilness, so harmless. This time of year, everyone up there on earth is sending them to their friends. Many of us were wondering why...couldn't—"

"Shut up!" snapped Satan, stepping on the fingers of the prostrate demon, who let out a piercing scream. "Sound general quarters!" the Devil commanded." Call all the workers and demons to an immediate community meeting." At once, ear-shattering, shrill, wailing sirens filled the steamy air of hell. With their hands over their ears demons and sinners were running madly to the area directly beneath Satan's office.

With a sweep of red satin, Satan stepped onto an iron-railed balcony. He was followed by the two giant demon guards dragging the convicted Christmas card user by the hair. Satan raised his arms high in the air, signaling for silence.

"Brother and sister demons, children of chaos and confusion, and our distinguished, and permanent, guests—sinners all—today this demon, second class tempter, division 14-B, was caught red-handed writing Christmas cards!" In unison an angry roar shot upward from the crowd below like an atomic mushroom cloud, echoing repeatedly off the iron walls of hell.

"And this dumb demon said that others of you also wish to be involved in this activity of the Enemy, this bourgeois decadent custom!" Pockets of guilt appeared in the crowd as the heads of some demons drooped, while sweaty sinners anxiously whispered to one another. "You there," screamed Satan, "yes, you, the demon with the word *hate* tattooed on your forehead. I see into your heart. You, like this idiot here, are also tempted to use some of these smuggled birthday cards dedicated to my little brother. And you, over there, and you...and you. Why must I be surrounded by such weak-headed incompetence? Why do my vocation directors send me only the dregs of society and its stupid misfits?" Enraged, Satan began pounding his fists against his forehead. Then, taking a deep breath, he regained his composure and continued.

"I have something to say to all of you about Christmas—but don't sit down, remain standing; it will be more uncomfortable. Many of you desire to send Christmas cards and be part of what's happening up there in the world at this time of the year. True, most of it has very little to do with the Enemy, with any real desire for Emmanuel. Also, many of you have suggested that we need our own celebration so that we can rejoice as much in hate and evil as the Enemy does in the coming of love and goodness into the world."

The crowd began a chant: "Yes, yes, we want a celebration of our own!"

Stomping his foot, the Devil silenced the chant, "Some of you have even proposed songs that yearn for the coming of Emmanusatan, Satan among us, cleverly dropping the last two letters of Emmanuel, *El*, which means 'God,' and inserting the Hebrew *Satan*, meaning the 'accuser,' the 'liar.' But brothers of evil, sisters of hate, we have no need to set aside a special day to celebrate the coming of hate into the world. For us every day is such a celebration!"

A polite round of applause rose from the crowd, although it was obvious that most of them didn't understand what Satan was saying. Leaning far out over the iron railing, the Devil, with obvious zest, continued, "Now, if Emmanusatan were to come in the flesh, how should that happen? Some have proposed that evil become incarnate as a full-breasted, olive skinned, dark-eyed woman. Still others have suggested an incarnation as war, greed or slavery. But I say to you that these are the suggestions of simpletons!

"Some have proposed that I appear as a dictator, spreading seeds of exercising power over others or that we implant in the heart of each earthling an extra dose of the hunger to be highly rewarded, held in esteem by his or her peers, to be respected, yes, even admired! But I say to you that these are stupid suggestions. Any thinking ones up there," and he pointed upward toward the ceiling of hell, "after even a brief reflection, would see these incarnations as diabolic. No, none of these are the way in which I have chosen to compete with my little brother. Being the elder, I am wiser and—"

A great cheer and loud applause thundered from the vast crowd below as a chant began: "Tell us, tell us, O Satan. Tell us your secret plan of Emmanusatan. Tell us, tell us—"

"Silence, sinners! I will do just that. But first, as to your craving for Christmas cards: If any of you want to send those token greetings, go ahead. It really does no harm to our efforts. In fact, we should promote it! In all the extra work of addressing envelopes and writing notes, we can make that activity fester with resentment, stretching nerves to the point of frustration."

More applause rose from the crowd, which began to

chant, "Cards stretching nerves, cards stretching nerves—"

"Shut up! My dear condemned ones, I'm not finished! Let us rejoice, for this whole jolly Christmas holiday season is harvest time for us. Yes, yes, all those sentimental songs and make-believe stories about love, family and home only invoke depression and loneliness in many people on earth. And those stores crowded with people and those long lines at checkout stands—why, they feed one of our very choicest virtues: impatience! In this season of good cheer, of Christmas gift-giving, those foolish mortals' inflated concern about gifts only nourishes false desires and unnecessary needs. It fosters competition, disappointment and poisonous guilt. Ah, my ugly, sinful friends, 'tis harvest time!"

The crowd chanted loudly, "Harvest time, harvest time—"

With a loud clap of his hands—which echoed like thunder—he silenced them and continued with a grin, "Ah, but these are only minor victories. I will now tell you, my stupid servants of sin, about the real coming of Emmanusatan. It was a stroke of genius on my part, and it works as well today as it has for millions of years. I come as the hate of evil! The work of my kingdom is to foster war against all evil, encouraging mortals to hate the sinfulness of their own bodies, to hate the sin and evil in one another! I come as war against injustice, as crusades against pornography, sin and heresy! Yes, my evil ones, you heard me correctly. The best way for Satan to incarnate in the world is as the *mortal enemy* of sin and evil!"

The crowd was clearly confused by this, but a few felt they had to make some response, so a spray of weak applause rose up from below.

"You dumb dodos and diabolic dipsticks! Use your brains! What better way is there to encourage hateful division among them. How true is the statement, 'What you war against, that you become!' And the greater the intensity of the crusade, the deeper the hate. By my coming in this way, I, the great Satan, will accomplish what my little brother, the Galilean, only promised: 'I will be in you, and you will be in me.'" Turning with a flourish of his scarlet cape and roaring with laughter, Satan disappeared in a puff of orange smoke.

After a time of silence, I began, "Amazing, Igor, absolutely amazing! Of course, I see the point. I was struck by that part about how you become what you war against. But, with so much darkness around, how can we *not* wage war against evil?"

"The issue, Martha, is not whether you're for or against evil and sin! There's no question about that. Rather," Igor said, "it's *how* you're against it. If it's going off on some 'holy' war, whether it's called a crusade or a just cause, you're in trouble because any kind of war is playing into the hands of evil. For the weapons of those wars are judgment, hate, self-righteousness and divisiveness."

"I need time to think about your parable," I said leaning back. "I need to chew on it."

"I agree. Besides, it's just about time for me to be on my way, time to *vamos*," he said. "Tell the tale of Emmanusatan to George and see what he thinks of it."

"He'll enjoy it. He's not into decorating like I am. We're very different in a lot of ways, and yet we do agree on many things. And, especially since you encouraged him to be more human and less machismo, we're able to communicate well with each other and understand each other."

"Ah, yes, Martha, understanding, reverence and respect are essential for all companions on the quest, especially for life-partners on the quest. Even if partners share the same spiritual tradition, all marriages are ecumenical. Each person has a unique spiritual path; the trick is to make those paths parallel and complementary. And whether it's marriage or a friendship, real mutual reverence is required for graceful *communication* to happen. Without that key ingredient there can be no true ecumenism; differences are merely tolerated instead of celebrated."

"Well, Igor, respect, reverence, a better ground for communication—whatever the ingredient is—it certainly has assisted our mutual journey. Thank you for your part in it."

"You spoke of George having changed; haven't you also changed? I've detected more balance in you; you seem less a prisoner of emotional issues—more free and open. Is that observation accurate?"

"I think it is, Igor. When I first began to seriously pursue the spiritual path, women's rights, or the lack of them—especially in the Church—was really a pressing issue for me. And feminine spirituality has been extremely important for me; it's helped me embrace the beauty and mystery of my womanhood as well as the need to stand my ground. On the other hand, I'm glad to have moved past the edge of hostility that's at times been part of the women's movement. Your Emmanusatan parable about righteous crusades creating division strikes a chord. I think that what George and I have been fashioning since we've begun sharing this hermitage space is more a *human* spirituality. It's a healthy balance of the masculine and feminine without sacrificing either. Our group also seems to be finding that kind of balance."

"I'm glad for both of you—and the group. The more balanced we are, the more godlike we can become. And to address your original question about what makes a secular activity sacred: Has not your increased inner freedom allowed you to create sacred space? You've found the inner spaciousness to savor some activity enough to make it holy, to truly ritualize it.

"But now I must really be going, Martha. As I said, share the story of Emmanusatan with George—and with the group, if you wish. While it has a Christmas theme, I assure you it's about much, much more than this Yuletide season. I'll see you again, Martha, in two weeks." As he closed the door to the hermitage, Igor winked and blew me a kiss, "*Bon jour, bonne amie*, and this year do I get a Christmas card?"

# Ship's Log

**Vessel:** *THE HERMITAGE*

**Officer at the Helm:** *GEORGE*

**Date:** *SATURDAY, DECEMBER 16*

**Time:** *1900 HOURS – 7:00 P.M.*

Snow has been falling off and on most of the day. Several inches have fallen and have covered the lawn, trees and fences, creating a peaceful and prayerful effect. As I look out my window here in the hermitage, it's as if our backyard has been draped in a white prayer shawl. On these last days of autumn, which feel more like winter, all creation seems to be praying.

Martha's been busy decorating and sending Christmas cards. I try to sneak in a little gift shopping after work, but I've always thought it easier for women to get into the spirit of Christmas than for men. I wonder if I'd even put up a Christmas tree and go through all that decorating if I lived by myself.

Entering these notes in the log gives me an opportunity to pore over some of my recent reflections on the Christmas season at home and at work: Is Christmas a sacred feast or a secular one? And if it's really a sacred feast, what is its meaning?

Two tough questions shadow these two: Will I be any farther along my pilgrim's spiral journey, my quest for the flaming pearl, because I celebrated Christmas? Will I come any closer to understanding what it means to be a prophet and how I can really change the world—even my small part of the world?

At this point I happened to look up for a moment and noticed designs forming in the frost on my hermitage window. One by one, the letters SOS were being traced in the frost by a finger. I stood up and opened the door, "Come inside, Igor, you'll freeze out there!"

"Thanks, captain, it's bitter cold out here today on the weather deck," he said as he entered, covered with snow. "I'm glad you got my distress signal so I could come inside the pilot house and on to the bridge to warm up. I know it's late in the day so I won't keep you for long. Just wanted to stop in to say hello and de-ice my wings." Igor stomped his feet and blew on his hands. "That's a nice-looking Christmas wreath in your pilot house window, mate. I'll bet Martha put it up."

"Yes, it gives a holiday touch to this place. Martha's been busy. She did all the decorations both inside and outside the house. Christmas around here would be rather drab and simple if I were left in charge of decorating. With the children grown and gone, there's little incentive. I guess I just don't know the meaning of Christmas, or I'd get more into the festivities.

"Also, Igor, I was talking with a friend at work last week about the Christmas season. He went into a tirade about how Christmas is just a convenient excuse for businesses to make big bucks. I had to agree with him. At the same time I wanted to say something about what Christmas really means, but at the moment I was at a loss for words."

"The meaning of Christmas? As *magister bibendi*, toast-master and master of the revels, allow me, kind sir, to play with your problem." Settling cross-legged into the cozy old easy chair, Igor began to breathe out some toasty warm air along with his tale:

a few days away, and the child lay snuggled in bed, dreaming of toys under the tree. Suddenly she was awakened by the sound of a drum. It was not the "rat-a-tat-tat" of the Little Drummer Boy, but rather a great "Boom-Boom-Boom!"

Climbing out of bed, the girl went to her window and saw something marching out of the woods behind her house and across the newly fallen snow. It was a large white rabbit pounding a big red drum! The rabbit was as tall as her father; he wore a scarlet coat with a golden bow at his neck, blue striped pants and long white knee stockings. Tiny bells jingled at his coat sleeve, from which also hung a couple of sparkling stars. The rabbit was really something to see, and the child stood breathless as he approached her bedroom window.

Opening the window, she was surprised, for it wasn't cold winter air that blew in, but a warm breeze with the scent of flowers and, of all things, sawdust! In wonderment, leaning out the window, she asked, "Who are you? If you're the Easter Rabbit, you're either very late or very early. Christmas is only a week away!"

"Child of wonder, I'm not the Easter Rabbit. Oh no, I'm the Christmas Bunny, sometimes called the Holiday Hare!" With that he began singing, "We wish you a Merry Christmas. We wish you a Merry Christmas..."

Now the girl's parents were sleeping in the next room, and she was sure this drumbeating, singing rabbit would awaken them. But she heard not a sound from their bedroom. "Easter...oh, I mean *Christmas* Bunny, why have you come to *my* house?"

"Child of wonder," replied the great white rabbit, "I have come to get you! The others are waiting for us out by the road."

"To get me? To do what?" she asked, puzzled, wondering who the *others* waiting at the road might be.

"Child of wonder," said the rabbit, "I've come to get you not to do anything but to take you somewhere!"

Warily the girl replied, "To take me somewhere? But my parents have sternly warned me *never* to go with strangers, which surely must include strange rabbits!"

"Oh child, you've nothing to fear. I will not harm you;

I've come to reward you! I've been sent to show you the meaning of Christmas and to take you to the Show of Shows. Quickly, child, jump out of window. We've no time to lose."

The Christmas Bunny's reward sounded exciting. The girl had always wondered what Christmas meant, so she climbed out of her window and followed the rabbit "boom-booming" on his big red drum until they reached the road. There, to the girl's amazement, was a large crowd of children eagerly waiting for them.

The white rabbit gathered them together and announced, "Now walk this way—there are only six *hopping* days left till Christmas." So hopping down the road, they all followed the rabbit to the beat of his big red drum till they came to the top of a hill. Below them was a valley of snow-covered pine trees in the center of which was a giant tent filled with lights. The tent looked like a great glowing mountain rising out of the snow-covered forest. The children all stood in awe. Then with a wave of his paw, the great white rabbit said, "Chosen children, behold: The Great Christmas Three-Ring Circus!"

They marched down the hill and straight into the towering circus tent filled with people. The crowd all stood and cheered wildly as the Christmas Bunny led the children to a reserved section right down in front. Then there was a brass fanfare and a drumroll, and into the spotlight's white circle in the center ring walked the ringmaster. It was Santa Claus himself in his bright red suit trimmed in white fur. He was wearing a tall black silk hat, and with him was the Christmas Bunny.

"Ladies and gentlemen, and chosen children," Santa announced through a large, old-fashioned cheerleader's megaphone, "welcome one and all to the Great Christmas Three-Ring Circus, the most amazing show on earth. Tonight, for your wonderment and absolute amazement, you will be treated to a show of breathtaking beauty, feats of magic to stun the mind and stir the heart. Friends, direct your eyes to the first ring for a spectacular show so marvelous to describe as to have escaped the ingenious powers of the world's greatest poets, painters and musicians."

A spotlight filled the first ring. In the center of the ring was a small stable to which were tied a donkey and a cow, while flocks of sheep grazed about. Then, as a blue- and gold-uniformed circus band played "O Little Town of Bethlehem," in the top of the tent there appeared trapeze artists wearing golden wings. They were swinging back and forth over the stable. At the same time clowns dressed as ragged shepherds ran into the ring pulling large wagons with cages of wild animals. They opened the cages, and out sprang ferocious lions, leopards, bears and growling wolves who ran straight for the stable. But to the surprise of all, the lions became as playful as house cats, while the wolves and lambs played together like little pups, all to the "oohs and aahs" of the crowd.

The walls of the stable suddenly rose upward on wires, revealing a father, mother and infant child. Trumpets sounded, followed by Oriental music, as into the big top came a grand parade of camels led by men in flowing desert robes. As the circus band played "We Three Kings of Orient Are," there followed huge Indian elephants ridden by richly robed kings. From high atop the tent a gigantic sparkling star swept down and came to rest directly over the peasant couple and child. Then, as camels, elephants and their attendants knelt in humble adoration, the three kings bowed their heads into the sawdust, and the spotlight swung back to Santa Claus.

"Is that the meaning of Christmas?" the girl asked the child who sat next to her.

Before he could answer, Santa announced, "Ladies and gentlemen, and chosen children, marvels never ever end, especially here in the greatest show on earth, the Great Christmas Three-Ring Circus. Please give your full attention now to the center ring." In it was the Christmas Bunny pounding on his drum, singing, "There's no business like show business, like no business I know. Everything about it is appealing, everything the traffic will allow. Nowhere else do you get that happy feeling...."

Into the tent rushed hundreds of merchants shouting, "Buy this! Buy that! Buy this!" The people jumped to their feet and began handing over their money to the merchants who ran up and down the aisles, eagerly stuffing the money into large, black garbage bags. As the band played "O Come All Ye Faithful," tumblers and clowns rushed about bumping into one another with shopping carts overflowing with boxes. Christmas Bunny was singing, "There's no business like Christmas business, like no business I know. Everything about it is a profit! Everything the traffic will allow. No other time is so busy. It makes you dizzy...." A great pipe organ then began playing Handel's *Messiah* as into the big top came a parade of prancing white horses on which stood Las Vegas show girls in pink swimsuits with tinseled angel wings. Behind them came choirs of little children carrying lighted candles and singing carols. They were followed by other children dressed in their parents' flannel bathrobes, their heads wrapped in bath towel turbans.

"Is this the meaning of Christmas?" the little girl next to her asked.

Before she could answer, Santa announced, "Ladies and gentlemen, and chosen children, cast your eyes up to the heights of the big top, where, without the benefit of any safety nets, stands the world's greatest acrobat, the Fearless and Astounding Jesu, Mary's grown, handsome son: the Star of Bethlehem!" High in the tent on a tightrope stood a young man clad only in a loincloth. In one hand he held a large globe of the Earth, in the other a great luminous halo. He juggled the globe and halo from hand to hand as he swayed back and forth, all the while keeping his balance, to the crowd's loud applause.

Then into the center ring raced jugglers dressed as priests, juggling the Ten Commandments and countless other lesser laws in the air, without dropping a single one! The young man on the tightrope shouted down: "You hypocrites!"

The priest jugglers stopped and shouted back, "Who do you think you are? Come down from up there!" Then they quickly climbed on top of one another's shoulders, forming a human pyramid. The priest at the top of the pyramid shouted to the crowd, "This man tinkers with our religion! He's an enemy to all who love God and home. Pull him down

194

from his high-and-mighty perch!"

To the girl's surprise, the crowd began to chant, "Pull him down, pull him down." Then a priest knife-thrower, with perfect aim, threw a knife upward, severing the tightrope. To the loud applause of the crowd, the Astounding Jesu, like a fallen sparrow, came crashing to the ground.

The priest-jugglers ran from the tent while in the center of the spotlight's white circle lay the lifeless body of the fallen acrobat. Out of the shadows ran Mother Mary followed by a dozen sad-faced clowns who lifted up his dead body and placed it on her lap. The twelve clowns gathered around the sorrowful Madonna, singing, "What Child is this, who laid to rest on Mary's lap is sleeping? Whom angels weep with anthems sweet, while shepherds watch are keeping." The clowns then wrapped the dead body in a white sheet and carried it away, singing, "This, this is Christ the King, whom shepherds guard and angels sing. Hail, hail, the Word made flesh, the Babe, the Son of Mary." Then the big top was plunged into funeral darkness.

After a long, dark silence, a spotlight shone on the third ring, revealing a gigantic black iron box bound in hundreds of great chains with padlocks. "Behold, ladies and gentlemen, and chosen children," cried Santa, "the world's greatest prison from which no one has ever escaped and in which Jesu is held bound. Watch now as the Astounding Jesu, the greatest Houdini, shall escape!" From outside the tent top, a blinding laser beam focused on the strongbox. In a great explosion its chains were shattered and the black box flew apart. Jesu the Astounding, the human cannonball, shot out of the box and upward into the high rigging of the tent. He grabbed a high-wire, flipped himself around it and up on top of it. He stood with arms wide apart, bowing to the roaring applause of the crowd, as below in the sawdust, laughing clowns were turning somersaults.

Pounding his big drum, Christmas Bunny began to sing, "There's no business like Christmas business, like no business I know. Everything about it is amazing! Everything your faith will allow...." Then, to a drumroll and brass fanfare, into the ring swept Santa's sleigh pulled by seven reindeer and surrounded by dwarfs and midgets dressed as elves. He climbed up onto the seat of the sleigh and announced, "Ladies and gentlemen, and chosen children one and all, you have just seen the greatest show on earth and have learned the true meaning of Christmas. Now our beloved Christmas Bunny will introduce the grand finale of the Great Christmas Three-Ring Circus."

As the entire circus company of animals and entertainers filled the three rings, the great white rabbit, accompanied by the circus band, began to sing, "We wish you a merry Christmas. We wish you a merry Christmas. We wish you a merry Christmas and a happy Easter!"

"Dear, wake up! You must be dreaming," came her mother's voice as the girl suddenly found herself back in her own bedroom! "You were shouting something or cheering; it must have been a nightmare."

"Oh, no, mother, it was the most wonderful of...of..." She wanted to say *adventures*, and to tell her mother about the great white rabbit, but she was old enough to know that it was really only a dream.

"Get dressed, dear. I have a warm bowl of Cream of Wheat ready for you." The girl slipped on her bathrobe and went to the window. It was a beautiful winter morning. The rising sun made the snow-covered yard glisten like a field of diamonds. Then she gasped, for in the glistening snow were very large rabbit footprints!

"Talk about a psychedelic parable, Igor! But isn't it kind of dark and heavy for a Christmas story?"

"The story of Jesus Christ around which Christianity orbits is a three act play, my beloved George! The scene of the Blessed Bambino, the infant Jesus, and his loving but poor peasant parents is a classic: beautiful, soft and sweet." Igor began singing in a choirboy, high, falsetto voice, "Oh Little Town of Bethlehem, how still we see thee lie..." as he rocked in his arms an imaginary baby. "Touching, eh, George? Nothing difficult to embrace in the opening act. Anyone, even those who have no faith, can enjoy act one. Ah, but act two! Now the story grows dark and deadly. And act three! The final act is holy hokum—fakery, a clever trick played on the audience! At least a growing number of folks believe that death is the end—The End—no curtain calls, show's over, *ultimum vale*, the ultimate farewell, the great and final period." At that point Igor jabbed his big finger outward toward me, repeating, "The great *period!*"

"Long answer to a short question! I'll grant all that about the usual sugar-sweetness of the Bethlehem story, but why introduce the grim, dark side into such a charming celebration as Christmas?"

"Short but pregnant question! It takes time to run all three bases, George, on the way to making a home run. Indeed, lad, why a disturbing and dark tale, unless Bethlehem's Bambino was *El Nino!*"

"*El Nino?* I know that's Spanish for 'the child.' Let me see if I get your flow: you're connecting Jesus with those oceanic phenomena of unusually warm tidal currents? That Pacific Coast current which has caused such widespread atmospheric disturbances and changing patterns in the distribution in marine life?"

"Correct, Captain of the Hermitage! *El Nino* and the Babe of Bethlehem are interchangeable names! Recall old Simeon's prophecy: 'This child is destined to be the downfall and rise of many in Israel, a sign that will be opposed.' Mary's *El Nino* caused more than atmospheric disturbances! He changed the patterns of life for centuries to come! He was one of the

197

greatest disturbances—mind you, a divine disturbance—in history."

"This is beginning to tie in with my dream and with my questions about being a prophet. There's nothing more disturbing than being a prophet! But Christmas is the celebration of peace, the lion and the lamb lying together and all that. Have you looked at our crib set? What's so disturbing about that?"

"How can you celebrate *El Nino*'s birth and be blind to the disturbances he caused and *should* cause today? Recall, George, that before I began the parable, I said it was more than a Christmas story. You're on a questventure, a pilgrimage, a lifelong *haji*—not to Mecca but to the mystic heart of the cosmos. This Christmas story is your story."

"My story? My mother wasn't a virgin and no great star appeared when I was born!"

"Ah, but you're a son of God, aren't you? The angels sang at your birth, only you and your folks couldn't hear them. Yes, the Bethlehem birth is the mystery of every child's being fertilized in his or her mother's womb by the Holy Spirit."

"I'll have to think about that kind of prenatal theology."

"Do! And remember that the birth and childhood—yours and Jesus'—is only act one. Act two moves us from childhood to adulthood and act three takes us to priesthood. It's a rare priesthood in which you are both the priest who offers the sacrifice *and* the sacrifice. Who wouldn't want life to be only a one act play, an innocent journey with no conflict, no suffering, no pain, no sacrifice? But since you and Martha are on a great questventure, Christmas can be an important port of call. It can be a calm harbor, festive with lanterns, song and feasting, where you take on essential supplies for your voyage. Or Christmas can be a *fata morgana*, a mirage on the high seas."

"This mirage," I added, "is a distortion of light created not by hot and cool air, but by shopkeepers, TV specials and churches!"

"'There's no business like show business.' And the sad part is that this modern mercantile mirage is a distortion of Light! It distorts the holy lights of Hanukkah, and the Light of the World, Jesus, for the sake of profit—big profit! But that brings us back to your personal questventure, George. What would you say now to your friend at work who had similar sentiments?"

"Even though I have a better understanding about the meaning of Christmas, I'm still not sure I'd say anything. I guess I don't want to become a disturbance, an *El Nino*, because I wouldn't want to come off like I was trying to convert him. How do I turn things around and upside down without becoming a false prophet, a hollow reformer, like we talked about the last time?"

"Ah, George, very good question! How do you exercise the priesthood I just talked about and make Christ incarnate in the world? How do you *make* Emmanuel rather than just wait for Emmanuel—and do it without distorting the light? For starters, I would refer you back to the Advent Ax prayer you wrote. It gives some clues about how to exercise your priesthood and bring light into the world by consecrating the stuff of daily life."

Then, raising his hand Igor said, "Speaking of light, look: there is none! It must be close to 1800 hours. We've talked so long that the day is gone. Look how dark it is out there. *Feliz Navidad*, old friend, and as the Russians say, *do svidanya*."

Igor departed, walking into the darkness across our backyard, singing loudly, "Hark! The Herald Angels sing..." As I closed the door, I saw that indeed it was 6 o'clock. Now that I've recorded the Christmas Bunny parable, it's time for me to depart as well. As I conclude my entry in the hermitage log, I'm aware that my pockets during these coming days till Christmas will be full of questions about Igor's parable and his insights about *El Nino*. And I have a lot of reflecting to do about my "priesthood."

P.S. I add this prophecy postscript, a P.P.S., to my log entry. As I return to the house by the moon's light, I'm sure that I also will see footprints in the snow: large dragon footprints!

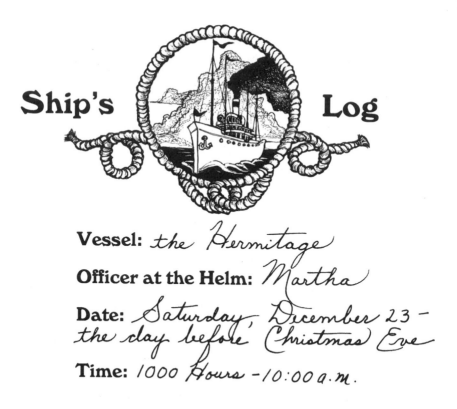

# Ship's Log

**Vessel:** *the Hermitage*

**Officer at the Helm:** *Martha*

**Date:** *Saturday, December 23 – the day before Christmas Eve*

**Time:** *1000 Hours – 10:00 a.m.*

I'm opening an early Christmas gift as I make my entry in the hermitage log. Since tomorrow is Christmas Eve, I've given myself some solitude time. I felt as if there was too much left to do and too little time left. However, after some debate between me and me, I decided to allow myself a half day of quiet before all the celebration begins.

I've had a growing awareness—and now feel convinced—that hidden in the midst of all the hustle and bustle, the revolving door, of these holidays lies the flaming pearl. It would be a shame if I missed it because of being distracted by all the glitter of the holidays—perhaps a better name would be *labordays*.

George and I have talked about Igor's last visit, and Christmas is like *El Nino*. Talk about disturbances in normal patterns—with all the work that goes into preparing for it, Christmas causes a complete rearrangement of normal patterns! Ah, but such a delightful disturbance! I really do love Christmastime.

I also love so many other things, like George and the children, my home, my friends, the "luxury" of the time here in the hermitage.... That's all great, but it's also a little disturbing. I must confess to you, ship's log, that lately I've been feeling a touch of guilt about all my attachments. In my spiritual reading, especially in some of the saints and mystics and some of the Eastern texts, I keep being confronted with the call to detachment. They all seem to be saying the same thing: If you wish to be holy, to be enlightened, you have to be detached from this world and its pleasures, even human love. If that's a requirement for—

"*Joyeux Noel*, Martha," Igor sang out as he entered the door strumming his *balalaika*. Its three strings sounded like the entire violin section of the Boston Pops playing the Christmas carol "Noel."

"Merry Christmas to you, my Russian *rebbe*, teacher of tall tales and merry *maharishi* of bittersweet wisdom."

"My, my, *ma chere*, aren't we poetic this morning!"

"This quiet morning in the hermitage has recharged my soul's battery, I guess. It's almost sinful to be doing nothing while an avalanche of tasks is ready to topple down on me."

"'*Volare*,' as the song goes: be carefree! *Volare* actually means to fly, and flying from care is what you've done. A little *volare* before the feast is essential. How else can you decorate your soul? I've peeked in your windows, Martha, and you've done a magnificent job decorating the tree and the entire house. It's so festive and beautiful."

"Thank you, Igor, but there's more to do. Anyway, yes, you're right; this morning, I did fly. I flew the coop!"

"I promise that because you did you'll enjoy Christmas more, and it will be a holy day as well as a holiday. As a bonus I'd like to present you with a surprise package that may be an answer to the riddle that's been nibbling at your soul of late."

"Oh, you shameless shaman who listens in on a woman's heart-talk! But I forgive you because I can't think of a better gift than an answer to my Christmas riddle. It baffles me: If

Christmas is the enfleshment of God in the world and in history, then how can the flesh be a roadblock on the way to heaven? Igor, I'm ready for your Christmas parable."

"Excellent, Martha, but first let me ask you a question: Do you want a Christmas story for the holiday or one for the holy day?"

"George shared with me your Christmas Bunny parable, so I'm tempted to say one for the holiday. I'm such a romantic; I really enjoy the sweet side of Christmas. It's such a family feast, what with the crib and tree and wrapping presents. Yet since the parable is your gift, it's only right, Igor, that you should choose the gift."

"Careful, Martha! I might choose the kind of gift that loving, but not very rich, parents give to their children on Christmas. You know, practical and useful presents, like socks and warm pajamas."

"I did get gifts like that when I was child, but Santa also brought me toys."

"Ah, toys! Now there's a place for leaping off into a good parable." Leaning back into the old easy chair, Igor began rubbing his hands together. Then, raising his right hand high in front of him, he slowly swept it across the space between us, and large snowflakes drifted down from his arm as he started his story:

On one of the twisting narrow streets

in the old medieval part of the city, out of which also rose a great, towering Gothic cathedral, was the toy shop of old Hans. The night before Christmas, as giant flakes of snow fell slowly like white goose feathers from the gray skies, the only light still burning on the street came from the back room of the toy shop. While all the other shopkeepers had gone home to be with their families, old Hans was still working. Bent over his workbench, Hans was lovingly putting the finishing touches on a toy. No ordinary toy, this was to be his masterpiece! Yet, with only a couple of hours left before Christmas, it still wasn't finished.

As he worked, old Hans sang to himself, "Hail, Hail, the Word made flesh, the Babe, the Son of Mary!" Ever since he was a child, he had sung in the cathedral choir; he would do so again this night at the midnight Mass. Slowly, the cathedral bells rang out ten times. "Ten o'clock, friends," he said to the toys in his shop. "My, oh my! With choir rehearsal at eleven o'clock, I must hurry or I'll never finish in time! Think of it, ten o'clock on Christmas Eve; yes, any moment now he'll be arriving!"

The one who would soon arrive was none other than Santa Claus. Hans had generously arranged that if Santa ever needed more toys, he was free to stop by and help himself to whatever he needed. Even though a large number of the toys had already been purchased by his customers, many wonderful toys still were left on his shelves.

The small bell that hung on the toy shop door jingled as three snow-covered men entered the shop. "Hans, aren't you ready to go? Don't you remember, the choirmaster set the rehearsal forty-five minutes earlier this year?" Old Hans groaned, since he had forgotten. He rose from his workbench, muttering, "Old age, old age," as he took off his work apron and put on his greatcoat with the fur collar. He paused and picked up from the workbench the toy on which he had been working. "I'm sorry, Michael! I forgot choir practice was forty-five minutes earlier. It's a shame that you will have to be left unfinished! Ah, but next Christmas!"

The four men left the toy shop singing. As the sound of

"Hail, Hail, the Word made flesh..." was soaked up by the softly falling snow, the silent toy shop erupted into clamor as all the toys began talking at once. "I can't wait!" said Black Teddy Bear. "While none of the customers took me—perhaps because I'm a *black* bear—I know for sure that Santa will want me." With a loud blast from his tin trumpet, a tall toy soldier in a red British officer's uniform of the Bengal Lancers shouted, "All right, chaps! Everyone into parade formation. Spit and polish! Bold as brass, any moment now old Claus will be arriving! Double-time, lads and lassies."

"Oh, Major General Wellington," said the unfinished toy laying on the workbench, "that's all well and fine for you toys whom old Hans has finished, but what about me?"

"Well, puppet, it's like many years ago when I served in Ind'ja with the Bengal Lancers—originally, you know, it was called the old 35th Foot Royal Sussex Regiment—those who couldn't keep up on a forced march, Michael, well, they just had to be left behind! Bloody bad luck for you!"

A sad groan arose from the workbench, then a feisty reply: "Major General Wellington, I am not a puppet—I am a marionette! A hand-carved, hand-painted marionette!" Indeed, it was a beautifully carved marionette that lay on the workbench. He wore a red jester's coat and cap, had white tights with striped stockings and, of all things, Texas cowboy boots! On the boots were painted large gold stars and on the toes, two small red hearts. Certainly a work of art, it was indeed unfortunate that Michael the Marionette was incomplete. He moaned, "Why did that choirmaster have to have practice forty-five minutes early this year? If only old Hans could have had just another half hour, he would have attached my wires. Look at me, I'm good for nothing!"

A chorus of whistles, bells, horns and tiny voices from the other toys in the shop expressed their sorrow for Michael. Black Teddy Bear, who knew what it was like to be overlooked, tried to comfort him, "When the Master does complete you, Michael, you'll be among the first toys chosen by his customers for next Christmas. Who of us here can claim to be among the 'first chosen'? Even if Santa takes all of us with him this evening, we'll each still be 'second choice.'"

Major General Wellington added, "Look at it this way, soldier! Being unwired, lad, so to speak, you're free and unattached. Wondrous state of life! Yes, you can do anything you wish, go anywhere you wish. Good show, old man! You're just like a soldier of fortune, foot-free and, as they say in Piccadilly, fancy-free."

Michael began weeping, "I may be foot-free, but look at me! All I can do is just flop about. I can't even stand up! It's no fun being unattached, regardless of how fancy-free that may make you!" Large tears trickled down his cheeks, moistening the two small red hearts which old Hans had painted on them. "All I ever get is kisses on the cheeks! I long for a real kiss, the kind that those who are attached give."

"Please, don't cry, Michael!" came a small voice from behind a paint can.

"Oh, hello, Church Mouse," said Michael, wiping his nose on his coat sleeve. "You're here to visit your cousin?"

"Yes," answered the small gray mouse, "there's so much commotion tonight in the cathedral, what with the crowds of people and that loud organ. I came down here to the toy shop for a little peace and quiet. But, Michael, why are you crying?"

"Look at me, Church Mouse, the master had to leave before he had time to finished me. I'm unattached!"

"Michael, wipe away your tears! Blest are you," said Church Mouse. "That's a holy state! As Buddha said, 'Be still; be free from attachment; know the sweet joy of the Way!'"

"By Jove, Mickey," said Major General Wellington, "Church Mouse is right, old chap. I remember hearing that years ago in Ind'ja from one of those wandering half-naked holy men! 'Be free from all attachment!'"

"All the holy mystics have said the same," continued Church Mouse. "St. Theresa, the Spanish mystic, said, 'The wise have renounced every selfish attachment.' Oh, Michael, without even having to try, you've attained holiness! Praise the Lord!"

"I don't want to be holy, or to know the sweet joy of the

Way," wept Michael. "I want to be attached! Just look at me—I'm not connected to anything or anyone!"

"Quiet, everyone; listen," cried Black Teddy Bear. Faint at first, louder and louder grew the sound of sleigh bells, until they stopped outside the toy shop with the shout, "Whoa, Dancer and Prancer, whoa!"

Like a hand grenade, excitement exploded in the toy shop. As Santa Claus entered the front door, he shouted to his elves, "Be quick, friends, we're late. To fill my long list tonight we'll need every toy in this shop." With the speed of bank robbers the elves began to empty the shelves of all the toys.

In the midst of the excitement Michael lay weeping on the workbench. Coming closer, Santa said, "What do we have here? This won't do; no tears on Christmas Eve. Who are you?"

"I'm Michael the Marionette," he moaned.

"That's Hebrew," said Church Mouse, "for 'He who is like God'! And Michael's a saint!"

"If he's a saint," replied Santa, "then why is he crying?"

"Oh, Santa Claus," wept Michael, "I want to come along with you, but look at my hands and feet. Old Hans didn't have time tonight to finish me before he left! I'm no good to anyone—I'm unattached!"

"Well, well, we do have a problem here," said Santa as he slowly rolled the tip of his long white moustache. Then, suddenly, his blue eyes sparkled. "I've got it!" he shouted to an elf. "Run to the sleigh and bring me that black bag from under the front seat. Be quick now, we've no time to spare." The elf hurried back into the toy shop with the bag, and Santa began to dig around in its depths. "I'm sure it's in here somewhere. I used it one Christmas eve several years ago when the reindeer harness broke. Ah, here it is," he said, removing a long, thick steel needle with leather thread. The needle looked very sharp and was as long as your foot!

"Sorry, Michael, but if you're to go along with us tonight, it's the only way. I'm also sorry that I don't have any pain-killer. Quick now, hot water and plenty of it," Santa said to an elf, removing his red jacket and rolling up his sleeves.

"Here, lad, bite on this bullet," chirped Major General Wellington. "When I was in Ind'ja with the Royal Bengal Lancers, for surgery in the field all we had to kill the pain was whiskey and a bullet!"

"I'll pray for you," said Church Mouse sweetly, and Black Teddy bear said, "I'll hold your hand."

Michael took a strong shot from the tin soldier's flask as Church Mouse began whispering prayers and Black Teddy Bear clutched his hand tightly. Michael closed his eyes as Santa Claus dried his hands. Then, taking the needle, Santa said, "I'm sorry, but it's necessary. Major General, hold the lad down."

Church Mouse cried out, "Oh, Santa, can't you use glue or tie the cords to his hands—'tie the knot,' so to speak? It wouldn't hurt then!"

"No, this is the only way," said Santa. He inserted the long needle into Michael's right hand and drew the leather thread through the wound, saying, "Now you're attached to suffering and sorrows." Next, with the skill of a surgeon, Santa pushed his long needle through Michael's left hand, saying, "Now you're attached to joy and happiness. Major General, pull off his boots, please, his feet are next." As the long needle pierced Michael's left foot, Santa said, "Now you're attached to laughter, and you can dance with delight." As the needle pierced his right foot, Santa said, "Michael, now you're connected to foot-dragging weariness and exhaustion." Each time the needle pierced him, Michael gritted his teeth but made not a sound.

"We've finished the easy part of the operation, Michael," said Santa. "Now comes the truly painful part. I must pierce your heart." Black Teddy Bear gripped Michael's hand tightly while all the toys looked on and prayed with Church Mouse. As the long needle pierced his heart, Michael screamed in agony. "I'm sorry," said Santa, "I know it hurts, but now you're attached to the heartbreaking pain of separation and the loss of those you love." When Santa pierced his soul, Michael screamed loudly and fainted from the pain. As Santa pulled the long needle out the other end of Michael's soul, he said, "Now he's attached to death and life, to great ecstasy and to total abandonment."

Then, wiping clean the long needle, Santa said, "It's over! Now he's connected; he's a completed masterpiece! I'm sorry for his pain, but you cannot be attached without great pain and suffering. That's at the heart of what Christmas is really about! Major General Wellington and Black Teddy Bear, give my elves a hand and carry him out to the sleigh. Be quick, though, we have no time to spare." With gentle care they wrapped the unconscious Michael in a blanket and carried him outside. Santa took one last look around the empty toy shop, waved good-bye to Church Mouse and closed the door.

Wrapped in the blanket, Michael was leaned up against Santa. The sleigh, loaded with toys and elves, raced rapidly down the empty snow-covered streets. Then it easily ascended. In seconds it was flying high over the rooftops as it sailed into the night sky above the city. Major General Wellington took a big swig from his whiskey flask and cried out, "I say, jolly good night to go flying!" Santa banked his sleigh to the right, making a wide circle-turn around the twin towers of the great cathedral whose bells were now jubilantly pealing. They were joined by the beautiful music of the choir rising upward from the cathedral. All the toys leaned over the edge of the sleigh and listened, readily picking out the beautiful tenor voice of their maker, old Hans.

The cold night air had revived Michael who looked up and said, "Thank you, Santa. I'm so grateful that you didn't leave me behind. The pain is almost gone now." Michael looked down at his hands and feet and saw the holes in each of them. Looking up, he said, "Tell me, Santa, now that I'm attached, to whom are you going to give me tonight as one of your gifts?"

Snapping his whip with a loud pop high above the heads of the flying reindeer, Santa pulled out a very long list containing thousands of names. Looking down at Michael with a big smile, he said, "Well, Michael the Masterpiece, I do have something special in mind, but, ah, to whom would *you* like me to give you?"

"What a beautiful story, Igor, a beautiful gift! Thank you, it was a perfect gift for both the holy day and the holiday."

"And for any day when you're on the quest, Martha. As you travel the Way of the Dragon in search of the flaming pearl, it's easy to feel that you should be detached. Being unattached is a quality that's admired by many spiritual seekers, and a virtue often promoted by spiritual writers. And, of course, the willingness to die to self, the ability to let go of attachments, is necessary along the way. Detachment is a great aid on the journey, as long as it's not gained at the expense of being truly attached. It's only when you're really attached that you learn how to love. Because of that 'theology' of being attached, many would like me to wear this yellow T-shirt," he said as he pulled a yellow tunic from his famous tail pocket. "*Ecce*, behold, my *sanbenito*!"

"Your *san*—what?"

"A *sanbenito*—it's a Spanish tunic worn by those accused of heresy. See the label: 'Made in Spain by the Inquisition.' Yet it is they, not I, who should wear it. It's holy heresy to teach that one must be unattached in life, the belief that one reaches God, finds the flaming pearl, by not becoming attached to anyone or to the good things of life."

"It hurts to be attached. That part of your parable made sense to me. I guess that's why so many resist it. But why have so many saints renounced attachment?"

"With attachment, the key word is 'selfish,' as Saint Theresa used it: 'The wise have renounced every selfish attachment.' There's a difference between clinging, clutching attachment—which leads to jealousy, greed, violence and a host of other deadly vices—and being attached in the sense of being connected. The sayings of the mystics and of Jesus are easily distorted. And religion, Martha, has often justified and sanctified the fear of and the refusal to be connected to another. *Sans souci, la dolce vita,* the sweet solo life is *the* way to holiness. So some claim! Bah humbug! The great holy day that begins tomorrow night shouts loudly about the pain of being attached, about God becoming flesh so as to be pierced, wounded, again and again."

"Those are powerful words, Igor! And thank you again. Just as the Christmas story you told to George was about more than Christmas, so is my gift. One more thing, though. Would you explain the ending please? What did Santa mean by that cryptic remark, 'I have something special in mind, but to whom would *you* like me to give you?'"

"A parable, Martha, is a present containing more than one gift. Why not unwrap your question with George?"

"Sorry, it's an old weakness to want everything to be neatly wrapped—or in this case, unwrapped. Yes, George and I will play with it like a grand and wondrous toy under the tree. He'll enjoy it, I'm sure."

"Well, *mon cher*, it's time for me to say *hasta la vista*. Time to go before the *la commedia e'finita*. Merry Christmas to both you and George." Igor stood up and tucked his *sanbenito* back in his tail pocket.

"Igor, what does *la commedia e'finita* mean?"

"It's from the opera *I Pagliacci*, but you'll have to wait a week to discover its meaning!"

"I respect your wishes, Igor. Now, one more thing before you leave. I have a gift for *you*. I hope you realize dragons are difficult people, I mean—ah—well, whatever, to buy gifts for, especially since you seem to be able to produce anything you want when you need it. George and I have a little something for you, more a token, you know."

"Well, thank you! Martha, you've touched this old dragon's heart. Do you know that this is my first Christmas gift! Do you mind if I wait till Christmas to unwrap it, or would you prefer that I open it here?"

"You sound like Santa Claus. If it's your first Christmas gift then, by all means, please open it on Christmas. Merry Christmas, Igor!" Leaning over, I gave him a kiss.

"*Grazie, grazie*! I won't wash my face for a week!"

With that, blushing like a teenager, Igor fled out the door. As I gathered up my things to return to the house, I reflected on Igor's parable of the toy shop. What a Christmas gift he gave me, the gift of a new meaning for Christmas. I am grateful.

My usual closing prayer is more a simple petition:

Please, God, give me the grace
   to make all the necessary work
   of preparing for Christmas
   into a prayer of love.
May my work of baking, cooking,
   and the last touches
   of decorating and gift-wrapping
   all be prayerful, done as a contemplative.
May those acts—and all my ministry—be acts of love
   truly connecting me with those I love
   and with you, my God.
'So let it be written, so let it be done,'
   to echo the Egyptian pharaohs.

P.S. I see from George's last entry that he concluded with a postscript. I'll do the same. After having concluded my entry in the log, and about to close its cover, a thought flew like a wild crane across my mind. The haunting thought I wish to record is something I felt in Igor's Spanish farewell, "*Hasta la vista*"—and the way he said, "Time to go." My intuition tells me it was a loaded good-bye. I wonder... I shall share my fear with George.

**Ship's Log**

**Vessel:** THE HERMITAGE

**Officer at the Helm:** GEORGE

**Date:** SATURDAY, DECEMBER 30

**Time:** 1330 HOURS – 1:30 P.M.

I'd fallen sleep in the easy chair after my simple lunch when I was awakened by Igor singing "Auld Lang Syne" in a thick Scottish accent, accompanied by the music of bagpipes.

"You're a one-man band!" I said as I stood up and opened the door. "How do you sing and imitate bagpipes all at the same time?"

"Trade secret, *La Serenissima*"!

"*La* what?"

"*La Serenissima*, the most serene, a title given to Venice at the peak of her power in the late fifteenth century. You looked so serene, so peaceful, as you napped that I hated to awaken you."

"I like that. I wish I was *La Serenissima*, the most peaceful, all the time. It's easy to become *La Unserenissima*, if the Italians have such a name for being stressed out. It seems that the holiday season puts added strain on life."

"For some, it's the straw that breaks the you-know-what."

"Right, Igor. These days are supposed to be so filled with

joyful activities, the loving family camped out in front of the fireplace watching the sparks dancing amidst the flames. Instead the sparks usually fly among the family members!"

"Did you have a good Christmas, George? I hate to ask that question, since everyone at work and on the street asks it."

"I could give you my recorded reply, 'Wonderful, thank you. And how was yours?' but I won't. Your Super Dragon Decoder would have unscrambled that one before I finished. Actually, Christmas was different, and interesting, even good, thanks to your parables. Both Martha and I felt Christmas was a powerful meditation for our spiritual journeys. Yes, I do believe it was a good Christmas."

"*Danke schon*, my Christmas was too. Thanks to you and Martha. Thank you for the wonderful gift—I shall treasure it always. And you know, George, *always* is a very long time for a celestial dragon! Since we're still in the Twelve Days of Christmas, how about a pre-New Year's Eve gift, a fortune cookie parable?"

"Before that year-end gift, Igor, I'm curious about the end."

"The *end*, George?"

"Yes, Igor. Martha and I are concerned—not worried, but concerned—that you're getting ready to leave again. Your *hasta la vista*s of late seem to have a double meaning. Are you trying to prepare us for your departure?"

"Something like, the end of the year means the end of the dragon?"

"Both Martha and I really rely on you to guide us. You're our mentor, our shaman, not to mention our MOO!"

"The pearl, the flaming pearl, will lead you—and it has been!" Igor said as he looked deeply into my eyes. "The pearl will be your compass, your navigator, if you are truly on the questventure. What's really important isn't me or any other mentor. Rather, the key is your fidelity to prayer, your fidelity to spending time in solitude. Why else do you think that Jesus was always sneaking away to deserted places?"

"Yes, but he returned to his disciples."

"George, I don't want any disciples, nor should you. Gandhi said that he didn't desire disciples but only fellow seekers of the Truth. That's the second key you've been learning on this stage of your journey: seeking the Truth with others, especially with Martha and your friends in your group, letting the flaming pearl lead you. I've only been a symbol of the pearl; your fidelity to your mutual process of growth with Martha has led both of you deeply into the Divine Mystery."

"OK, Igor, I can't match wits with a dragon. But let's delay any plans about your early retirement as my mentor. For now, how about that New Year's fortune cookie parable that you promised."

Igor sat down in the chair at the desk. He tilted the chair back so that it was resting only on its back legs, the front two high in the air. It was quite a feat, especially since the positioning of his weight should have caused the chair to tumble instantly backwards. Igor flashed one of his large draconic smiles, aware that I was admiring his magical skills. Then he began:

She stood beside the gutter,

next to piles of trash, just another of the thousands of ragged and pitiful homeless. She had not always been among the forsaken.

But allow me to begin at the beginning. She had volunteered to come to the city from the high country, where she had grown up and was so much at home. Like so many other young volunteers, she had been an idealist, a romantic with stars in her eyes, eager to change the world, eager to make a difference. The enthusiastic recruiter had spoken to them with words that inflamed their hearts to leave home and security, and by their service to make the world a better place.

Along with other idealistic youth, she had eagerly stepped forward and joined the Movement. Like those who had joined Habitat for Humanity, they were eager to help the homeless. Like volunteers to the Peace Corps, they had offered their unique gifts in service to those in great need. During their training course the instructor had told them, "Just be yourself! Just be there among them, and you can help them rise out of their poverty." Following training they were driven down to the city, where they were assigned to various staging areas. Here the poor and needy came and chose one of the volunteers to live in their home and help lighten the family's life.

She was chosen by a very poor family of three. She was surprised at the size of their car, but then again the instructor had told them that the poor often had large cars. As they drove home, she concluded that their sad state of poverty was the reason they seemed to constantly argue with each other. All the way home they were always talking about money, especially the need for more of it. She felt sorry for them since she had come from a wonderful and happy home in the high country.

As she rode to the poor family's home, she realized that they would present a real challenge, but that was why she had joined the Movement. She also recalled what she had learned in the volunteer training course, "Just be yourself. Just be there among them, and you can help them rise out of their poverty."

When she entered the family's house, she couldn't help turning up her nose—the smell was terrible! She wondered if this was the smell of poverty. Perhaps it was actually radon gas, which she had heard was so deadly.

But something that was even more baffling, and more disturbing, was the fact that when the family had chosen her they seemed eager to have her come to share their life, yet once she was there no one seemed to be interested in her! She was left alone standing in the living room as each member of the family rushed off to various activities. "How rude," she thought to herself, "but then again, I shouldn't be taken aback; after all, they are poor people."

The man of the house was the first one who really noticed her. As he went out the door he whistled, "Wow, this one is really a beauty! See you later, I've got a golf game with the guys." The woman of the house quickly snapped back, "She's practically naked! Typical male response." Turning to the volunteer, she said, "Now, dear, don't you worry, I'll find you something decent to wear. We'll spiffy you up so that you'll look like a million. Let me go and see what we've got to dress you up."

When the woman left, the volunteer heard growling. It wasn't from a dog or any other animal that she had heard up in the hill country. She peered around the corner and saw strange black boxes with long tails that were connected to the wall. The bigger black thing had one great eye. In the kitchen she saw several smaller white things with long tails that also were connected to the wall. "Perhaps," she thought, "it's these things with long tails that are the source of the terrible stench in this house." Feeling like an alien, she again repeated to herself the advice given to the volunteers, "Just be yourself. Just be among them, and you will help them rise above their poverty."

The woman returned with several large boxes, "I've found some things to dress you. A few friends are coming over for coffee, and I wouldn't want them to see you like..." Her sentence ended like a freight train without a caboose when the poor family's daughter came into the room.

"Mom, I'd like to give you a hand, but I've got a date," she said. The volunteer sighed; anyone could tell the girl was a victim of poverty just by looking at her.

"Honey, you promised me you'd help me with this. We can't just leave her this way! I thought this was going to be a family affair. Your father ran off to a golf game, and now you're going out?"

"Sorry, Mom," and the front door slammed shut.

"Now I want you to try on these beads," the woman of the house said to the volunteer. "Ah, you're looking better by the minute. I don't understand how he could have thought you looked beautiful—being so bare, I mean. Now, dear, let's try this star for your head. Lovely! Now some strings of lights."

Just then a bell rang in the house. "Who could be calling me?" the woman said as she left the volunteer and began a long newsy conversation on the telephone.

As the woman chatted away, the volunteer moaned to herself, "'Just be yourself,' they said; look at me! I look so silly wearing all these trinkets, cheap beads and junk. What bird would ever come and nest in something like me, or what rabbit would want to hide under my lower branches? I feel like I've lost all my power to help them. How can I heal them now that my beautiful body has some of those long black tails connected to the wall? Oh, I'm starting to stink just like those other things do—like this whole house does! Why didn't the woman listen to the man; I was so beautiful when I was naked!"

She began to weep great tears that trickled down the looped strings of fake cranberries and artificial popcorn. "I had volunteered to give my life to come to the city and to help make the lives of the poor more natural—so they could be more human! But now look at me—I couldn't feel more *unnatural*. I've become a prisoner of their poverty." She sighed so deeply that all her decorations trembled. She looked out the window at her cousins and longed to be with them again. Seeing her image reflected back to her in the glass of the window, she moaned, "They've cleverly made me powerless to heal their home or their lives. How can I 'be myself' when now, like everything else in their lives—including them—I'm artificial, made up to be something that I'm not?"

The volunteer had realized that once she joined the Movement, she could expect to live no more than three or four weeks. As Christmas approached, she knew her days were numbered. She felt death creeping over her, and she lamented, "This Christmas will be no different for this family. Family? It only pretends to be a family—at least the kind that I knew back home in the high country."

Briefly on Christmas day the house was free of the stench as they opened the presents that had been piled under the volunteer. The very day after Christmas, they divested her, without any ceremony, of her beads and fake jewels. After being ruthlessly stripped naked, she was tossed out by the gutter along with the trash. Across the street she saw another volunteer, who had also been discarded, but in shame they both kept their eyes downcast.

On the second day of Christmas, the volunteer found herself sticking out of a mountain of trash in the city dump. She was a naked, bent tree, high atop a pile of tin cans, plastic jugs and old broken appliances. Around her swirled gray-black smoke from burning rubber tires and trash. While naked and bent, she tried to stand as straight as possible with her face turned upward toward the sky. All that remained of her former adornment was a broken plastic star dangling in the wind from an upper branch. Once called a "beauty," she was now old and ugly. Oh, the shame, the pain, the sense of failure! A sudden gust of wind engulfed her in a cloud of smoke, dust and blowing trash. Out of it she cried, "My God, my God, why have you forsaken me?"

I sat in silence, pondering the parable, as Igor slowly returned the chair's front legs to the floor. Standing up, he walked over to the window. We both remained in silence for a moment. Then he spoke as he gazed out the window.

"December 30th. Tomorrow's the end of the year. *Fin*, as the French say, 'the end.' A good day to take inventory of where you've been, before looking ahead to where you're going in the New Year. I propose, as part of that inventory, this question, George: Why do people so quickly find Christmas trees boring and out of place in their homes?"

Igor turned, facing me with an expression like a large question mark on his face. All I could think of at the moment was the obvious: "I guess, Igor, because Christmas is over!"

"Perhaps there's more, George. Is it because once they stop being a source of gifts, or the hope of gifts, people find them expendable? Does that parallel the attitude toward Jesus? Once he no longer worked wonders for the crowds, they lost interest in him. One more question, George. Did your Christmas tree in any way change your lives?"

Igor turned toward the window again as I pondered his questions in silence. Then turning around, he added, "Did your Christmas tree make you or your home any more beautiful, natural or holier than before? And a larger question: Was Christmas a turning point for anyone in your culture, a conversion like that of old Scrooge, or was it just an intermission in people's soap-opera lives?"

"Tough questions, mentor. The answers to those questions would probably reveal why for many of us Christmas is over before New Year's Eve."

"Over the day *after* Christmas for some! But, again, move the parable closer to home. If because of old age or hardship you were no longer a provider, no longer gifted or talented, would others find you uninteresting or inconsequential? Christmas trees are decorated with more than ornaments. They're decorated with hopes and dreams of gifts; they hold a promise of rewards."

"The day I become useless is a day I dread to think about. But you're right, Igor, when people stop being a resource, stop being productive—"

"George, what is the purpose of Christmas trees: to anticipate or to celebrate Christmas? One way to have them grace your home without looking useless would be to give a gift on each of the twelve days of Christmas."

"Twelve days of gifts—that makes sense! It would mean Christmas day wouldn't be a big gift blowout but only the beginning of giving gifts. I like it: giving a gift on each day of the season!"

"And the gifts could be small or large, tokens or real treasures. For you and Martha, it would mean that on Christmas night there would be at least twenty-two gifts left under your tree!"

"Great idea, Igor! Then the Christmas tree wouldn't be trashed a day or two after December 25th. From Christmas all the way to Epiphany would be a time for feasting and fun."

"And savings in your piggy bank, George. You could add those gifts as the twelve days go by, picking them up at those fantastic after-Christmas sales!"

"True, especially for me, Igor, since I'm usually late buying gifts anyway, and I love to catch a good sale. Having gifts under the tree till Epiphany would also make Christmas trees electric with more than lights—they would be charged with anticipation. The twelve days of anticipation could be—"

"Be careful, George, the idea might spread. Beware, because twelve days of giving gifts could wear you out! Indeed, so much gifting could make Christmas into Crucifixion—particularly if you truly give gifts of yourself!"

"Wow, Igor, that's quite an exclamation point to your Christmas tree suggestion, but I think I get your point! Spending yourself in gifts of service to others inevitably leads to some kind of death. All your recent parables say that. The thing that bothers me about this parable is the *tragedy* of the Christmas tree."

"Not all such deaths are tragedies, though, George. Remember the Robin Hood parable I told to Martha? Robin wasn't diminished by his death, nor did it matter that no one was being changed by his service of song—the important thing is that *he* wasn't changed. And as it turned out, he didn't sing in vain. Neither did Jesus. Neither will you if you stay true to spending yourself in love."

"That's a tall order, Igor. But at least I can say that I love your twelve days of Christmas idea. Martha will love it too. Next holiday season when you come to visit, we'll show you our Reformed Christmas festival."

"Yes, next year. Time now for this old dragon to *vamos*, to get out, hit the road, be on my way. So *sayonara*, Sent George—and happy New Year to both you and Martha."

"This is beginning to sound like curtains, Igor. I hope you're not going to abandon us like orphans on the road of the questventure."

"Impossible, George!" Igor said, stepping toward me as I stood up. He embraced me with great affection. "Good friend, the pearl will guide you. You've already glimpsed it in your daily lives and even bathed in its glow. Continue to search for it daily. Be alert! Yes, be watchful since you live in a *shower* of pearls, and the very brilliance of their glory can blind you to the fact that you're surrounded by them, drenched in them! How sad it is when spiritual pilgrims exhaust themselves, running to sanctuaries and shrines, searching for what is right in their midst, hidden from view only because it is so obvious! No, George, you're no abandoned orphans. The flaming pearl is eager to lead you." Then Igor stepped back, saluted and said, "Permission to go ashore, sir!"

I was so touched by his affection that I found myself speechless. I managed to utter, "Permission granted." As I lifted my hand in a halfhearted salute, Igor whirled around and began a fandango dance step, clicking his fingers together like castanets. Before I could say anything, the old dragon danced passionately out the door of the hermitage and vanished before my eyes.

The music, the castanets—all of it—prevented me from asking him what he meant when he said that the flaming pearl would lead Martha and me. Like Martha, I have a feeling of dread about the imminent departure of our beloved teacher, the Master of the Occasion. As I enter this account in our hermitage log, I am aware that mentors have a short life span. They are an endangered species. It's rare to find a good one, and once you find one, brief is the time together. The very nature of the special relationship makes it limited. I know all this, but I don't want our relationship to end.

Igor's told me on a couple of occasions that it would have to end someday. I think back on the parable about Lucky Lux and his mentor, Photon. Indeed, Igor disappeared before, years ago, and I was on my own for some time. Then he magnificently reappeared this summer, and the adventure was even more exciting and more challenging than before. I feel ready and eager to escalate Igor's role as a mentor into that of a friend. I wonder if that's possible. On his next visit I'll ask him about it.

I conclude this last log entry for this year with a sense of gratitude for the year that is ending and of great anticipation for the new year about to be born.

# Ship's Log

**Vessel:** *THE HERMITAGE*

**Officer at the Helm:** *MARTHA & GEORGE*

**Date:** *SUNDAY – MONDAY*
*DECEMBER 31 – JANUARY 1*

**Time:** *200 HOURS – 2:00 A.M.*

Both of us are together here in the hermitage. It's two hours after midnight, and so much has happened. Martha and I have sat here recounting the order of the events from last night and this morning, looking at their meaning.

Last night we had a New Year's party for our friends in the "group" and two other couples whom we've known for years. It was a wonderful party. The work we have done together and the consequent bonding helped make it special. Unlike previous New Year's Eve parties we felt free of the *need* to have a good time, and so we were really free to have fun. There was a sense of simply and enjoyably sharing the evening while waiting for something truly new to begin. Everyone brought wonderful things to eat and drink, and so it was a feast to be shared on many levels.

At midnight we stepped out on our patio to welcome in the New Year. Off in the distance church bells were ringing. Here and there across the neighborhood we could hear shouts

225

and laughter and fireworks. We were in the midst of raising our glasses in a toast to the new year when suddenly the back of our garage exploded! Or rather, as Martha more correctly stated, from behind our garage in the hermitage there was a tremendous series of explosions.

Roman candles and aerial bombs raced skyward at a dizzying pace. Gigantic cluster bombs and fiery showers of star shells combined to create thunderflashes high above our backyard. The frenzied whooshing of skyrockets soaring into the midnight sky made it seem as if our garage area had become a mini Cape Canaveral. From behind this fantastic pyrotechnic display came what sounded like the combined Boston Pops and Russian Army Band playing a complex melody of "Auld Lang Syne," "It's a Long Way to Tipperary" and "Somewhere Over the Rainbow."

"Wow! George, Martha!" gasped our bewildered guests. "What a New Year's display," Paul exclaimed. "Are all those fireworks legal?" Betsy asked, "And what's that stringed instrument I hear in the band? It sounds like an entire chorus of them."

"*Balalaika*," answered Martha, casting me a sidelong glance.

"Gee, George, this is great!" said Frances. "How long did it take you to rig up this thing?"

"A better question, George, is: How much did it cost?" countered Jack.

"You guys, don't be so practical. Just enjoy it!" said Betsy. The words were hardly out of her mouth when a series of explosions rocked the garage. Skyward roared a fusillade of rockets that burst over us to form an American flag. Then it turned into a great red Chinese dragon that lingered in the air with one eye giving a big wink. This was followed by another series of rockets that exploded and spelled out, in rainbow colors, *Till we meet in Paradise*.

As our guests oohed and aahed, Martha and I noticed that the windows of the hermitage were glowing so brilliantly that you'd have thought the sun was rising inside the old toolshed. We both knew who had arranged this.

226

Finally the smoke began to clear, and quiet returned to our backyard. But suddenly, with a great roar, a large rocket shot heavenward, and a great cluster bomb exploded over the patio. It was breathtaking; it looked as if a giant star had burst into pieces directly above us in a blinding splash of colored sparks. The New Year night sky was filled with what appeared to be red-orange, flaming, luminous ping-pong balls slowly drifting downward in clouds. As they showered down upon us, Frances cried out, "Wow! Look at that—they look like flaming pearls!"

Martha and I tilted our heads, shrugged our shoulders and simply looked at one another. As quickly as they had begun, the fireworks ended, and the lights inside the hermitage dimmed. With laughter and small talk, we all went back inside the house. After a cup of coffee, our guests departed for home. Both of us were eager to go to the hermitage, with the hope that Igor would be waiting for us.

Entering the hermitage, we found only a faint afterglow of the original brilliance. The source of the faint light was nowhere to be seen, but we did see something. The logbook was open to the pages before the entry I am now making.

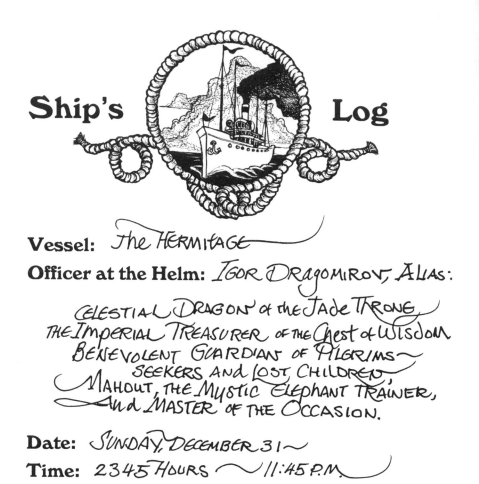

# Ship's Log

**Vessel:** The HERMITAGE

**Officer at the Helm:** IGOR DRAGOMIROV, ALIAS:

CELESTIAL DRAGON of the JADE THRONE,
THE IMPERIAL TREASURER, of the Chest of WISDOM
BENEVOLENT GUARDIAN of PILGRIMS
SEEKERS And LOST CHILDREN,
MAHOUT, THE MYSTIC ELEPHANT TRAINER,
And MASTER of THE OCCASION.

**Date:** SUNDAY, DECEMBER 31

**Time:** 2345 HOURS 11:45 P.M.

Dear George and Martha,

Know of my great affection for both of you. While my visits here to your hermitage have been wonderful and enjoyable, you no longer need a *mahout* mentor. You are well schooled in all that you need to walk this stretch of the path without falling into a ditch! You've renewed your spiritual practice, having taken your voyage through and past the doldrums. You've expanded its boundaries into a companion quest. You've dealt with the difficult and ultimate issue of death. You've come to a greater understanding about what it means to be a prophet and about the way of self-sacrifice and loving attachment.

All mentors are mirrors of the One, the Divine Mystery, who is the best—and only—guide anyone can find. MOOs or *mahouts* like myself are only temporary teachers. Keep your eyes open and you will find many a *mahout* with even bigger elephants eager to enter your life.

Now you must become spiritual directors for one another as hand in hand you follow the path of the flaming pearl. Remember that the best way to learn anything is to teach it. This is especially true of the spiritual path since if you try to teach what you're not putting into practice in your own life, you will quickly find yourself and your student in the ditch. Share—mirror the Mystery—with each other and with your friends in your group. Become mentor mirrors that reflect—without judgment or blame—who the other is at the moment and also who the other *really* is. Praise what is good and holy in each other; be patient with that which is still being converted.

Enjoy—yes—have fun on your quest. As I depart, I leave you a parable written in my own hand.

It was midnight,

right on schedule, when the night nurse appeared in the doorway. "Your light's still on? You should have been asleep hours ago."

Ed lowered the book he was reading. "Just doing a little nightcap reading. You know, Mrs. Hennessy, I'm going home tomorrow," he said, glancing at his bedside clock, "which is just about now. Thanks for what you and the others have done for me while I've been here."

She smiled. "Now, Ed, we both know you can't go home. This is your home." Holding a finger to her lips, she added, "Let's not wake up Mr. Jarrowitz in the next bed. Good night. See you tomorrow." She turned off Ed's bed light, looked in on Mr. Jarrowitz and then left the room.

"Mr. Jarrowitz," Ed said to himself, cocking his head toward the curtain that separated their beds. "Old George, you mean! Don't worry, he's beyond waking up. Poor George is hooked up to so many gadgets and machines, he's only half alive, let alone awake." Blowing a kiss toward the curtain, Ed whispered, "Good-bye, George, sweet dreams. I'm going home."

Ed had felt that call in his bones for several days now. He knew that tonight was the night to go home. Quietly, he slipped out of bed and collected from the drawer of his bedside nightstand his only belongings: his rosary and his billfold, with its precious photos of those he loved. Rolling up two blankets, he carefully placed them in the center of his bed, covering them with the sheet and spread. He dressed in a white shirt, his best tie and his blue suit. From a secret place he removed his special equipment, which he had hidden away just for this occasion, and placed it in his overcoat pocket.

Taking his cane from behind the door, he peeked out the doorway. The hallway was deserted and dimly lit. Ed knew it would be at this hour. He had studied meticulously the habits of the nurses and aides, aware that people are creatures of habit. At the far end of the hallway, the night nurses were gathered with the early morning shift over their coffee and reports. Ed knew they would be occupied for some time. Like a fleeting shadow, he slipped out the side door and quickly began walking downtown toward the bus station.

Stopping to rest after a few blocks, he checked his special equipment. Its presence in his pocket reassured him, and he began softly singing, "Give me land, lots of land, under starry skies above. Don't fence me in." His walk switched into a soft-shoe routine, and he twirled his cane just like Fred Astaire in those old movies. If you had seen him out on the street at that early morning hour, you'd never have guessed his real age.

Ed walked up the dark alley till he reached the rear of the Greyhound bus station. Standing in the shadows, he checked his watch. "Just about now, the 2:15 from Tulsa should be arriving." A few minutes later, the bus came rumbling up the street and pulled into the bus station. Several sleepy-eyed passengers stepped down as a few people waited their turn to board. Ed emerged from the shadows and fell in behind those departing from the bus as they entered the station. Looking like a passenger, he walked straight through the lobby and outside where a couple of taxi cabs were waiting.

He climbed inside a cab, announcing to the African-American driver, "Holton, please. I'm going home."

The cabby turned around, saying, "That's over thirty miles from here! You can catch a bus in the morning for Holton. It'll cost you a bundle to take a taxi way up there."

Ed flashed a big smile, holding up several twenty dollar bills. "I've got the money. Besides, at my age, what's money? I want to go home in style." As the driver pulled away from the curb, he mumbled, "As they say, 'A fare is a fare.'"

Ed checked his watch. It was 2:30. His timing had to be precise in an operation like this. They wouldn't be checking his room till 3 o'clock. He smiled a big grin, which grew even larger as they left the city limits and headed out into the countryside. Ed and Sammy, the cabdriver—they were now on a first name basis—swapped life stories. Like luminous, golden threads woven in and out of Ed's story was his gratitude for how rich had been his life and his joy at going home. Several times as the cab drove northward, he carefully fingered his special equipment in his overcoat pocket.

In those early morning hours there was little traffic. Halfway to Holton, as they passed through a heavily timbered, deserted section of the highway, Sammy felt a gun barrel in the back of his neck. "Pull over, Sammy! This is a stickup!"

The cabdriver muttered aloud, "Oh God, I should'a known better, but who'd have guessed—a geriatric gunman!" Pulling the cab off the highway and into the woods as he was instructed, he pleaded, "I've got a wife and kids—don't shoot! I ain't got much money—fares and tips have been terrible tonight—but it's all yours. Please, don't kill me."

"Don't try any funny business," said Ed. "If you don't want me to give it to you, give me what I want! No, check that, I'm sorry, I got it all wrong. If you give me what I want, I'll give it to you."

Clutching the steering wheel, Sammy moaned, "Are you crazy? What'do you mean: if I give it to you, I'll get it?"

Ed tapped his shoulder, saying, "Here, it's my favorite fountain pen. It's a calligraphy pen; it's got a gold point!" Removing the fountain pen's barrel from Sammy's neck, he handed it to him.

"Don't be fooled by my gift. This is a real robbery, even if it is a special stickup. I've been planning it for years. I'm gonna rob you of your memory. That's right: hand over your memory of everything since I got in your cab at the bus station, and I'll give it to you. I've had it hidden until this moment—it's my special equipment for going home." Before the driver's unbelieving eyes, Ed unfolded five one-hundred-dollar bills! "Sammy, if you give me your memory of the past two hours and promise never to tell anyone about it, this tip is yours. Is it a deal?" Sammy promised, and the two shook hands on their deal.

Sammy pocketed the full fare, and the generous tip. The two sat visiting philosophically about life until the sun began to rise in the east. Then Ed patted Sammy on the back, wishing him luck, got out of the cab and walked off into the woods. Sammy shielded his eyes from the blinding glare that flooded through the trees. His last sight of Ed was the old man walking straight into the blazing rising sun. After a few moments Sammy drove his cab out of the woods and headed back to the city.

The sun was full above the horizon when Sammy turned on the radio. After the national news and the weather, there was an announcement: "Edward Nye, a longtime resident of this city and lately a patient at the Sunset Nursing Home, disappeared from the Home late last night. The police and nursing home authorities have been searching for the elderly man since early this morning. Anyone having any information concerning his whereabouts should contact the police at once by calling—" Sammy's fingers tightly squeezed the steering wheel. Then, with a big grin, he relaxed his grip and reached over to switch the radio to another station.

P.S. *La commedia e'finita*

Dearest Martha and George,

Indeed, my good and dear friends, "The comedy is ended!"

# Ship's Log

**Vessel:** *THE HERMITAGE*

**Officer at the Helm:** *GEORGE*

**Date:** *MONDAY, JANUARY 1*

**Time:** *1730 Hours - 5:30 P.M.*

Martha is fixing a light supper, and we agreed that I should come here to the hermitage and enter in our log what's happened over the past fifteen hours.

When we finished reading Igor's final parable, I closed the logbook, and Martha and I simply looked at each other in silence. We both had tears in our eyes, and the unspoken sentence that passed between us was, "He's gone!"

"It's been a long day, George. Time to go to bed," Martha said, breaking the silence. Slowly I closed the hermitage door, and we walked back toward the house. The unique smell of fireworks still lingered in the early winter morning air of the first day of a new year. Somewhere not far away, a dog's barking broke the silence.

We went to bed New Year's morning somewhere around 4 o'clock and slept late into the morning. Both of us awoke wondering how much of our memories of the previous night and early morning had been a dream and how much was reality. We agreed as we had our late-morning coffee that our recollections were indeed all made of the stuff of reality.

The TV parades and bowl games that are so much a part of New Year's day were part of ours this year. We decided not to go anywhere or visit anyone, spending the day at home. It was as if a funeral pall had been draped over our home—after all, a good friend had left our lives.

Around 4:30 in the afternoon, the doorbell rang. We weren't expecting anyone, but as I went to answer it, I must confess that I secretly wished I would open the door to find Igor standing there with his *balalaika*. Instead, there was a stranger at the door, a young man in his early twenties. Rather nervously he asked, "Excuse me, sir, is your name George?"

"Yes it is. What can I do for you?"

"They...the people at that church down the street, they sent us." With a nod of his head, he motioned toward a young woman who was seated in the car at the curb in front of our house. "They said you and your wife Martha might be able to help us."

"Help you? How?"

"My friend and I—she's kind of shy, sir—we're...ah, looking for some assistance."

"Assistance?" asked Martha who had joined me at the front door. "What kind of assistance?"

"We went to the church, but they said...well, they were too busy. They told us to come and see the two of you, that you might be able to help us. You see we're looking for, ah, spiritual direction. We're both interested in meditation-type prayer, but we don't know how. We're interested in going on a spiritual quest. We were hoping that the two of you, might, if it's possible, become our..."

Martha had graciously invited the man's wife into our house and was now ushering the youthful couple into our living room. The young woman, her eyes big as full moons, said, "And we understand that behind your garage you have a hermitage!"

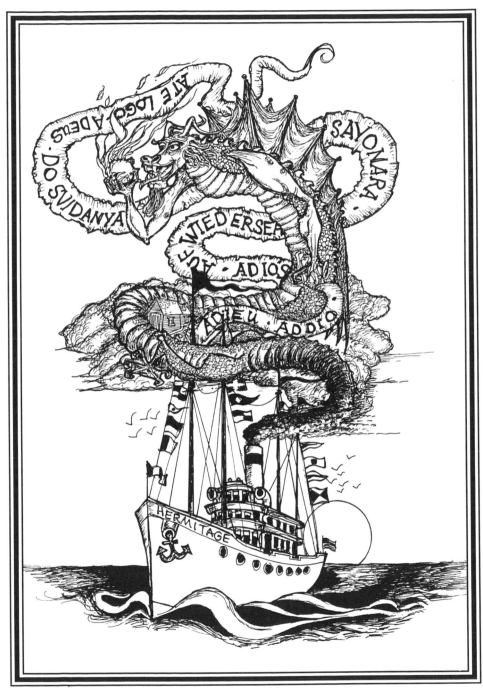

237

# Parables

Lucky Lux..............................................................11

Robin Hood...........................................................25

Doctors Franken and Stein.....................................36

The Holy Mountain...............................................45

Land of the Perpetual Rainbow..............................60

Angelus.................................................................72

The Lighthouse......................................................82

Fred, the Fire Truck Driver.....................................93

Bury a Grudge.....................................................100

The Last Easter Egg..............................................111

The Toddler Timepiece.........................................120

The Deathday Party..............................................129

Isabella Veracruz..................................................143

Nineveh Beach.....................................................153

The Second Coming Landing Strip.........................162

The Wal-Mart Ax Nightmare..................................171

Emmanusatan......................................................180

The Christmas Bunny............................................190

Hans' Toy Shop....................................................202

The Volunteer.......................................................215

Time To Go...........................................................229

# About Edward M. Hays

While *The Quest for the Flaming Pearl* is not so much a book as the third act of a play, the author is not a playwright. Lacking formal education in both writing and art, he enjoys being a play-writer and play-artist, creatively playing around with both.

The occasion of his birth in his parent's bed in Nebraska was overshadowed that same year by the invention of *Alka-Seltzer*. His outlook on life was formed early on, growing up in the 1930s depression years which spawned songs like "Every Time It Rains, It Rains Pennies From Heaven," crammed with evergreen hope. Coming from a deprived childhood without TV or the regimen of Little League, he was forced to use his imagination or die from boredom, the Sahara of the soul. After high school, he was taken in by a monastery of Benedictine monks at Conception Abbey in Nodaway County, Missouri. In 1958, after eight years of education, the good monks kindly threw a cloak over his intellectual faults, and he was ordained a Catholic priest. Hays also holds two doctor's degrees from the University of Mistakes, which has been the source of numerous insights and occasional surprise attacks of wisdom.

Some say his middle initial *M* stands for *Mahout*, Hindi for elephant driver, reflecting his interest in the East and the circus. Others claim it is for *Mercury*, the Roman god and patron of messengers and thieves. Still others, especially his former professors, claim it is for *Merope*, dimmest of the seven stars in the Pleiades, of the constellation Taurus. Known to wear various disguises, his activities are difficult to confirm. Akin to UFO sightings, there are, however, reliable reports of frequent sightings over the past twenty-some years of the author wandering in the timbered hills west of Leavenworth, Kansas.

# Author's Acknowledgments

An author, unlike a painter or poet, creates with others. This *art work* would have been impossible without the help of **Thomas Turkle,** who encouraged its creation and made significant suggestions and who as my publisher was responsible for the many aspects of its coming into print. As editor, **Thomas Skorupa** creatively performed plastic surgery on the original manuscript, spending long hours with a hot iron smoothing out word-wrinkles in the work. **Madelaine Fahrenwald**'s insightful reading further contributed creative suggestions; like a needle, her third-eye threaded the loose ends and wove them into place, giving the text a rich texture. She, **Immanuel Eimer** and **Johnny Johnston** then provided magnifying-glass proofreading of the final manuscript to detect errors hidden like stowaways in its sentences. To these companions of creativity and to all my other friends who encouraged and supported the writing of this book, I am deeply grateful.